This Crooked Way

Also by Elizabeth Spencer

Novels

Fire in the Morning
The Voice at the Back Door
The Light in the Piazza
Knights & Dragons
No Place for an Angel
The Snare
The Salt Line
The Night Travellers

Short Story Collections

Ship Island and Other Stories
The Stories of Elizabeth Spencer
Jack of Diamonds and Other Stories
Marilee
On the Gulf
The Light in the Piazza and Other Italian Tales
The Southern Woman

Nonfiction

Landscapes of the Heart

Drama

For Lease or Sale

THIS

CROOKED

WAY

ELIZABETH SPENCER

University Press of Mississippi   Jackson

www.upress.state.ms.us

The University Press of Mississippi is a member
of the Association of American University Presses.

Published 2012 by University Press of Mississippi
Copyright © 1952, 1980 by Elizabeth Spencer
All rights reserved
Manufactured in the United States of America

First printing 2012

Library of Congress Cataloging-in-Publication Data

Spencer, Elizabeth, 1921–
  This crooked way / Elizabeth Spencer.
    p. cm. — (Banner Books.)
  ISBN 978-1-61703-218-9 (pbk. : alk. paper)—ISBN
978-1-61703-219-6 (ebook) 1. Plantation life—Fiction. 2.
Mississippi—Fiction. 3. Visions—Fiction. 4. Psychological
fiction. I. Title.
  PS3537.P4454C76 2012
  813'.54—dc23
2011043919

British Library Cataloging-in-Publication Data available

For DJK

CONTENTS

Now, sirs, quod he, if that yow be so leef
To finde Deeth, turne up this crokéd wey. . . .

GEOFFREY CHAUCER, *The Pardoner's Tale*

The Wandering

IN THE early 1880's one August Sunday noon there was a rain storm up the Yocona River. The bridge at Yocona washed away and the ford flooded, so that half the people gathered at the Yocona Baptist Church for an all day Sunday preaching and sing couldn't go back home. The other half thought it only sociable to stay. There was another round of singing and another round of sermons and so on until late at night. Not counting conversions, a number of small miracles happened, and one big one. Two boys who had slipped off to go swimming just before the river rose, were feared drowned and so were being prayed for by crowds on the river bank when they appeared, riding down the yellow current, happily straddle of a section of bridge.

All summed up, the day touched off a two and a half week revival meeting. By the end of the first week so many people were coming that the church would not hold them, nor would the church yard. They crowded the steps of the church and pressed their heads in the windows. The dinner tables and benches were heavy with them. The church floated in them, as in a great sea of bodies and song, and some preachers held forth inside and some on the steps and some on the dinner benches, though mostly the people wanted to sing and when they sang the church got up and walked as conjurers can make a table do. They say you could hear them all the way to Oxford, and that people along the Trace stood still to listen.

When the meeting closed at last (the preachers sweated hoarse and played out), they saw there wasn't a plain between Yocona community and the river big enough to hold them in comfort the next year. So they crossed the river and found a ten-acre pasture which a brother praised God was his to give them. When the next meeting came in late summer between laying-by and cotton picking, they threw up a brush arbor big enough to shelter two thousand. Families more than three hours away by wagon built shacks out of scrap pine from the sawmills and carted in hams and souse and pigs' feet and live chickens and canned vegetables and fruit and Lord knows what. There was even a sizeable herd of milk cows every year. They called this Tabernacle. It went on like that for fifty some-odd years.

In 1900, during what was afterwards referred to as "one of the strongest meetings," when the turn of the century like all events that have to do with time and space had stirred people to wonder how much longer the Lord would suffer a wicked race, Amos Anderson Dudley, a boy of sixteen, who had been coming to Tabernacle as to a big annual picnic since he could remember, overheard his father talking with some other men about "the year of the Lord."

"They claim the world wasn't much over nineteen hundred year old when Jesus come," one said. "If any."

"That old? Is that so?"

"Then this year brings it back around?"

"So I been thinking. Signs in the sky." He looked up.

In the enormous August sky, the stars flared in chunks of light, like wind-blown lamps. A brilliant one passed unhurried from the center downward, trailing curved fire. "Last night I lay and seen them pass the window."

"It don't worry me none, though," said Clyde Dudley, Amos's father. "Things like that. A little thing like musket fire, now, that worries me. But the world burning? There aint nothing a man can do about that but hold on to the floor and pray." He did not seem an old man yet, but he had fought the war as a boy.

Young Amos crept away. He went to the side of an empty shack, keeping a close watch on the sky. His father might not be worried by what the men said, but he felt he was not good like his father. His father was an even man and for Amos life went up and down like the hills across the river. Last night he had been up. Jessie Beckman had let him kiss her, the first girl to let him kiss her like he wanted to kiss, in a way that he thought he made up himself, out of his heart. Out of the evil of my heart, he thought. And all night long he was way up, thinking about Jessie Beckman. But in the morning he was groggy and it was hateful to help his father milk and feed. He kept slopping milk out and once the cow kicked filth off her feet into a bucket and it had to be thrown away. "Go on back in the house," his father said at last. "I can do better without you. Go on back." But as soon as he was out of sight on the path, he quit being sorry about the milk and began to think about Jessie Beckman again. She had said she would let him sit by her in church that night.

There in the shadow of the shack, he remembered her and what she said and the taste of her mouth. He guessed she was waiting for him, but he did not go. He was afraid to go. He was thinking hard about the end of the world and what his father had said: Hold on to the floor and pray. He felt how it would be to hold on to the floor which would be rising and falling beneath your stomach like a boat in rough water, and how through the windows you could see the fire and black smoke billowing up, each flame as big as the barn, the fire circling every horizon, the fire and smoke gushing inward, and trees in the yard bending and lighting easy as sage, and how when the roof went flaming, you could see the sky and how the last stars were tearing from their sockets and the heavens were black, enormous, and blind.

He was covered all over with sweat. And then there would be hell. Hell for him, for Amos Dudley, forever.

He thought: I just can't go to hell. There ought to be some way, there's got to be some way. If it just holds off a while, I ought to be able to figure some way. If it just aint tonight.

He was afraid to be alone. He was so afraid it would be tonight, the fire, the blind stars, the hell for Amos Dudley, that he was afraid even to hope that it wouldn't be tonight, as though by hoping against it he might provoke it. But as long as he stood alone, he stood desperately hoping anyway, and was afraid.

In the lantern-lit clearing under the brush arbor, he could hear the singing begin, the roll and vibration of it, the curious sweet lilt of the upper notes that the women sang, the rich, under-curving of the men's part. The singers drew him, trembling, to their company.

He found a small vacant section of bench toward the very back and fitted himself into it. Way up front he saw Jessie Beckman sitting; she kept turning to look behind her as though someone twitched her head with a string and everytime her tight blonde ringlets jumped. But she could not see him. That was all he cared about her now. He pushed a swallow down his dry throat while hell chilled him to his toes. He sat rigid, his voice dumb, and let the music flow into him like a great wave.

> *"Whe-un we-e've-uh be-un there-uh te-un*
> *thou-ou-sa-und years,*

Bri-ut shi-uni-ing a-as the-uh sun,
We-e've-uh no-o le-uss time-uh to-o
si-ing-uh Hi-is praise
Tha-an when-uh we'ed ju-ust begun."

They were praying now. He hardly heard. He waited for the singing to start again. Only the singing was as big and billowing and strong as his big image of the fire. It came again.

"Hide me, O my Sav-i-IOR, hide,
Till the storms of life a-ARE past.
Safe in-to the har-bour guide.
O receive my-y soul at last."

It went on for a good while, with the people crying the numbers of this one and that one and the men rising to pitch them right, the sopranos and tenors carrying at first, then the basses and altos surging in, and all soaring together; but now that they were silent all the singing had done was clear the air for one man's voice, and with so great a cleared space to sound in alone that voice had better tell the truth. Because Amos Dudley had to listen to the voice. He had to listen because he was afraid to think. It was the first and last voice he ever paid close attention to in his life, and it took hell itself to make him listen. The voice told him about Jacob who went out from his home.

". . . And the day that he went out, the Lord was with him, my brothers, and the Lord showed him a ladder of angels. When Jacob saw the ladder of angels what did he think? Was he afraid of God's wrath? Oh, yes, he was afraid of God. And what man and what woman of you, in the secret guilt of his heart can stand and say, I am not afraid of the wrath of God? Stand up, if you can say it. Rise, I say, and declare it to us all.

"Not one."

"Amen," the people said, far and near.

"Yes, Jacob was afraid. Jacob who cheated his brother, Jacob who lied to his father, Jacob who contrived evil in his heart. Oh, but he was afraid! And then— And then—! What fell on the trembling ear of Jacob? The CURSE of GOD? Oh, the frailness of your human heart that would answer me and say, But Jacob had earned the curse of God. For what have you yourselves earned with all the might of your hearts, but the curse of the living God?"

"Amen," the people said.

"Oh, when will the day dawn upon you, my brothers? When will you learn, my brothers and sisters of Yocona Community, that the great God whose voice you tremble to hear in that unknown day, is longing to bless you, is eager to call you His own? Praise God, I say!"

"Oh, praise Him!" some said, soft and deep.

"It was NOT the curse of the Almighty that fell on Jacob's sinful ear! It was blessing, my dear friends of Yocona Community! Blessing! For I will be with thee, He said.

"Oh, wayfarers upon the earth, learn well the lesson of Jacob.

"Oh, lonely and despised ones, seeking to and fro upon the earth a resting place for your hearts, remember Jacob.

"Unto Jacob the shining ladder came down, my brothers.

"Not to ESAU!

"Way back at home there, over there with Isaac and Rebecca, plenty of food to eat, surrounded by his wife and his kindred, what need had Esau, my brothers, to see the watchful angels of the living God?

"It was to Jacob, alone, despised, there on the rocky hill, locked in the sins of his heart, that God's voice spoke, that God's angels came clothed in shining light. Oh, when you are lonely, my dear friends, when you are fearful, when it seems that the night will never pass into the sunrise, oh, then, my brothers, remember Jacob. How in the night of his despair, in the night of his going out, God waited not for the sunrise. God waited not till he reached the land of his distant kindred. God came in the hour of departure. God came in the hour of his loneliness. God came in the night.

"Oh, the beauty of the host of heaven, outshining the sun in splendor! But, oh, the glorious beauty of the host of heaven, pouring out from the darkness of the night. . . ."

The people were singing again and Amos Dudley stood singing with them. He stayed until his family were all gone home, moving in with the dwindling crowd that cried for hymn after hymn, until the lanterns went out in most of the shacks and the singers were hoarse. When he saw the preacher coming down to shake hands, he slipped away. He did not want to see the preacher close. It was no human hand he wished to touch when he took the dark way home alone.

Instead of going home across the bridge, he took the short cut over the ford. The narrow path dipped steeply into a wild ravine. He almost stepped on a rabbit that scutted away ahead of him. A fat possum ambled into the fallen leaves. But he moved steadily on. For he owned something now that was greater than the fear that was in high going of the night wind, or the movements of half-seen things, or the chuckle of unseen ones, or the stillness of those like the owl who watch and nothing else. The owl could look down now with eyes aflame like the windows of hell; he did not care.

The path twisted to the crest of the ravine, then broke gradually down toward the river. He could feel the scuff of the sand under his shoes. The trees gave way to blackberry bushes and these opened suddenly and he was on the river bank. He could hear the murmur of the water and see a faint light that glanced out of the center of the stream and the dim line of woods that ran down from the Dudley pasture to the river bend. That was all he could see, for the sky was overcast and all the stars were hidden. He knew that the ford lay straight ahead, but he stood before the blackberry bushes and waited. He did not know what he waited for. He did not much think it would be another ladder. He did not think either that it would happen by the ford. The ford was the wrong way for him on this night. He moved on.

Downstream where the river curved, willows and cane lashed with vine, drift logs half-buried among the cane roots, came down to the water's edge. There the sand turned to mud. A clump of three pine trees crowned the bank across the river. Against the low sky their trunks and heads were plain; they were the only things darker than the sky.

He took off his good shoes and tied the laces together and hung the shoes around his neck. He rolled up his pants and his shirt sleeves as high as they would go. Mud heavy with sand coated his bare feet and lay in a thick crust over the sand in the river bed. Alive, the water curled against his ankles; he could feel it speaking. He was up to the waist before he stopped and took his direction from the pines. The water flowed stronger against him; it thrust and pushed about his knees and thighs, separating his clothes from the nakedness beneath, exploring his secret parts.

It was then he understood.

This is why they baptize, he thought; this is why they lead you into the water and say words over you because the words keep you in the water a spell longer. And they won't ever do this to me. I will do it to myself and for myself, and that way it will be right, he thought, and I will have it forever.

The water waiting to take him, moved alive and talking under

his armpits, around his neck, pressed insistent as a mouth
against his closed lips and loosened the hairs from his scalp. It
is flowing above my head, he thought, and walked on, buried.

He might have drowned there if the strong under-current
had not lashed, sudden as a whip, about his knees and thrown
him, so that he kicked at it and came up swimming. He snorted
and coughed; his forehead blazed inside where the water had
got up his nose. Again the current flung him. It pulled him
against himself, thigh from shoulder, and angry now with the
fury of outraged innocence, he twisted and fought away, swimming with the strength of rage. He gained the foot of the high
bank and clung there by a root. Resistless as a weed, his spent
body trailed in the long current.

He thought: Put your trust in something and look what it
did: tried to drown you.

Cheat, he thought bitterly, spitting the water, the thin muddy
taste, from his mouth. And that included not only the river
but the preacher's words that had stirred him, the singing that
had comforted him, and the men who casually talking of the
day of fire had made him afraid. Nothing to it, he thought.
Nothing to any of it.

He looked back accusingly over his shoulder and saw something with a head and legs turning dreamily toward him in
the current. He clave to the bank, staring, his free hand buried
in mud to the knuckles. End over end it came; he saw the black
hoof and one stiff ear and two water-cold eyes like white door-
knobs. The current slacked against his body as the thing went
past: a dead calf. He laid his face against the root and the chill
mud and said, aloud and defiant: Cheat! Cheat!

On the very sounding of the words it came over him Who he
was talking to, that it was not the river, the preacher, singing,
or men any more, but the One who stood in back of them all, a

little off to the side, and was never seen by any that lived to tell about it. It came over him too, with certainty, that this One was close and had heard him and was about to be seen by Amos Dudley with blasphemy choked filthy in his throat.

He made a desperate scramble against the twenty-foot bank that arched over him, for he had to get in open ground. From his fingers the mud fell on his face like hard rain. He slid back falling into the water, trapped by the bank and the current, his cornered heart plunging in him, his fear mounting in the face of the darkness that thickened terribly as though pressed from without, closer and closer to bursting.

But he did not see it burst, slash open by the sword that flamed, either side of the dark curling back like paper in the fire. He did not see anything. Whatever came to him came from behind, unseen by him forever, a hand stretched down from behind to lift him up. He felt the strike and pull of fiery pain in his right shoulder, the lightening and lift of his whole body. He saw, as he passed upward, the high bank fleeing by, with every streaking of mud and clay and all the small roots and tufts of thick grass. Then mud, bank, and water dropped far beneath him, like stars falling under the earth instead of over it, and there was only the fire in his shoulder and the easy sweep of the round earth.

He could not remember coming back down again. His next consciousness was of sitting calm as mid-afternoon at the top of the bank with his feet dangling off the edge toward the water and his hands crossed idly in his lap. His clothes were dry and there was no mud on him anywhere. He touched the bank and steadying himself with both hands on the soil stubbed with grass, he settled back into the world. He was not trapped anymore, and he was not afraid. It seemed days since he had been in the water, yet he knew that no time at all had passed.

It was the same night, the same hour, even the same minute as before.

He turned his head and the ache in his shoulder came alive. He rubbed the ache, and shoots of fresh pain ran along the nerves like fire in dry sage.

Upstream, the clump of pines stood plain against the low sky. The darkness had spread out again, relaxing. Below him the river went on. It was all the same, and even the way he now felt was not unfamiliar. He had felt somewhat the same that very morning when he spoiled the milking and got sent back home. He had been scolded and he knew it. He had been impudent to God and God had snatched a knot in him. He rose slowly and still holding his hurt shoulder, he studied every nook and crevice of all he could see. Nothing showed. He guessed that he would have to go farther and do worse before he got the ladder and the angels. He unslung his shoes. The dry knot loosed easily.

He went home, quietly, without hurry, a child of God.

2

The next evening, after he had separated the calves from the cows, Amos kept on out the back way and went seining for minnows with Letty's boy, Nig. Ephraim, his oldest brother, had said he wanted all the Dudley's to be at Tabernacle that night. When Ephraim said that at supper, all the Dudleys immediately wished they had somewhere else to go besides Tabernacle. Their father had to threaten three of them with a whipping to make them dress.

When Amos came back to the house it was good dark. He had no more than hit the front porch when he knew there was somebody in the house. He went on into the dog trot and stopped, trying to place the footsteps in the kitchen. It scared him to think this might have something to do with God again, and it aggravated him a little bit too. He wondered if he had got himself into something that wasn't going to stop.

This is one saw I aint going to catch aholt of, he thought. I'll holler and if nothing answers back I'm going right straight out again.

But when he hollered a voice said, "Whyn't you come on back and see?"

"Ned!" he cried and ran. "Oh, Ned, how come you home?"

A big man stood in the middle of the kitchen floor drinking a gourd full of water. He had washed his hands and face; his sleeves were turned back on his wrists and his shirt was open half to the waist.

"Everybody's down to Tabernacle, Ned."

"Down praising the Lord," laughed Ned and threw the drops in the gourd in Amos's face. "And you jumped the pasture. Just like I used to do. Mind you don't grow up favoring your brother Ned." He grabbed Amos by the chin, said, "Show your teeth, sir," and poked him. Amos, like every other Dudley except Ephraim, couldn't help but laugh at Ned.

But he was older now and he felt all right to say: "Tell Ephraim on you. You come to pay off that gambling money, Ned? Ephraim aint going to like it you don't pay off that money."

"Hush, boy." Ned stuck his head in the kitchen safe.

"Mama's teacakes," chanted Amos. "Saving for Sunday."

"By Sunday, boy, teacakes won't be in it. Chicken pie and coconut cake by Sunday."

He thrust Amos a handful of cakes, blew out the lamp and walked through the house with the rapid sureness of an owner. Amos, trailing, found him sitting in his father's rocking chair;

his big, coarse, florid face showed plain in the dark, not laughing anymore, but fixed on the empty front gate. Under Ned's belt around above the back pocket, Amos saw the bulge of something rigid, something as important to Ned as what bulged his crotch in front. None of the other children would come striding out and sit in Clyde Dudley's chair. But it was all right for Ned. Amos ate the last teacake, squatting in the shadow by the steps.

"Where'd you come from, Ned?" he ventured.

"From out of the Delta. Crossed through the big woods."

"They got roads through? Roads through the Delta to Yocona?"

"Sawmill railroad, boy. Where you been? Roads, too, bad ones. Buckshot and snakes."

"How come you home, Ned?"

"Home? Oh, home to see Mama. Home to see the place. Home to pay my debts and let old Ephraim rest."

"Where you going to, Ned?"

"Going? How come you think I'm going anywheres?"

"You always go off somewhere, Ned. Mama says, Ned never—"

"Hush, boy. Just hush."

"Then you going to stay, Ned? Oh, if you'd stay—"

"If I'd stay what? What about if I'd stay?"

"I don't know."

"That's right, boy. You don't know."

And that was all Amos could think of to mention. For when Ned came home he brought what he always brought, the sense of having come out of something not to be talked about, unpleasant to know, and as long as he kept things humming around him you forgot it, but when things got quiet you saw it in the house, plain as an old rope-tied suitcase sitting unpacked over in the corner. Amos had wished a thousand times in the whirl of shouting and teasing that Ned brought, the cries over the favorite dishes Ned could get cooked for him, that he could have Ned just to himself for a little while. For whenever you asked Ned a question somebody interrupted or Ned made a wild answer, and you never knew. But now that he could ask Ned anything, the unpleasant thing Ned had brought along, as bad as a wife, sat with them, a silent listener, and Amos had to be quiet.

From the road he heard at last the creak and strain of the wagon on the hill below the house. It's over, he thought despairing. My chance is gone. He tried to think of something quickly. "Is that a gun you got under your belt, Ned?"

But Ned jumped up. "Well, if it aint the folks," he cried. "The folks home from preaching and me in Papa's chair."

Ned stayed a week. During the days he would go to Yocona and come back again, but what he did there no one asked. Amos knew now that it was a gun and that it lay beneath the pillow when Ned slept. He knew that Ned paid up his debts while he was there—even worked out one of them, hauling wood and sweating like a nigger, looking strange and temporary in a pair of Ephraim's overalls.

The day the two youngest Dudley boys, Durley and Mason, fell in the swing right after dinner, Ephraim blamed Ned.

"You just as good as pushed them," he said, "setting on the porch making them show out."

"He never said a word!" the girls cried.

"Durley's arm is broken," Clyde Dudley said. "Ride for the doctor, Amos."

"Ned never said a word!" the girls wailed.

"Never had to," said Ephraim.

"By God, Ephraim," said Ned, "I paid off that money today, but there's one more note I owe." He drew back his fist.

But his mother was at the door. "Boys!" she cried. "Boys!" But it was to Ned she cried. "Aint it enough to have one child with a broken arm?"

Three days later Ned went to Yocona and did not come back. The younger ones blamed Ephraim, until they heard Ephraim say Ned owed twice as many people as when he came. Then they weren't sure. All of them knew in their various ways about the unpleasant thing that Ned carried along with him. Still, it was so tiresome for Ephraim to talk about the debts, they would almost have swopped having to hear about it for Ned's unknown portage. Ephraim waited and grumbled for five years; then he paid. "Ned is proud," said their mother, who loved Ned so much perhaps she never sensed the unpleasant thing. Whenever the train blew at Yocona she would wait just the time it took to walk from town to the house and she would be out on the front porch looking toward the road with her face fixed for them to think she had her mind on something else. "You wouldn't allow a word to none of the rest of us for what he done," Ephraim said. "You never knowed the way of Ned," she answered. She was not a demonstrative woman and the counsel she kept was continually her own. She had nine children in all, not counting two still-born, but their father said she had been taken harder with Ned's birth than with all the rest of them.

When Amos told her he was going away from home, she said, "You aint stirring a step from here till I get these new britches stitched up for you," and he saw a little way into her because she was thinking maybe if she delayed him a while he'd change his mind, all the time knowing he wouldn't. She made him wait four days for the britches, giving up at last, working all day at the machine, and the night she finished them, while she was steaming the creases in the kitchen, he overheard her say to his father, "The two that's my heart are the two that leave." He did not know before that his mother cared specially for him. She hid it from me to keep me, he thought. She showed it for Ned, and lost him, so she hid it from me. He went off in the woods and cried.

3

But just the same he left. He went to the Delta with Arney Talliafero. Arney had been deputy sheriff at Yocona when Amos caught the Negroes. A store back up the road at Toccopola had been robbed of a lot of work clothing during the night and the county officers had been on the lookout all day for anybody with a sack or box. Amos was clerking in Ephraim's general merchandise store at Yocona and from the barred windows at the back he could see the railroad. Ephraim was at his dusty desk back of the flour sacks totting up the books. Amos, who was supposed to be watching the store, was sticking his hands to the wrist in a bucket of lady peas, feeling how they crawled on his skin, and wondering if he dared slip over to Mrs. Fremont's house for a glass of cool buttermilk. He saw the Negroes go by on the railroad track, but they weren't carrying anything. Folks took the tracks for a road lots of times. The Negroes drew near the long curve he liked to watch the train make, there where the weeds sprang up higher and the two tracks sank together to a single line and slipped away behind the bluff.

The next thing he knew he was calling Ephraim. "There they are!" he cried, pointing.

Ephraim craned to the window and came up shaking his head.

Amos saw he was going to have to stand there and prove it to Ephraim by arithmetic and the Bible and every other kind of way, and by that time they'd be gone. He ran out of the store. He stood in the middle of the wide road between the two stores and the blacksmith shop and the postoffice, none of which showed the least sign of mortal habitation, and yelled at the top of his voice: "Them niggers just went by!" When he reached the tracks, running, a half-dozen men and ten or more children were streaming behind him.

One of the Negroes, the younger, tried to run away but he couldn't go very far or fast in two sweaters, three pairs of over-alls, and five work jackets. The other one, an old strong bent Negro with a wise face, commenced to take off one jacket after the other while Amos was still thirty yards away. He thrust out a wad of clothing into the boy's arms, so that when the men caught up, Amos stood up to the ears in new-smelling denim. Three men and all the children leaped the culvert whooping and like dogs on a rabbit fell on the younger Negro who lay curled up in the grass giggling, as if it had all been a game.

It was later yet before Arney Talliafero, the deputy, came sprinting full steam up the track with the cinders spraying behind him and made the arrest.

"How'd you figger it?" he asked Amos when he got his breath back. He was a tall loose-jointed man who had shot up so fast as a boy he had got into the habit of leaning over to listen. When he leaned you saw the sharp blue eyes and hook nose that made him look older than he actually was. He wasn't really much past twenty. He didn't marry and he never worked at anything steady, so the sheriff made him deputy which pleased him for a while, then it wore off. "I seen them two myself," he said, "but I never thought nothing."

Amos spit like a grown man and dumped the clothes back

at the old Negro to tote. "Aint nobody going to wear that many clothes in June," he said.

"Well, I swan," Arney said. His eyes were very bright and pleased. It came over Amos with a kind of shock that big Arney Talliafero was not concerned with taking trouble to act smart. He stood out in front of everybody admiring that Amos had outsmarted him.

Amos went back into the store. "There's some stuff called hair grease that the niggers are using to take the kink out," he told Ephraim. "I seen Letty using some of it when I was over there borrying coal oil. I thought maybe we ought to put some of it in stock. That and them iron combs you heat over a lamp to make it take."

Ephraim climbed on the counter to put up a new spiral of fly paper. "I aint heard tell of it," he said, and stopped to let his head swim.

"She had a bottle of some kind of medicine on the mantelpiece. Called Peruna. It's supposed to cure rheumatism, malaria, toothache, grip, heart burn and a whole lots of other things."

"Folks aint going to buy that kind of stuff," said Ephraim. "Not around Yocona they aint. What folks can't cure at home they call the doctor to look at."

"Folks must be buying it somewheres," said Amos.

"Aint enough niggers around to keep a stock in for them," said Ephraim.

"There's niggers around," said Amos, "but they go up to Johnston's at Toccopola. They going to go where they can get what they want."

"I aint going to lay in a stock of worthless merchandise to please nobody. I don't care if you did catch them niggers."

"You could try just a little bit of it," said Amos. "Bet you they'd buy it."

"Buy it!" Ephraim cried. His brown mustaches jumped up savagely from his mouth. "Don't make no difference who buys it. It's still worthless." He climbed off the counter with the intention of talking down into Amos's face, but he had to talk eye to eye instead and that made him mad. "You mind you don't start getting too big for your britches around here. You tend to your business and I'll tend to mine."

"I got no business to tend to," Amos said under his breath, heading toward a woman before the piece goods counter.

But that's the way it goes, he thought, and the next day when Arney asked him to go along fishing, he walked out of the store and went. Ephraim gave him a good going over. "Folks don't like to wait to get waited on," he said. "It don't pay."

"Well, you aint paying me nothing to make it pay," said Amos. Gritty worm-slime was stinking on his hands. He was drawing water to wash and go clean the fish, a two-foot string slung out on the slab bench near the well. He felt the rope jump and slack as the tin pipe struck water. Now he could hear the suck of the water filling in. He was tired from the long day of fishing. Out there on the hill-locked lake with Arney he had felt very distant from Ephraim. On the way home he had told Arney long stories about Ned. Some of them he made up.

"Paying you!" Ephraim cried. "Didn't nobody ever pay you to git up and milk in the mornings either. You was wanting to quit that so bad, I'd a-had to hog tie you to keep you out'n the store. Go on back to milking then. Durley's getting big enough to work with me."

"I aint going back to milking either," Amos said and turned a gush of water into the bucket.

"Then you can get your own store and land and start working for your vittles," said Ephraim. "You shore done outgrowed us."

"Papa aint said nothing," Amos reminded him, and walked away with the bucket.

Amos showed up at the store the next day, mainly to dog Ephraim, but it was evidence of something you were liable not to mark up for Ephraim that he spoke kindly to Amos and helped him open up some crates of cheese and flour and canned goods that came in on the train. That afternoon Amos was back on the lake, glum and short-tempered, with luck that Arney could only swear at. There was fish on the Dudleys' table off and on all summer.

Amos's father had not been well since a spell of typhoid two summers back the year after Ned left. Elida, the youngest girl, had died of the same fever. Clyde Dudley, mild-tempered and congenial with the neighbors who were always dropping in to swop stories and talk, developed a curious way of looking at Amos every time there was fish for supper. He would cut a big portion of fried cat fish and turnip greens off onto his fork which he held in his left hand, tines downward, prop his knife blade on the edge of his plate, and take up the hot cornbread yellow with melted butter, and while he was chewing all this together, he would look at Amos and half close his eyes as though he were about to commence on a sad little hum. He seemed not to be able to gather strength for settling his sons' quarrel, and Amos would believe that his father sided with him in secret until he recalled there had never been a compliment yet on the fish.

Just before Tabernacle that summer, Ephraim went down with malaria and Amos kept store alone. There was some talk of money being short—last year's crop had suffered from rain. One afternoon a drummer came through. Amos made a large order on credit. The shelves and counters of Dudley & Co., Yocona, were piled up to crowd the ceiling the day before

Tabernacle opened. Amos walked back and forth in the store
aisle and wondered what would happen if he shipped it all
back. On paper nothing had seemed so big. He turned his back
to the shelves to get them out of his mind and scaling Ephraim's
stool, he began to write out a list with prices. He thought for
a minute, then threw it away. He made out another list without
the prices. At the bottom he printed in large letters: ALL JUST
ARRIVED AT DUDLEY & CO YOCONA FIRST STORE BY
THE RAILROAD. At the top of the page he put: CHEAP.

He worked all day making copies of the list. He stuck one
copy in the window with some glue, and the next morning
early when the Tabernacle wagons began to roll past the railroad, he gave a Negro boy twenty-five cents to spend the day
handing a list into each wagon.

An hour before any of his folks would arrive for preaching,
he locked the store and went down to Tabernacle. He thanked
the Lord it was a hot, close night and he sold six dozen fans
at a nickel apiece. Each of them had Dudley & Co., Yocona,
printed on them, and the drummer had said it was a good idea
to give them away, but Amos couldn't see the sense in that.

Three days later when he came home from work, he looked
up the hill to the house and saw that Ephraim was up and out
on the front porch bundled in a blanket. His face was as yellow
as the inside of a bordock tree and it was a deeper yellow in the
long seams that ran into the corners of his mustache and out
again, like lines drawn on for a play. He held a copy of Amos's
list crumpled in his hand.

"I am ordering you," he said, "to go down to that store and
pack ever' last thing on this here paper back into the boxes it
come in, and mail it right straight back to whatever folks was
fool enough to put it on the market. If that don't give you
enough to do, you can set your mind to drawing up 'umble let-

ters explaining how you got to send it back because you aint nothing but a nobody Mr. Ephraim Dudley was obliged to leave tending the store. Being ill."

"I can't," said Amos. "I done sold it all."

"Sold it!" Ephraim's thin fever-wasted body sank back into the blanket and he hitched it tighter around his shoulders. "The infernal fools," he murmured and turned his eyes away as a ray of sun struck through the trees and hurt him.

"Listen, Ephraim," Amos said. "Ever'body knows I done it. Aint nobody going to credit it to you. I done paid off the drummer and—listen, Ephraim—what I cleared come to $96.84. I didn't want to leave it up at the store, so I brought it home to you. I don't want none of it." He lifted up the sack of money.

"I don't want to see it," said Ephraim. He held the list out from him, squinting. "Pinkham's Vegetable Compound, Peruna, Hood's Sarsaparilla, celluloid collars, fancy bow ties, ladies pink and blue celluloid dresser sets, powder rags, ladies genuine gold-plated jewelry, sterling silver rings, men's hair tonic—aint there even one thing you got that aint the work of devils and crooks?"

"Don't none of that medicine hurt nothing," Amos said. "I took some myself to make sure. Even that ladies complaint stuff. Aint nothing but some kind of whisky sugared up."

"We got honest whisky to sell to folk that wants it," Ephraim said.

"Some of that other stuff was good merchandise," said Amos.

"You better get to bed early tonight," Ephraim said. "You got to get up early and milk. After that you can go ask Mama what stuff she wants brought in out of the garden. She's likely to think it's due for a good chopping. First thing after milking, take Durley down to the store and tell him anything he wants to know. As for that money you got there, when they pass the skillet around tonight, you can drop it in."

"All of it?"

"Ever' last cent."

"I aint going to do it," said Amos.

His father was standing in the door. There was a dead silence.

"What is it you aint going to do?" his father asked.

"I aint going to put this money I sweated for in anybody's collection plate."

"How much is it?" his father asked.

"$96.84."

"Then there's nine dollars and sixty-eight cents of it due the Lord," said his father. He saw Amos draw breath and he cried out: "Hush!" At the thunder of his voice, it was as though the hill clove in two. Even the children playing out by the well were silent. The effort cost him. He stood there calmly, but somehow smaller and Amos saw how frail he was. Then he turned back into the house.

That night Amos put nine dollars and sixty-eight cents into the collection skillet, seeking with some embarrassment to hide the size of the sum in his fist and then look as though he had done nothing out of the ordinary. He came back earlier than the others, cutting down through the woods to wade the ford. In the middle of the ford he stopped and spread the mouth of the sack wide. Downstream, bright under the moon, the river curved and the clump of pines stood over the deep water where he had baptized himself and known the hand of God. He drew from the sack a fistful of coins. They made a thin shine under the moon.

What was wrong with it? he wondered. What made it bad?

At Tabernacle they were singing still. Their voices came in the wind, sweet and clear over the water. Money in one hand and money in the other: he wondered, What if both hands offend you?

He let two coins drop through his fingers into the water. His quick eye saw them pass, a silver dollar and a two-bit piece. The brown surface flicked as though two small fish had passed. Then they were gone as though they never existed, as though all the hours of worry and decision and making lists and more worry and clerking and talking and peddling fans had never been thought of, much less done.

Throw it away? he thought. I might as well be Ephraim.

He dropped the silver back into the sack, and leaned down. The quarter was easy to find for it lay on the surface of the sand bottom, but the silver dollar had either sunk down or been pushed away by the current. He dug for it a long time, and waded about in a circle staring down at the river until his feet shrank. But the river told him nothing.

Waste, he thought bitterly, going home. Shameful waste.

Three weeks later he had just milked and let the calves in to suck when Arney Talliafero surprised him by the lot gate in the dusk.

"I'm going down in the Delta tomorrow," Arney said. "They done already started picking down there. I thought maybe you'd want to go along."

"How much they give you?" Amos asked.

"Same as anywheres else. Forty cents a hundred. But it works up fast. I cleared twenty-two, three dollars last fall in something like three weeks."

I cleared four times that much in three days at the store, thought Amos. Now I can't set foot in the store.

"That place down there," Arney said. "It's a sight. Things go on the like you never seen."

"What things?"

"Well, there was this here woman come down in the cotton last fall. Went from one row to the next."

"Picking cotton?"

"Oh Lordy, Amos."

"Aw, Arney. You swear? Black or white?"

"They claimed there was both. The one I seen was white. Then one night we was setting in this saloon over in Greenville down by where the boats come in, and this man he come in with a top hat on and a ves' and this coat down to here—" he speared his fingers into his thighs—"and he says, I bet ever' one setting here five hundred acres of land I can shoot more ducks than you can on Lake Washington come sunup in the morning. Them that loses got to pick my second stand of cotton for me from tomorrow on till she's cleared out.

"Five hundred acres of land, Amos! Five hundred acres of land so rich all you got to do is throw cotton at it out the back door and go on up to Memphis. And when you come back you can't stand along side of it and see over it. I says to myself, That man aint had that land long. It aint been long since that man been setting round in overalls drinking corn likker same as me."

"You didn't shoot ducks with him, Arney?"

"Sure I did. We all did. Shootin'est son-of-a-gun ever I seen. We all picked for him two-three weeks," Arney said complacently, as though this were of no consequence. "But five hundred acres of land!"

"That you didn't get," Amos said.

He drew a long dizzy breath out of the limp air. It was early September, the summer's deadest hour, the worn-out time, when the heart lies like a heat-curled leaf, the hands move at work from habit, and nothing will do to think about but the cool weather which never comes.

I would have got it, Amos told himself. For five hundred acres of Delta land, I would of out-shot Buffalo Bill.

"I'll go with you, Arney," he said.

4

In the Delta the land was black and tough. There were fields and swampy woods and nothing else. The fields, toothed with smoking stumps in the middle of the cotton rows and continually threatened with wire-hard vine, had the tattered look of having been rent from the woods. Wild and jungle-like to the edge of the fields, the great trees stood, oak and sycamore and elm, and always in the marsh and swamp water, the cypress, pillared spider-like among its great knees and ragged with moss. There were pickers and planter and nothing else. The pickers, white and black, dragged dirty eightfoot cotton sacks behind them and burrowed down the rows of black-green cotton like moles. The planter rode through on his horse at a fast walk that he would not check even to ask questions and give orders. He wore a gun openly at his hip and a limber black whip coiled around his forearm, the handle at rest in his grasp. He spoke to the white men like niggers and to the niggers like dogs. Amos would rise to his feet when the horse went by along the edge of the shallow drainage ditch by the field, and watch the long regular swinging shuffle of the horse's walk (not such a fine horse, he thought) and study the slump and curve of the man's seat and the stain of sweat down his back and around his belt line and the forward thrust of his head, as though he were getting there in thought long before the horse. He would stand watching while he bent his burning shoulders back till the blades touched and think: He's shore going after it; he's getting it done.

The planter's name was Mays Johnson. Arney hated his guts and said so, but Amos did not hate him or like him either. He

and Mays Johnson stood on exactly the same emotional footing:
Mays Johnson hired and paid; Amos Dudley worked and got
paid.

For a week the weather was hot, calm and so dry the black
dust stayed gritty between your teeth all night even after you
washed. Maybe too hot, thought Amos. Maybe too dry. (He
was feeling his way into the weather question in the strange
country where the clouds bulked over no hill and the sun, setting in no valley, dropped red and single into the woods.)
Maybe that's what's dogging Mays Johnson.

He and Arney and five other white pickers slept in a pine
slab house on the edge of a burnt deadening. The trees had been
ringed to kill them in the winter and sage fire had got loose
amongst them. Charred black and thin, they stood by dozens,
close together, yet every one alone, like a crowd of city folk.
To see the moon through them was frightful. One of the men
in the slab house picked a guitar. They called him Drew. Amos
never knew any other name but that. There was the vague hint
of hard times about him, and he never talked much about his
home folks, though he was from the hills like the rest of them.
After supper had been sent to them and eaten, they would sit
by the fire that Arney would build at sundown like a rite, something he couldn't stand being without, and Drew would sing
songs, more to himself than to the others, though if they listened
he didn't mind. One song Amos remembered for a long time.
Drew had got it from a Negro he was picking by one day. It
went soft and stepping and eager:

> *Green corn! Green corn!*
> *All I want in the whole creation's*
> *A little bitty wife and a big plantation.*
> *Green corn!*

Drew was a young man with something ravaged about his smooth round face that was always sunreddened, as though like his songs, it stayed innocent in continual harshness.

One night there was a waning moon that you couldn't see plain because the sky had been shrouded all afternoon with a dark haze, more like high dust than cloud.

Mays Johnson had snapped his whip above a cotton row to make a picker answer him. The picker was Arney.

"I hope to tell you," Arney said straightening, "you better thank the good Lord you never touched me with thatair thing."

"Beg your pardon," said Mays Johnson. "I thought you's a nigger."

"That aint no thing to think," said Arney.

"How much you reckon you picked so far?" Mays Johnson asked.

"I don't weigh in till dark," said Arney. He shifted the sack off his shoulder and held the strap up to Mays Johnson. "You want to go weigh it now, you can."

The horse, unusually nervous, jumped back from the gesture. Mays Johnson took advantage of the few feet between them to shrug and ride on. Three rows over a Negro sang soft scornful words, as though to himself.

That night Arney sat silent by the fire and Drew trailed a mournful minor key off the strings again and again and did not sing.

Amos lay on his stomach to keep it from hurting. It hurt anyway. He had got too hot in the field and drunk too big a bait of cold artesian water afterwards. The Delta water had a flat sulphur taste. He found the same taste later in the greens and stew that they all grubbed up together out of a pot the Negro brought, and in the coffee. He could taste it in his mouth now while the wind rose and blew against his cheek. The wind tasted of the water too. He went off back of the house to the edge of the woods and threw up. Arney came looking for him.

"I want some good water," he said, almost a child's plaint in the tone, as though Arney were to blame.

"I can't get you none," Arney said anxiously, accepting the blame.

The others had gone inside. Through the deadening Amos could see the foggy moon lying sideways. To the left of the house the fields spread away, falling downward into the dark. Off to the right and back, the woods were sucking the wind off the fields. You could hear it going thin and silky in the treetops. The night noises were still.

Amos thought: There is no hollow nor ravine nor valley nor gully nor bluff to hide me. There is no hill to watch from. There is nothing to do but wait.

The men had not gone to bed. Three were sitting in the corner around the lantern playing seven-up. One of them swore constantly, hurling the limp cards down with his whole arm as though he swung a hatchet. Only Drew was lying on his pallet of loose cotton.

Pickens, an older man with a bearded face, looked up from the game. "I reckon we aint going to get that rain," he said.

Drew rose quietly, picked up his guitar, and walked toward the door. Every eye followed him. Then they heard it too. "Lord to God," one said, low, and they all five plunged after Drew in what was immediately the dark, for the lantern went crashing first thing. Amos jammed through the door with them and for a maddening moment whatever his feet was striking would not let him run. Then he knew he was running across a man. He shoved frantically at the dark fallen shoulders lifting in front of him, and jumped clear. He landed hard on his heels on a thin surface that splintered drily and broke beneath him, so that he tore away in a heightened panic, thinking for a minute he was in Yocona walking to the privy on a black night and had fallen through the old well. But when he thought this he was far back of the slab house toward the woods and the wind was striking. He caught hold of an oak shoot as tall as his shoulder and went down with it, pasted to the ground like a worm. His stomach heaved drily and his mouth lay open against the ground. He could not see the others, or where they'd gone, what refuge they'd found without him. He believed that he lay alone under the storm. In the corner of his eye he saw strange shapes hurtle past. A moan and crash came from the deadening and a heave and crash from the woods. Rain was in the wind, great ropes of driven water, and his face was blinded in a drench of mud. He bit the mud back from his tongue, smelling the stench of the black over-ripe earth, thinking: It's bound to give out sometime. It can't last forever.

Then it passed. Arney was beside him. "I swanee," Arney said. Amos looked. The slab house was gone. It did not look as if anything had ever been there.

Later, Amos was to see bigger houses floated away in flood water, trees and fences and stock going quietly away like rubbish, and it always gave him the same shock as when he looked at the ground where the slab house had been: that something could turn into nothing that fast.

One at a time, the other men drew near through the rain.

"Well," old Pickens said, "I was a-laying out chonder a-wondering what if the rain had done blowed through on my bed."

"Reckon that's a thing can't nobody vouch for, Pickens," said another.

"Some fellow in the next county going to wake up to a mighty handy pile of kindling wood," said Pickens.

"If Mays Johnson aint already sent a nigger to gather hit up."

Amos called Arney aside. "I'm going in to Leland," he said. "This aint no way to live."

And he took Arney and left them standing by the ruined deadening, making jokes in the rain.

In Leland, in the deep dark along towards dawn, a sensation of falling woke Amos out of an exhausted sleep. He sat up, his mind working away of its own accord. He shook Arney.

"I got to go back out yonder," he said, groping for his overalls.

"Crazy," Arney said. "Three miles out there in the dark. What for?"

"I broke Drew's git-tar when I run," said Amos. "I just now recollected. I got to pay him for it."

"Give it to him tomorrow," said Arney. "Give it to him when you go to work."

"I aint going back to work out there," said Amos.

"You got to go to get paid," Arney said.

"That's right." He sat on the edge of the bed and thought. Sleep weighted him into the pillow.

I seen him lift it . . . it was to stop me, I thought . . . being scared . . . I hit and jumped . . . he was just a-walking along when we run . . . I heard it break . . . heard the well cover busting open . . . I never meant. . . .

The sun blazed out dry the next day and by afternoon Arney was picking again. Amos went to Mays Johnson to collect his wages.

He found Mays in the commissary weighing in cotton sacks at the scales. "Get on back to the field," Mays said. "You're late."

"I aint going back," Amos said.

"You're signed up to pick on through."

"I never signed nothing."

"Your friend signed you up."

"I never knowed nothing about it."

Mays Johnson laid down his pencil on the ledger and came around the high desk, just barely shifting his pistol as though it galled him. Amos saw him do it, yet it never really entered his head that Mays would use any force on him.

"You better get on back to work," said Mays.

Amos said nothing.

"I'm paying good enough," Mays said.

Now I got him, Amos thought.

"I reckon not," he said, and looked absently out of the window.

Mays turned angrily to the safe and pulled out a cigar box heavy with cash. "You aint getting a cent more than I hired you for," he said. He flung the money down across the ledger and turned back to the safe, saying in an undertone, "Damned hillbilly shyster."

Amos gathered the money into his hand, spit on the open ledger and walked away. He felt the chill walk up his back as he reached the door, just before the open hand whaled him on the shoulder and he pitched sidelong down the steps. The big man towered thigh and shoulder above him. From the ground Amos regarded him with the same lack of feeling he had felt toward the whip, the gun, the horse, and the sweat-soaked shoulders passing.

"Never set foot on my place again," Mays Johnson said. "Unless you want a bullet in your god-damned belly."

He meant that, Amos decided, walking away. I reckon that's the way they do down here, every fellow grabbing for himself. Like every fellow running for himself when the wind—

He stopped in the middle of the road. He had forgotten about

Drew. He weighed the importance to himself of squaring with Drew over the guitar against the possibility of getting a bullet in his belly. Arney could tend to it for him, he decided.

By spring he owned a grocery store in Leland. He sub-rented the place to start with from a lawyer who drank all the time and was not at all disturbed by the sight of canned tomatoes and flour barrels pushed up next to his law books. By the first of the year the lawyer needed money so badly that he moved the law books into his room at the boarding house and sold the office to Amos for a small down-payment.

Arney had gone back to the hills soon after picking was over. He went to Greenville for a few days with his cotton money and spent it all on a girl who sang with the showboat. He came by to see Amos before he took the road to Yocona.

"What you want me to tell your folks?"

"Tell them howdy," said Amos. "Tell them I'll be along some time soon to visit with them."

"S'posing you go broke?" Arney asked.

"I aint aiming to go broke," Amos said.

"They aint going to think kindly of me," said Arney, "taking you over here and not bringing you back." He fingered a fancy bow-tie with a snap band. "How about one of these on a credit, Amos?"

"You don't want to go toting that thing back," said Amos, "when you can get one just like it up at Johnston's at Toccopola."

"I reckon not."

He was going then, not even offended, not even catching on that Amos didn't think his credit was any good.

"Arney?"

He turned back.

"Tell Ephraim—"

"What, Amos? Tell Ephraim what?"

"I forgot what I set out to say," Amos said and went back to winding odd scraps of string on a big nail stuck between the stocked shelves.

Alone that night in the rooming house bed, which he shared on some nights with drummers or other travellers, he lay and cried like a child. He cried because he missed big Arney Talliafero who was admiring and good to him for no reason, and from Yocona. He knew as a foregone conclusion that Arney was not worth a nickel and never would be; if it came to a choice he would rather be Mays Johnson than Arney any day; but he did not think any of these things when he lay missing Arney and crying. He had not cried since the night he learned how much his mother loved him.

5

In the Leland boarding house, Newt Simpson, the lawyer who drank and needed money, would stick his head out the door every time Amos came up the stairs and call: "How about a little toddy, little Dudley?"

Amos always refused. He knew that Newt Simpson had friends he could drink with any time at the saloon, and he figured that Newt just wanted somebody to stand for the whisky. Once Newt said to him when he refused: "A man's got to have somewhere important to get to if he won't drink whisky. Where you got to get to, Mr. Dudley, suh?"

He used the voice on Amos that he saved for law cases, a shrewd, mannered drawl that put Amos in the box.

"I don't know, sir," Amos answered quickly and shut the door of his room between them. He did not like to be spoken of lightly. It scared him to be asked that. He would have to lie down for a minute every time. At last he would decide: he wants me to feed him whisky; that gave him the strength to get up. It never occurred to him that Newt Simpson liked him.

He worked early and late, and loneliness crabbed him like age. The only nourishment he could afford to offer his heart and stay on was the thought of Ephraim, a thin gruel, but it kept him there. And the heart, ravenous and patient, ran the fences night and day. In the spring it escaped straight into slavery.

He saw the man first, then the girl. The man was heavy-set and rather short, with thick graying hair above an inattentive face. He wore a light tan riding coat, comfortably soiled, and high boots that he had not polished for himself. Amos stood by the rail at the mule auction. Other odds and ends of the growing Delta town stood near him: a Jewish merchant with two sons attached; two Chinamen, matched to the eyeball; a Syrian with meaty bared forearms rammed across the fence; and many the likes of Amos Dudley. But the men who were like the man in the riding coat stood down a ways, shifting about with talk and laughter in no unfriendly group, yet they let you know that they had money in their pockets and land over somewhere, not far. They had come to buy, not watch. The man whose boot heels set careless and deep in the earth did not bother with much talk and hardly at all with laughter.

Amos punched the Syrian. "Who is he?"

"Don' know. Him there? Don' know."

He tapped the Jewish merchant. "Who is the fellow yonder?"

"The gentleman in the tan coat you are speaking of? Morgan. Mr. Ross Morgan. Of Lake Washington. Very important man. You have connections?"

"No," said Amos and stared on, more dreamy than covetous,

anonymous beneath his hat brim. But when Mays Johnson
strode in amongst the planters, looked over a dozen mules and
voiced the high bid for five, Amos knew that with enough land
he could stand there too, and look big and talk small and punch
mules in the rump and bid, that they had all grubbed in the
ground once, same as him, and oughtn't to forget it. Them or
their daddies, he thought, and studied Ross Morgan again who
wouldn't quite fit in with the run of his mind.

The horse with the girl on its back stepped right past him:
its hoof flung dirt on his sleeve.

He was shocked. He didn't think a girl ought to be out here
with nobody but men. Then he saw how the auctioneer tipped
his hat to her and waved the crowd back from the rail and
blocked out the other riders who also had horses to show and
sell. Tagged and tied at a fence over in the green pasture beyond, the mules stamped at the new grass, eating right up to
the pants of the Negro boys who sat with the lead ropes, watching. The planters drew nearer the rail. The wind died down
and the smells of sweat and manure smoked sunward with the
dust. Everything watched. Once again the arrogant hooves trod
past him. He saw the clean undersweep of the girl's chin, the
small gloveless hands easy and sure on the reins, and the small
taut shoulders retreating.

He learned a lot from her in the moment that was just beyond
the moment where the crowd might have laughed or swopped
glances, dismissing her in some little way. He concluded rap-
idly: In order to get in where you didn't belong you had to be
good enough first, and next you had to be sure enough. She was
good and she was sure, and his heart which had feared for her
discredit, beat proud and quiet within him in time with the
proud tread of the hooves.

It was a mare she rode, bright bay and nervously alive in its feet and neck, with a strong narrow head that swung and flicked dangerously. But she was not going to fall off, Amos thought, and the smell of sweat and leather came heavily by again with the sound of the saddle, and bit foam lay on his cheek. She drew in, tightening, shoulders leaning; her heel touched and the black hooves lifted, slow at first, the eyes and mouth in outrage against the bit, then faster—they pounded in his head with the leap of the dirt and foam and swung away, pounding fast; above the leap of the black mane and the bright bay withers churning, above the flying dirt and the speed and the shrunken ring spinning like a little disc, her face bore down upon him, a point of absolute stillness, was whirled by and returned, white and alive, but more still than ice. He became the face, whirled as the face was whirled, immediate with all speed, skill and rightfulness.

As suddenly as a ball hurled against wood, the face from a point rebounded, ricochetted out of his vision so that he turned his head dizzily twice before he found her. The horse was still plunging, but now only in one spot. He found himself too, fallen across the rail, his hat in the hand that had snatched it off his head, and the echoes of his own Comanche yell of delight still ringing horribly in the air.

He was right about her. She wasn't going to fall. She had kept her seat by the barest margin of skill. She rode away from the men who had run out to help. The horse went round again slowly, nostrils flared. Of everybody there, the girl was the only one who did not look at Amos Dudley. She was not going to look at him either. A man was pulling him back from the rail. "What the hell's the matter with you, fellow?" The planters pointed. "Something ought to be done to him." "Is he drunk? Who is he? Crazy fool." "I know his name, now wait a minute."

She was not going to look. They clapped for her. She was

never going to look. He struck off the arm that held him, drew his hat down to the ears and fled. Leland was all but empty. He passed down the muddy main street, over the plank sidewalks, past the locked stores. Just off the main street sat the newly white-washed one-room building he had turned into a grocery store. He stood in the door and checked the shelves with his eye.

"I'll have to sell out at cost," he thought. "I've got to get straight back where I belong."

He locked the door and went back to the boarding house. The afternoon was softly bright, just aging, and very still. He wanted to see Yocona more than ever then; he wanted the shapes of the hills. He came to the boarding house instead which, like everything else in the flat land, was without size, neither large nor small, and he himself entering took on that quality, and sat down on the bare white-enameled bed, miserably ashamed, and not knowing if he in his shame was large or small. Then he heard a grunt and a throat-clearing from the stair, and in the hall the thump of old feet coming down, not heel and toe, but altogether, like a hoof. A door slammed.

Amos went down to the saloon and bought a glass full of whisky.

Newt Simpson was asleep, lying clothed on the unmade bed with a shelf of law books that smelt like old wallpaper, perilously atilt above his head. Amos held the whisky to his nose and shook him.

"I'm not asleep," Newt Simpson said and opened his eyes. He saw the whisky. "To have so much sense, Mr. Dudley, you show precious little judgment. You think I walked all the way from out yonder for you to ply me with this accursed bribe?" He clothed his naked face in glasses.

Amos set the glass on the table, to which Newt Simpson

presently returned it empty.

"Who is she?" he asked.

"Ross Morgan's daughter," said Newt Simpson.

He was outraged. "No wonder!" he cried at once. "I reckon she did belong there. I reckon she can do anything she gets damn good and ready to do. She don't have to care where the horse shit falls. She don't have to clean it up. He's rich, aint he?"

"Ross Morgan? Yes. That is, he has always given the appearance of being rich."

"I thought she just had nerve. I thought she had more nerve than I ever saw."

"Is that why you scared the horse? To see how much nerve she had?"

"I didn't know I was doing that. I was surprised as anybody."

"Ary Morgan," Newt Simpson said. "She has got nerve. She has a beautiful sister, for one thing. That must take considerable nerve."

"Nothing takes very much nerve if you're rich."

"Never having been rich, that is a conclusion I have no means of proving."

"I'm going home where I belong," Amos said.

"There are stories of many battles," Newt Simpson said, "and fair ladies said to have caused them. But I doubt if you would be interested."

"What did you say her name was?"

"Miss Ary Morgan. Ary. Like Mary."

"Ary. That's nobody's name."

"It's hers. And her sister, a pleasure to see, has such an ordinary name. Louise."

"You know them, Mr. Newt! You've been there!"

"Steady a minute. Hold a point, my boy. Don't jump the gun. Have a seat there. Let me instruct you, little Dudley.

"The Morgans have, as you say, considerable means. But money is not the principal thing which the Morgans would list among their possessions. The Morgans are a family both old and proud, river settlers of the Delta before the Delta was named. Before Gray ever shouldered arms against the Blue they had housed themselves to the best advantage in a brick mansion styled with such classical grace that no one had to speak of its size which is phenomenal. At this place, which they named Dellwood, they have multiplied, thriven and entertained so generously that none but a besotted and worthless ingrate would dare to mention that beyond producing children, cotton, and food in comparable quantities, they have never accomplished one noteworthy feat. A great supply of energy they have, but self-absorbent—it proceeds from the Morgans and returns thereto. They make their best appearance in a pack, covey, herd—no, pride: pride of lions. Yet singly, alas, they have left no mark on our fair state for bad or good. A distressing thought. I suspect that they likewise are distressed and make all the merrier: their social graces bloom, perfect, my boy, as the finest summer rose. At dawn. Their visitors—and they number many young men since Miss Louise and Miss Ary have come to flower—enter those portals with the proper speech borne upon the tongue."

"I don't know nothing about all that," Amos said. "I just don't know nothing about it."

"I thought not," said Newt Simpson. "Reach back behind you for that bottle that's propping up the bottom row of books. A spot for you. And me."

"Will you take me there?" Amos asked.

"You have driven me out of my office, known of old. You have put pork and beans and Garrett's snuff on shelves I badly needed for my law books. It was money that I needed most.

Nothing but money."

"I paid you fair and square," Amos said. "I don't owe you nothing."

"And neither do I, young man, owe you anything."

They stared at one another across the room.

Amos said: "But she is more than owing is." He was not thinking of Newt when he said it, nor of himself; in fact, he was not thinking at all, he just opened his mouth and that was what fell out of it.

"What day," Newt Simpson asked, "would you like to go?"

"I don't close up till Sunday."

6

That happened in May.

On a Sunday in September, Amos and Newt Simpson cooked a chicken on the iron stove at the grocery store, and afterwards went back to the boarding house where Newt took off his shoe and sock, exposing a large swollen dead-white foot and heated his bunion over the chimney of a coal oil lamp.

"I am going to die soon," Newt said. "My bunion has ceased to respond to the weather. Little changes presage great ones. And you have ceased to respond to the call of the fair lady of Dellwood."

It was the first Sunday Amos had stayed in Leland since the mule auction. It was the first Sunday he had not risen at three to ride out the long dawn on a mule rented cheap from an Italian café owner. It would be the first Sunday night he would not spend half-asleep in the saddle, rocked crudely on the rutted buckshot.

"Don't you feel all right?" Newt Simpson asked.

"She don't even know I'm not there today, I bet," Amos said.

But that was not the real thing that worried him. What kept him from going was the company he had to keep on the way home. Along in July sometime (he couldn't be sure, for it seemed after the first time it happened it had been happening all along), a man began to ride back from Dellwood with him, misty at first and only for a few minutes, but of late plainer than daylight and every step of the way till dawn. It was a man on a horse, a tall man in handsome, casually worn clothes, and the horse he rode was twice as high again as the plodding mule. He kept in step with the mule only by reining the horse to a high-hoofed prance while the bit foam flew and the saddle strained. He rode with his eyes straight ahead and never spoke, forging into the dark with no eye for the snake in the road or the rabbit and only a glance for the deer. The sweat smells of his fine horse and the good leather smell ran like a stain across the night, and he turned Amos Dudley's heart to stone. It was not until the last time that he knew why. He cared nothing for the man himself, but Ary Morgan cared for him. He was the man she thought she ought to have.

"There aint really but one difference between me and them," Amos said to Newt Simpson. "Land."

"Did you tell them that?" Newt asked and wound back around his bunion a bandage which had been cut from an old shirt cuff and buttoned snugly at the undercurve of his toe.

"I aint said but three words since I been there. Four. Morning, much obliged, and goodbye. They don't do a blessed thing but talk and laugh and eat."

"You haven't got to talk with Miss Ary?"

"Every now and again. It comes hard to me too. Real hard."

"But if you had some land you'd know just what to say."

Amos saw the crooked old fingers methodically hooking his

shoe laces. The smell of old flesh waxed rank. Newt might be particular about his starched collars, but that was as far as it went. He never washed and his gray suit hung in a drab area of cloth from shoulder to cuff. He drank with anybody who would pay and hear him talk. He took little cases for Italians and Chinamen, and played poker with lumber riff-raff; and folks scratched off his debts saying, "That's Mr. Newt; I'll never get it"; and he knew it and let them and even traded with them again for that very reason.

"You aint worth a dime," Amos said.

The old man rose and stamped his foot to set the shoe. He regarded Amos from out a fortress of shrewd and untrustworthy dignity. "I never claimed to be," he said, and the gates banged shut on so much stone.

Driven to restlessness by a four-months' habit gone, Amos walked through town and out of it on first one side, then the other, and knew for the first time in his life how badly a man can ache to give up. Every time a street ended, land started, mocking him, corn dripping silks and half-picked cotton hanging, all Sunday quiet with settled dust, as though after rain. Other men's land. He knew that all over the Delta the banks were selling cut-over land for little or nothing an acre, but the thought of loans and debts appalled him. He had never been in a bank but once in his life and that was to change the forty dollars that were left from the money he made at Yocona into silver dollars which he carried with him today, twenty to each coat pocket. He placed a hand gently over each pocket and the Yocona River flowed round him again and Ned and Ephraim stood by a Leland gate, quarreling.

It was not the giving up so much as the finding somebody to give up to. He wouldn't have it known within himself that he gave up to the Morgans, or to Newt Simpson. Certainly not to Ephraim. And not to the man who rode the tall horse, either. Who was fit for Amos Dudley to give up to?

Dark found him out from town in the field where the mule auction had been, leaning alone over the rail, and by that time he had the answer, which was why he had come. A little moon floated out, thin as a coin's edge, and three bright planets burned near her. It was a strange sight. He hoped it would not be the world's end, with him so out of pocket. When Ephraim had his teeth pulled out, he buried them in the back yard so he wouldn't have to look for them here there and yonder on judgment day. Amos happily remembered that the moon had first to turn to blood. It probably took a big moon to do that right. He came back to the business in hand.

He thought at first that he would say simply to God in heaven that he wanted to be sent back home, and so he stood with head flung way back as though to let rain fall in his face, and his eyes plumbed the heavens with a certain confidence and familiarity, now that he had the moon business settled. He knew long before he spoke that God was aware of him, that he had, to put it one way, stepped into the cage; but he knew also that God had not looked at him yet and would not, as a matter of policy, until he spoke. So before he spoke, he thought twice, and pride stung him arrow straight under the sky.

He said to himself that he would not lie, asking for a thing he wanted only because he couldn't get what he wanted most; even if there was no good in what he wanted most, he would not lie, even if there was no reason for having it outside of wanting it, he would not lie. Then, quick, he saw that even if he would be wrong in asking what he wanted most, if he were only wrong *enough* that wrong would work to send him home; so in asking what he wanted most, he would have at least a crack at it, with home for sure if God angered, and home with peace at that, outdone not by Ephraim or Newt Simpson or the Morgans or the tall-horse one, but by the One whose hand had jerked him out of the river to the top of a twenty-foot bluff.

So he drew himself up and flung it out, saying (whether out loud or not he did not know): "I've got to have that land. I've got to have Ary Morgan. You've got to give me the land. I can't get it no other way. You've got to give me Ary. I can't get her no other way either."

He thought he saw the stars smoulder and the moon rock like a cradle.

His bravado was gone. He fell across the railing hands down, crying, loud and silent at once: "Why did you show me things I can't have? Why did you let that man come to ride with me?"

When he looked up, the night was bigger than his eyes dared see; it fixed him, flaming. He faced it out for a moment only, then he turned and fled again in naked shame across the field to town and behind him rang the silent scorn of heaven.

He locked himself in his room that night and lay in bed as stiff and wide-eyed as an unfound corpse. He hoped he hadn't overdone it.

It was his belief that blasphemy provoked catastrophe.

7

Except for the clothes on his back and the forty silver dollars of the original $96.84, the entire goods and chattel of Amos Dudley changed hands within a week. The suit and the valise he had bought with grocery earnings for visiting at Dellwood he had swopped to the Italian café owner for the mule. With the money left in the till on Friday night he had bought a pistol and bullets. The pistol rode under his belt next to the pocket where the store keys used to be. Since 9:30 Tuesday night, the keys along with the store and everything in it belonged to a Chinaman named Wang Tu Jones. In place of the keys Amos had a paper; in place of the store the keys said he had were six hundred acres of land the paper said he had. The paper was deed and title, won by Wang Tu Jones, who had never seen the six hundred acres, in a poker game from a one-armed saw-mill man, who had never seen them either.

It remained for Amos Dudley to go and see, but first he as good as tied the Chinaman in the back yard until Newt could see if the deed was clear. It was Saturday before the mail limped through. He told the Chinaman it was all fixed, and Wang Tu Jones, who had already snipped out things quite neatly in his head (possibly from the moment he crossed the threshhold and saw standing behind the counter where the lamp burned, the young man whose great preoccupation outburned the lamp and shrank the store to the size of a toy box)—Wang Tu Jones, in his sporty little white man's shirt and trousers, made no reply except to shake his hands delicately and jabber in shrill Chinese over Amos's shoulder to a customer. Chinamen seemed to have grown up out of the ground: Amos stumbled clumsily among them, getting out, and they glided aside like fish.

He went back to Newt Simpson.

Newt had done a lot in twenty minutes. He was collared and brushed, the bed was made, he sat in a chair wedged between his desk and the foot of the bed, and laid heavy black words to paper with a squeaky pen. It was a moment before he would glance up.

"Well, well," he said smiling and laid the pen aside. "Well, well, little Dudley. So he's a landowner now."

"I just come to say goodbye, and much obliged, Mr. Newt, taking me over to Dellwood and all."

"Oh that. Glad to be of service, Mr. Dudley. There's many a young man here and there, I make bold to say, to whom I have extended a glad palm, steadying him past the slippery rock or over the treacherous gulf. To whom did I first give such aid? To none other than that great statesman, my old classmate, Lucius Quintus Cincinnatus Lamar. He was poor in Latin. But he had the steady fire in the blue eye, my boy, the same that I perceive in your own, and in the years since last I saw him, I have learned the name of that fire. It is called Success!"

"You look mighty nice, Mr. Newt. All slicked up."

"Oh that." He hit a casual bullseye in the spittoon. "I am expecting clients. Momentarily. Nothing too important as yet, but I expect—developments." He rose unsteadily; his scaly old fingers shook across the page smearing the fresh ink. Amos took the stain on his own hand. He stood in the door. There were no clients coming; he knew that.

"What are you going to do, Mr. Newt?" He blurted it.

The old voice came back at him, soft and steady. "What do you suggest, little Dudley?"

From across the threshhold Amos looked into the small over-crowded room where crated books and trunks and canned rations called to mind a freakish sort of journey, not willed or even wished, but a progress just the same, like that of a river moving deeper and dirtier, more sluggish but stronger too, going downward with the tilt of the land, and one step retraced across the threshhold would have sunk him in it, and God, the deed, and Ary Morgan, that now so potently flanked him, all would slip away, lost along green banks. He pushed back from the door the length of his arm and answered:

"Nothing."

"So I thought," Newt Simpson returned with grave dignity and shut the door softly in his face.

So Amos rode out on his own journey alone to see what he alone possessed, and what he saw cleared the fumes of miracle from his head. There was no need for anybody to help him find it once he got near it, for the cleared and planted land of other owners came neatly to his borders on four sides. He circled it carefully, the matted wilderness, left to bloom and rot in ignorance of which was which, useless as the stone in the peach. The broad tail of a bayou lay in its center and flooded outward in swamp where the big trees grew and the heavy vine. It was easy to tell where the swamp stopped; the timber had been felled to the last tree and cane grew thick as grass, sixteen feet high.

On his second trip around Amos marked what looked like a hunter's road angling off through the trees. It had been a dry fall; through a break he saw the bayou, low as a branch and crawling with green slime. Among the trees the light was green and dim as dusk after a storm, and like dusk alive with mosquitoes and gnats. He heard the snakes thrash and slip away at his coming and once as close as his elbow the undergrowth leaped sounding as a large shape tore hidden away.

His face was wet as water and every thread of his clothes clung to him. He wiped his eyes to see ahead and batted the thick insects, thinking, Damn if you couldn't ride off in here and just never come back. But he went on.

The road twisted left, climbing up a little from the slope to the bayou. A sharper turn and the trees gave way to a clearing. Even the mule stopped to look. At the edge of the clearing was a house mounted on high cypress pillars, the whole trunks of enormous trees. A flight of steps ran steeply up to the front porch. Over the railing hung pieces of tarpaulin and an old seine; they had rotted together into one cloth that broke into dust at the touch. Under the steps a boat sat on the dried-out gray soil. Two lengths of plank lay in it, a tin can, and an old black boot. The porch ran the front of the house. The walls were of hewn logs chinked with white clay. The door had no latch; it swung inward at his touch. The large square room contained nothing but a fireplace, a broken chair, one-half of an iron stove that looked to have been sliced off from the other half with a knife, a piece of fishing pole, and some empty cans scattered about the room as though they had been hurled at the walls in a rage. The raw inner walls, like the outside ones, wore a clean look that no disuse could efface because it was born of soundness. The house did not shake under his step. He came out the door again, descended the steps halfway and sat down. The mule hung its head over the rail and breathed out, stirring a span of dust.

"Well," said Amos to the mule. "I guess we're home."

Later he discovered the narrow shed room and the flight of back steps with the landing. Below the steps he built a smudge for himself and the mule out of a rotten log. He was hungry and tired to the bone and any fool would have gone back to Cypress Landing for the night.

Ladder of angels, he sat and thought. Ladder of angels.

Between the first time he said it and the second time, deep night fell.

From every limb, far into the wood the tree frogs called for rain, and from every dry leaf the crickets sang, and frogs by the hundreds intoned at one another across the low bayou. Then stillness curled in close like a breeze and Amos, with knocking heart, went down the steps toward whatever it was that waited for him on the edge of the trees.

He had rushed in, silent with craft and desperation, when the moist gleam of a white tooth showed him what it was: a little old black Negro man, who cried: "Fo' Gawd, boss!" when Amos, reasonless with new disappointment, struck him down. He cowed on the ground until Amos scooped him up. He was light as a stick-man with small muscle and smaller bone laid loosely together beneath the flesh. He led Amos through the trees a little way to where a well spouted out of a pipe—the water was sweet and iron-cold without a trace of sulphur. Amos drank and plunged his head into the stream; the water ran down his neck and shoulders. He went to get the mule.

The Negro man took him through the wood to a cleared field between the trees and cane: ten acres or more it seemed in the dark, planted largely in cotton with a few rows of corn and a vegetable garden at one end near the shack. The Negro's wife was an Indian woman with large sagging breasts, a massive face, a quantity of greasy black hair tugging loose at the nape of her neck, and tiny feet shod with beaded moccasins. A poster big as a window was tacked on one wall. "See Ouida," it read, "Princess of the Savage Sioux. Savage Tribal Dances. Mysterious Rites of Sun Maiden Exposed. Secret Indian Herb Cures Revealed. Five Cents Only." This and a bright painting of a slim Indian girl sitting cross-legged, with big eyes beamed all around like pictures of the sun. A great many gaudy strings of beads hung on a nail and one whole shelf was laden with bottles full of liquid, some red, some yellow and some dark brown. While Amos ate, she opened a yellow one and drank it off like soda pop. Some black books, all alike, were stacked in one corner.

The Negro man, whose name was Eccles, told Amos that the two of them would work for him now. Up till the high water ran them out, he said. Amos said it looked like to him he would have found them living up in the other house, but Eccles shook

his head. "White folks house," he said. Amos asked who had
been there before he came. Eccles shook his head again. "They
comes and goes," he said. Amos turned to the Indian woman who
had yet to say the first word. "Ouida," he said. She sat on a low
chair with her chin in her palm, her dainty beaded feet set side
by side together, knees wide, cross-eyed from staring at nothing.
Eccles shook his head a third time. "Name of Nellie," he said
and grinned, ear to ear. He went to the sign of the Indian maiden
and drew a line with his finger under the lettered name. "Nellie,"
he said.

The black books were Bibles. Nellie had not left the travelling
show without loot. When Amos went back to the high house,
leading the mule close behind for company, he carried a Bible
with him and a coal oil lamp.

The house grew up out of the dark before him; the long back
steps fell down to meet him. He staked out the mule, climbed
to the landing, and lighted the lamp. In so much darkness the
little light seemed far too bold. He had drunk and eaten and still
his stomach caved like hunger and he was dry to the bone. He
dimmed the light till it was a bare excuse to see by and leaning
close, down on one elbow, he opened the Bible. He had to look
for a long time, here and there, checking a section at a time,
but at last he found it.

"Behold a ladder set up on the earth, and the top of it reached
to heaven: and behold the angels of God ascending and de-
scending on it."

He read through it again and noticed that it said Jacob
dreamed. That threw him for a minute. He did not want to be
caught fooling away time over a dream. Then he saw how that
was. Another man wrote it down; that man called Jacob "he."
To that other man it was a dream. But Jacob knew it was no
dream.

He read it over twenty times and though the darkness that sang on held steady about him, the unhurried words fell bright through his mind, going down golden through deep water, and when one passed another came, ceaselessly, shining.

8

For six solid weeks the weather held. Terrible dry thunder-storms split the nights and blew up out of towering clouds at odd hours of the day. Quick showers spattered the dust and passed on. The heat held until early November when the nights turned a solid windless cold and by day the sun came red through the dust. The woods and fields were everywhere a dark dust-coated green, hateful to the eye.

On a Wednesday morning Amos rode out at dawn to where the sawmill gang was clearing out the wilderness. He knew the weather was about to break. He rode with his ears pricked for the snarl and return of the cross-cut saws, the shouts of the work crew, the jangle of chains and harness and the pistol-loud blows of axes and whips. Hearing nothing, he thought resign-edly, Something's broken, and wondered if he'd have to fix that too. He had long since quit wondering whether or not he could fix anything that wouldn't work because he knew that whoever has to get a thing fixed will do it while the rest sit by and tell over the breakdown.

Two logging wagons were pulled up among the new stumps. Tall uncut trees stood naked to the cold; their grey trunks gleamed with dew. The work gang of some dozen Negroes sat in one wagon or leaned against it, talking a little. One who sat with his feet dangling out the back was whittling and humming to himself. Their breath smoked on the air and their black wrists below the sleeves of the blue denim work jackets were grey with cold. Amos rode into them.

"You aim to set here and freeze with that timber standing there ready to cut?"

Their eyes slid past his own.

"Naw suh," one said. "I'o'no suh."

"Sho ready to cut," said another and looked at the trees.

"Rain coming," Amos said. "I got up this morning knowing it, feeling it. Rain could start in the morning. What's the matter with you? You think you're going to get any timber clear of this mud once it sets in? Get a wagon caught in that buckshot and you won't have nothing left but a pile of kindling wood and a wind-broke team. What's the matter with you?"

After a while, one said: "Mist' Dubard."

"Yes suh," said the other, "hit's Mist' Dubard."

"Mist' Dubard aint here," said the one sitting in the wagon and he just barely looked over his shoulder toward the second wagon.

The woman Amos had not noticed sat on a wide board thrown across the front of the wagon bed. She was thus a little above them and a little off to the side, in just the relative position to them of a mother who sits out with some sewing and watches her children play, and Amos saw the reason why he had come on as mean a bunch of Negroes as you could find waiting placid and content together. She did not look old (as a matter of fact, he never did know her age; he never thought to ask probably because she appeared not to know herself), but she made him feel very young, either young or not in it, as though she surveyed his prodding the Negroes toward work exactly as she would have looked at a child playing soldier or at a man asleep fighting a dream.

He took off his hat and went to her. "I beg your pardon,

ma'am," he said. "I didn't notice you's here."

"I just come down to say that Pat aint coming to work. Him and Mr. Stacey had words last night and then Pat hops on this other man and cuts the side of his face off."

Amos waited for her to go on, and she saw him wait and added, as though from politeness: "Still bleeding."

"Who?"

"You don't know him. Eps Wilson. The man Pat lit into."

"Can I do anything for you?" he asked. He fenced around asking her exact connection with the men in the fight.

He thought for a minute she dipped snuff and that she was going to spit, not contemptuously, but simply to show that her own inner systems of control were working.

"I just come to say Pat won't be down to boss," she repeated. "Mr. Stacey will more than likely send a man on soon as one comes in. I reckon, though, you can give me a hand down out of this wagon."

She came at him slowly over the side of the wagon, moving her feet in the ponderous manner of the very old when they first get up. He saw that she was pregnant. She turned away from him, holding on to the muddy wheel with both hands and breathing hard.

"Will you be all right?"

She gave him a glance over her shoulder; her eyes were a warm blue and seemed about to laugh. Then she walked away. She wore black high-laced shoes that were perfectly flat and broad and looked to have been made for an old man. The shoes were cracked at the seams and crusted with mud, but her faded skirt was perfectly clean. She pulled her sweater about her walking, in a slow strong deliberate motion that separated the threads in the back.

Before she was even out of sight, Amos was up and at the

work gang and soon the chains were playing out and axes and crosscut saws and timber hooks were swinging. He waded right into the strange equipment, guessing the use of this and that before anybody had to tell him and by the time the new foreman rode out, the left-over logs from yesterday were trimmed and loaded and another big one was shaking loose among the treetops, forming in that high world an unsteadiness and outrage that would ever panic the birds and squirrels. A fleet of crows, atilt like a black sail, abandoned the whole area and with their leaving the loud work went on in an atmosphere of stillness.

At mid-morning Amos rode to the sawmill. It was set up at the end of a spur track about two miles away. Amos found Stacey loading lumber on the open rail cars. The spur track ran through the stacks of sawn lumber. Two Negroes stood on each stack and heaved the yellow planks to Negroes on the rail cars.

"Dudley," Stacey said, "I'm just a poor ignorant bastard from Alabama. Would you mind telling me if you folks over here know what rain is when you see it?"

"You must never been here in the winter," Amos said.

"Hell, boy. I been in Miss'ippi eight years come spring, cutting Delta timber. But I never seen nothing like this."

"It's just about ready to break," Amos said.

"Tomorrow or next day," said Stacey. "I felt it this morning time I woke up."

"Two more days ought to clear me down to the bayou," Amos said.

"Gawd," said Stacey and spit. "It'll take a good three days, then some bastard'll bust a gut. I done tole you time and again: you can't work that crew after sundown."

"Once the rain starts, they aint going to have nothing to do for the next four months but set on the front porch and study who'll lend them some money to buy some more likker."

"You tell 'em," Stacey said. "Sure, Dudley, go tell 'em that."

"If I get 'em to cut it, will you still pay 'em and buy it and saw it?"

"I aint standing back of no shootings and cuttings," said Stacey. "I had enough of that last night. Sure, Dudley. Bar shootings and cuttings."

"What happened to that woman?" Amos asked suddenly.

"Who? Dubard's wife? Oh, she just now got what stuff she had and left. Aint no place for a lone woman down here."

Beyond the rail cars a handful of shacks leaned every which way: one fairly good cabin they must have found there, the others with a scrap lumber base, square like a pig pen, and each covered with a tent canvas roof with a tin stove pipe plugged through. She'd lived in one of those, he guessed, and walked the plank walks across the dried chunky buckshot out to the road in front and to the privy and artesian well in back.

"Whereabouts she go to?" Amos asked.

"Into Cypress, I reckon. I seen her heading that way."

Amos climbed back on the mule. "She's five-six months on the way," Stacey said. "I never liked nothing I couldn't set in the saddle to ride."

Amos said quickly and honestly: "I just felt sorry for her," and the blood came up in his face against Stacey who saw it and laughed, and paid no attention to his words. For Stacey was like the big revolving saw that clove the tree trunks with a roar and spew of sawdust. You couldn't feed that saw anything but lumber. Stacey had two or possibly three reasons for doing everything he did. He thought everybody else was the same way.

"Pat Dubard come back he'll skin the bark off you, boy," he

hollered after Amos and laughed and shouted to the Negroes.

Amos rode away. To himself he mildly reckoned that Pat Dubard wouldn't do that.

He was back on his own borders before he made out, far up the road ahead, the squarish, bulky figure in motion so steady that no step could be made out from any other. He caught up with her. Under one arm she had a bundle wrapped together in an old flour sack washed soft. From her other hand swung a couple of boilers and a skillet and coffee pot wired together through the handle eyes.

"Mrs. Dubard," he called.

She turned and waited. The air was still sharp, but there was a light covering of perspiration across her brow, under the thick wavy dark blonde hair which she wore parted in the middle and pulled back. Her head was broad like all the rest of her. He wondered anxiously if she was perspiring from weakness, but then he reckoned she had never been cold in her life.

"What you going to do?" he asked.

"Going into town. I got to find some place to stay."

"You aint got nobody?"

"Pat left last night. That's my husband."

"How long before he'll be back?"

"He aint coming back."

"Not at all?"

"He's tried hisself," she explained. "He went off twict before. Trouble both times. It's the likker fastens on him, goes stir crazy. He says to me, Thelma, the next time you see me having to go, you know it's for good and you go on peaceful, any way you choose. I knowed unless there was trouble he wouldn't go. But there was trouble."

It struck Amos that she did not seem to mind or not mind either. She was not expecting anything now. It was like he'd stopped anybody to ask how their family was and they'd told him. If he had said, Well, goodbye, and gone off down the road, she would have continued toward Cypress Landing without once looking back. Good Lord, he thought, in a desperation for her which she ought to have been feeling for herself; what does she think she's going to do?

"You see that next cut off," he said. "You take it on down to the left toward the bayou and follow it on around through the trees till you come to my house. I got to see this timber cleared out tonight and tomorrow night too, it looks like. You can stay there till I find you a ride to town or till Mr. Dubard comes back for you."

She smiled. The shelf of belly under the clean skirt thrust up as the baby kicked. "It's mighty kind of you," she said and moved on. He didn't know whether or not she was going to do what he said until he saw her take the road toward the bayou.

He dressed himself up for the sawmill gang. He stuck his pistol in his belt and borrowed a whip from a planter up the road. He coiled the whip around his wrist the way Mays Johnson wore it. Then he looked down at himself in his soiled work clothes and split shoes that the toes stuck through and at the patient mule that asked him no questions and told him no lies, and he knew it wouldn't work. The whip and the gun were other men maybe and all right, but they were not Amos Dudley. He returned the whip to the planter's commissary and the gun to the croker sack on his saddle. For his was a slow violence that came out best in work, and it was by main force of being there and working too that he kept the Negroes felling trees for four hours after sundown.

Just before the trouble in the air came to life, he called a halt. They drew near him sullenly, blue Negroes to a man, naked under their overalls and lavish with sweat in the cold air. Axes, crowbars and timber hooks hung from their hands. They herded closer, in a rough circle. Animals, he thought, more afraid than he could think about, knowing that if even the thought of fear showed on his face it would ruin him.

"Tomorrow night," he said to them. "Yes, tomorrow *night,* damn your eyes, and listen to me—tomorrow night there'll be something extra for you, something you'll like. I promise it to you."

He rode home without once turning his head, his back crawling with fear in the dark.

The next day he went into Cypress Landing and bought a barrel of corn whisky. He had no wagon; the mule pulled it out to the bayou on a borrowed water slide. For every tree that came down that night he promised a dipper full around. By dawn the twelve Negroes were tossing the cut timber into the wagons as carelessly as match sticks; their eyes were rolling loose in their heads like floating eggs, and they seemed not so much happy or drunk as simply puzzled as to what was happening and why.

Amos stared into the wagon. One of the logs there bore the whittled initials, A.A.D. They had come to the line he had set. They had passed it. Through the remaining trees the early light picked out the bayou, gummed with slime, waiting for rain.

He drained off another dipper full of whisky. The dipper clattered into the barrel. He waved his arms. "Stop!" he cried, but a whisper came out, so he tried again, and you could have heard him to the Mississippi River. Arms still outstretched he whirled with wide revolving steps away from the bayou and the loaded wagons. The forest was a field. He ran into the field, in and out among the stumps. He thought he was going down hill and then up hill and just as it struck him that this was odd, he seemed to step into something like a sinkhole and the stumps were level with his eyes. He turned painfully over on his back and lay there with no will to rise, his hand idly caressing the rings and saw scars of a cypress trunk. Then he laughed.

"I found out," he shouted. "Hey, you black sons-o'-bitches! I found out what'll put hills in the Delta!" It was the whisky he meant.

From around the empty barrel, the Negroes roared.

When he got back to the house, the woman was still there. He had forgotten about her. Just as on the night before, she had a pot of turnip greens cooked and waiting for him on the back of the small iron range he had bought second hand in Cypress Landing, and a pot of strong coffee and some cornbread. She had taken the loose cotton that he slept on underneath a pile of second hand blankets and had sewn it into two mattresses. He didn't know where she had got the cotton-sack ticking. He ate and fell across the mattress and went to sleep with a smile of pride and slyness on his drunken, unshaven face. The trees were down. The God damn trees. He cursed a hundred he remembered and a hundred he'd forgotten. He was smart to get the woman here. He had known all along she would cook, make mattresses, pick up things that were turned over. Stacey said with his laugh, You're a dumb boy thinking you can make those niggers work. You're a green fool wanting another man's pregnant wife in the house. But Amos Dudley knew; Amos Dudley knew Amos Dudley was smart; Amos Dudley knew Amos Dudley a long time ago.

The tiredness and the drunkness swelled up in him, enveloping him and muffling him, like a great wash of mud, and if it was mud he didn't care.

Dead asleep he lay, yet he knew the very minute it began to rain.

9

For three days Amos Dudley and Thelma Dubard did not speak except to say, Thank you for the cornbread, and things like that. The fourth night, with the thin rain so steady it was like a sound that came with the roof, she turned them up a road. He was standing before the stove, wet and tired. His clothes smoked. He was working now to find Negroes for his land, and working with the Negroes he found to levee the bayou away from the cleared land.

"You better get into some dry clothes," Thelma said. "You're liable to catch cold."

He took his clothes back in the shed room where she slept and changed and combed his hair at the piece of mirror on the wall before he even thought about what she said. Then he grabbed at the dry blue shirt as though it burned him.

"Come on in and eat," she called.

He sat down on the mattress and studied what to do. When she called him again, he was still short of a conclusion, so he mussed his hair back the way it was and went in to eat.

"All this food from Nellie and Eccles still?" he asked.

"Some from them. Some from others. That Clay Pittman family you got on three-year lease, and the Turner family. You don't owe them nothing yet."

"How come I don't owe them nothing?"

"They bring it to me. Always do. They think I got a hex."

He looked at her sharply. She was licking the rim of buttermilk off her top lip. He suspected that she was trying to josh him.

"Have you?" he asked.

"Not that I know of," she said.

He was in the habit of falling straight down on the mattress after supper, but that night he sat over in the corner in the chair, not sleepy, but taking in the pleasant warmth of the room and the slow soft way she was moving about, keeping company with the life inside her and not needing even to know he was there. Yet she did know he was there. She was making him want to talk to her. It aggravated him, for he was like a man around whisky who doesn't want the whisky but wants the way the whisky makes him feel and doesn't know any way to feel that way but to drink the whisky which he doesn't want. He gave in.

"How come they think you got a hex?"

She poured boiling water into the dishpan and dipped cold water in from the bucket. "It was when I was over at the saw-mill," she said, as though they had been conversing all along, "and there was this mid-wife on Tad Elmore's place across the bayou. She needed some help with bringing a colored baby— young woman over there down below Cypress by the river and nobody within holler, so I went with her. The nigger man hadn't no sooner got us there than he put out again, and before her pains had time to get started up again, here he come back just at dark—he was a great big black nigger man—toting this little yellow nigger in his arms with his feet clamped together like he was carrying a little pig. He set him down on the porch real easy, like he might be a piece of glued-together china, and holds him by the elbows till it give you the back-ache to see. Then he says no louder nor meaner than I'm talking to you: I'm a black nigger and Kaydee she's a black nigger. If that aint a black baby I'm going to cut your little bitty yellow neck off. Only he didn't say neck. He talked real nice like he was talking to the baby already or to a little dog. The mid-wife went over to the window and said, Hush up, nigger, you know there's a

white lady here to birth this chile. So when the little yellow
nigger hears that, he starts whining top of his voice: Aint none
of mine, aint none of mine, sweet Jesus know aint none of mine,
Kaydee know aint none of mine, that white lady tell you aint
none of mine. And making so much racket the pore little nigger
on the bed commenced to call on the Lord. So I went to the
door and said: You niggers shut up. You don't shut up I'll call
on the Old Man hisself to make it albino, then you won't know
whose it is. So the nigger shut up and Kaydee got down to
business. Pretty soon I seen the head come and it was white as
a teacup."

"Albino?"

"Just as sure as I'm washing these dishes. The mid-wife
wrapped it while I settled Kaydee and the big nigger come in
carrying the little nigger and when he seen it he set the little
nigger down and aint nobody said the first word. I went to
fling a tub of water out the back door and I turned around to
say, Help me fling—and there wasn't a soul in the room could
move to get out of it. I went to the door and all I could see was
that puny little old piece of chunked-up road going into a
stretch of sassafras bushes, then the swamp out there black as
pitch. I hollered out, One of y'all don't come keep the buggers
off me through that swamp, I'll tend to you. I went out the
front gate and into the road. Sure enough, one of them followed
me all the way back, back way behind me till the swamp opened.

"I reckon it was one of them."

"What you mean, you reckon it was?"

She set the lamp off the table onto the mantel-piece and laid
the dishes out bottom side up as she dried them. "One time
back when I used to live in Arkansas, long days ago, it was down
below our big field on the other side of the spring in another
man's pasture on the edge of it. I come on the pasture and in

the middle was this big circle of buzzards lit around a dead horse. They'd ring-around-the-rosey first one way, then the other, stepping off the time, then they bowed and like it was one-two-three-go, they skimmed into that dead horse and covered him hair and hide. Did you ever see such a thing?"

"One time. It's just what they'll do."

"But what I set out to say, A bunch of six-seven little churen were up the hill and across from me watching too, colored and white churen both—town dressed. They pointed to me and run. We seen each other at the same time, right when the buzzards was dancing, and there was me and there was them and there was the buzzards acting such a crazy way and all of us just happened up. How come it wasn't me pointed at them and run? They was scared of me ever after, churen in town, the ones I never knew to name. They just got the jump on me, you see how it was. It ought to been me to run."

"Except it was all of them and just one of you. Folks do that way. Been one buzzard it wouldn't a-stepped off time."

She studied it out. "There's something in that. Another thing might be if there was something behind me they seen stead of me."

"Something *behind* you?"

"Like whoever, whatever followed me back through the swamp. Like whatever made me say albino in the first place. You believe in such as that?"

"If there's God to be known of, there must be devils. There aint no other way to figger on all the sights folks see."

"Devils?" she said. "Like in the Book? I never thought on it like that."

She was sitting in the rocking chair now, having covered the dishes spread for breakfast with a cloth, decent, same as the Dudleys did. She had got the rocking chair same as she got the mattress ticking and the food (until he asked) out of nowhere, like a child will come on things lost for years, the owner dead or gone. She had splinted and wired it to hold her up. She was all big soft belly and swelling breasts with a greater fullness in her face now, up around the cheekbones toward the temples and eyes. She was due to be big anyway; without the baby in her, she would have had that intricate, comfortable, befitting bigness of a cow. She would be slow like a cow and never awkward except when hurried or frightened, at once completely commonplace and completely mysterious. And thoughts and passions would ramble within her slow as food tunneling along its hidden way.

Her thinking surfaced at last. "It don't bother me none at all," she said. "Not for myself. I trouble some about the baby." A tear rolled out of each eye. "But if it hadn't been for me"— her thoughts passed in slow procession beyond whatever had caused the two tears—"them niggers wouldn't have stayed up all night chopping down the woods for you."

"I'll be God damn if that's so," he said.

She sat rocking, her hands in her lap. I reckon Pat Dubard beat the tar out of her for such as that, he thought. I reckon it takes more than words to jump her.

He went to bed without saying anything more, but angry just the same.

She had stepped on his territory. But he had strolled about on hers, had sat in the shade there and listened to a story, which is the beginning of error.

10

It kept on raining. Amos thought that if it had been God who stopped the rain for him so long, He had had to bargain with it when He did it.

Thelma kept on staying.

One cold fair day he came in at noon to the sound of women's voices snarling and as he hurried through the big room the whole house shook from a heavy passage down the back steps. He came to the door in time to see Nellie, the Indian woman, disappear among the trees at a crouching run like a bear, her black hair shaking out another length down her shoulders with every stride.

"They're leaving," Thelma said. "She won't give Eccles no peace."

"Just so they don't dig up all the turnips and pole beans. I don't like her and Eccles anyway."

"She came to get her lamp back, the one she said you borrowed when you came."

"So I did."

"Then she snatched the book and run."

"The book? I got no book." Then he saw in her hand the thin torn leaves each rimmed with red and the black fine print; she held a dozen sheets ripped half in two.

"Oh," he said, "the Book. Can't neither one of them read, so what you reckon—"

"Hit's against me," she said and laughed, wadding the torn leaves which she threw aside under the steps. "How come what makes a nigger stay would make a injun woman leave?"

"Hush that talk," he said. He bent quickly under the steps to recover the torn leaves and when he straightened she was laughing at him without mystery or rancour, as though at one who is the victim of some mild joke. He reddened, and hurling the paper from him, turned away up the steps.

Around New Year's Thelma burned her arm on the stove door. It was red hot and the smell of the burning lingered for a whole two days. A long brown brand, raised and scabbed, lay on the flesh to make you wince for a month after she took off the bandage, and afterwards there was the white scar whorled into the skin like acid-eaten stone.

Three weeks after the burning, a back step, third from the top, broke under her and she hurtled down, down forever right under his eyes, still clutching the dishpan while the water leaped out of it, every drop, sucked into one gray ball, and landed thump beyond her like another body fallen. At midnight in agony she gave birth to what reminded Amos of nothing so much as a medium-sized cat fish with arms and legs. A week more, the doctor said, and it might have lived. Amos sat up all night in the rocking chair and watched her sleep. He had never before in his life felt laden with another person's misery. He carried the lamp out twice and looked at the broken step, as careful as a detective hunting for clues. The step hung by the tip of one bent nail suspended over the water which had backed up around them from the bayou. He went back into the house and looked with equal care at the stove door and then he pulled back the covers from the cotton basket and looked at the dead baby. He simply did not understand it. His mind would come right up to it and be stumped. He was like a puny man trying to pick up a bale of cotton; he could get his arms around it, but he couldn't even wiggle it.

What has she come here and brought? he wondered. What

has she brought to my house?

He wondered if she would die. He held the lamp above her face. The covers fitted close over her flattened belly; her whole broad body seemed to have caved in toward the center; she looked as if she were lying in quicksand that sucked slowly and that each drawn breath inched her out of it and each freed breath inched her back in again.

But he did not think that she would die. Whatever she had brought with her was still there, alive, waiting for her to wake and get up again.

11

In summer—it was night, the first week in August—there were footsteps on the bayou road and a white man's voice called from the yard. Amos took his stand near the door and drew back the hammer on his pistol. Thelma sat over in the corner on the iron white-painted double bed Amos had bought back in the winter right after they had sewed the two mattresses together. She had the same look on her face she had worn the other time—the time it was just a hunter lost, the same as when Amos brought her a length of dress goods from town. It was a look of relishing what happened and all the time being more than half-way amused at the cause of it. It aggravated him to see her take it so, for they were both thinking it might be Pat Dubard out there calling up the steps for Amos Dudley, and they both knew it, though they never said. It aggravated him as being a little girl streak in her, wanting to see two men fight over her, no matter if somebody got killed. Amos Dudley, for instance.

The voice called again. Then he knew. He caught up the lamp from the table and held it high, peering down the steps.

"Arney! Arney Talliafero!"

He was so happy he stuck the gun barrel in Arney's hand. "Lordy, Amos," Arney said, and pushed the gun aside with his little finger, "them things go off sometimes."

"Arney, this is Thelma," Amos said.

"It's a pleasure, ma'am," Arney said and took off his hat.

Later he and Arney sat on the back steps where it was cooler and drank out of Amos's jug. He made a smudge of dried cow dung in a molasses bucket. When he finished telling about himself, Arney picked up the jug in the crook of his arm, and his big adam's apple pumped several times. He blew out the fumes and wiped his mouth on his sleeve.

"Amos, you have come over here and lost your mind."

"No, I aint."

"Look. Just because you run into one big strip of luck like that Chinaman walking in with a plantation in his pocket, that aint no sign ever'thing else you fancy is going to come racking up to your front door."

"I don't ask that. I work for everything I get. I don't ask nothing but her."

"Ask who? Ask what?"

"Nothing. Nobody."

"Look. That woman over there, that Airy—"

"Ary."

"All right, Ary. You aint been to see her in a year, let alone taken her nothing. But you going to marry her."

"I hope to."

"Then what in the name of all that's holy does that one in there think about it?"

"She don't know it."

"That there's a good woman," said Arney, sorrowfully, for he was hurt.

With his words, all of the Dudleys seemed to lean out of the cypress and watch, his mother tearful, Ephraim about to snort and charge, his father weak and accusing as a ghost. And they were all of them right, and he knew it.

"It aint none of your business," he said to Arney, to them all.

"It ought not to be none of yours," Arney said.

"You're a fine one," said Amos, happily recalling a whole dozen of Arney's escapades.

"I know it," Arney replied and gave up and whistled.

Then he said: "Look, Amos, I done put this off too long. I come bringing bad news. Your father died this morning early, just before day. I aimed to mention it before, but I couldn't get it out. I'm sorry, Amos. He was as good a man as ever walked. They sent me to tell you."

12

Amos left Arney behind and went to Yocona on the night train. In the mid-morning he stood by the tracks at Yocona until the train went around the bend. The still cluster of stores seemed to be shrinking under the increase of August sun. Every one, even to the blacksmith shop, had the bolt drawn and the Yale lock clamped in. Beyond, the big square white houses were scattered here and there over the hills, facing every which way, and every one empty. A week day and everybody off? He felt vaguely responsible, as though he might have known this was what would happen when he left. The side door of a small one-story house back of Dudley & Co., Yocona, slammed and a Negro boy came out. He unhooked the mail sack off the arm and his eyes picked over Amos in a way which he seemed to feel that a stranger, being not quite there yet, could not quite see.

"Where is everybody?" Amos demanded, and came into focus. "Don't seem like there's a soul around today."

"Naw suh, aint nobody home terday."

"It is Friday, aint it?"

"Yes suh, hit's Friday. Sho is."

"Stores closed. Houses empty."

"Everybody gone."

"Everybody."

"Nobody left but me, en-trusted to tote the mail sack."

"It's too early for Tabernacle," Amos said.

"Tabernacle two weeks away."

"Then where are they? Fishing? At a fire?"

"Ain' no fire, boss. You mus' aint heard the news."

"How you reckon I'd hear the news? You just now seen me step off the train."

"They's all out to Mist' Clyde Dudley's house. Mist' Clyde Dudley he died yes-tiddy."

All of them, thought Amos. He was so quiet, and all of them his friends.

"You know Mist' Clyde Dudley? Lives down by the river bend?"

"I'm his son," Amos said, and walked away home.

He had no more than rounded the curve of the hill than his mother ran out from among the horses and wagons and the mules that stood crookedlegged, knocking at flies. Light as a girl she ran to him, stirring a little low trail of dust, and he guessed she'd heard the train blow and had waited like any other day, counting the steps a man would take from the station home. He caught her. Tears had loosened her body; she bent to him, pliant as a girl.

"It isn't Ned, Mama," he told her. "It's me, Amos."

"I know it's you," she said, and clung tighter. "It's you I waited for, Amos. Amos Anderson."

He had to stop trying to talk then; but he could not give over utterly to sorrow, for already she had him wondering.

They asked him in the room right away, but he bided his time. He did not want to go in with anybody else. He knew he would not "take on" the way the women liked to repeat; he did not really know what he would do, but he did not think he would act in any of the ways they expected. Still, if they were there about him and watching, he might be tricked into acting the way they wanted and he had a profound feeling that if he acted a lie before his father's body some final gate would shut in his face, and he could never walk a straight road again.

He went in alone, at noon time when they had gathered out in the back yard around the long board table they had pieced together on carpenter horses and laden with hams and cakes and chicken and souse and fruits and pies and biscuits that the people had brought to the family. There were three mourners still in the room. Aunt Reesa, and two old ladies, one with a bristle of stiff whiskers, the other with a lip full of snuff, and they filled the room with the smell of old flesh, way past coffin time, overlooked or too deaf to hear their time called, left to play out any time at all—didn't matter when. They were there because they felt that a body should not be left alone until it was underground. And why they felt this way they could not have said.

He pushed the door open for them to leave.

"I'm his son," he said. "I'll stay."

"Amos," Aunt Reesa relayed, in a whisper. "His son."

"Amos?" one old lady said—Mrs. Fremont. "Of course, it's Amos. Hit's Amos Anderson, Miss Emma."

"Huh?" said Miss Emma. "Who?" She never understood, but she kissed him and patted him like the others, and went distrustfully out to the food.

He closed the door.

Clyde Dudley lay in the center of the bed, his head propped on one clean pillow, their best case, fringed round with tatting. The white sheet was pulled high under his armpits and folded back over the best quilt—the one that every man, woman and child in Yocona could locate their old clothes in. Amos saw pieces of his mother's dresses she had worn when he was a child, lying under the neatly folded brown hands. He looked at last at the face and the sight did not shake him. It was an even face and one side of the mouth was exactly like the other. He guessed not many a man could come to the end of his days with an even mouth. Arney had had a story from a man he had met off the riverboat once about a place in the middle of the ocean going to China where you go to bed and it's Friday and you wake up and it's Sunday. At some minute, some one tick of the clock, one whole day goes by, and when you cross that line you do not even bump. There are only the waves like before and the stars or the rain go on as though nothing had happened. Two days pass and there is no sign. So Clyde Dudley had come on such a line and had skipped a hundred, a thousand or so years, and was past the end of the world. He will never see the fire they talked of that night which made me sweat and shake and seek the God that I found, thought Amos. Yet he knows beyond the fire: he knows, oh, he knows.

Looking on the placid brown face which reminded him of no other thing except his father, but which was also the face of all men in their own houses who turn to no one for gain or with envy, Amos felt all the things he knew and had done and seen and wanted gather into one subject, whole and able to be talked about.

Suddenly he whispered to the still face: "Did you side with Ephraim, Papa?"

He leaned close, but the face defied him.

"It's true I left, but I tell you now what I've said to no man. My land was given to me, out of high heaven where they know about me for sure. The time's not come for her, for Ary Morgan; but if I get her too, wouldn't you take it for a Sign? A Sign I was right to leave, that I worked well, that Ephraim was wrong? It was you started me on this road, talking under the big elm at Tabernacle with Mr. Jess Maybry and them. You said there was nothing to do when the world shook but hold on to the floor and pray, and I took out after the good Lord like a cast hound. And what I found I found, no man's but my own. Papa, I can't forget how you used to look over the fish, the words you never got up strength to let fly. Was it siding with Ephraim you meant? Papa!"

His hand reached suddenly forward. But before he touched the face to part the eyelids, two witch-like faces, one on top the other, craned in at the window. He stumbled up and toward them, crying out in rage. The children ran.

When he turned back, the impulse was gone, and he was glad he had not touched the face that was for women to smooth. Yet desperately he still wanted to see and know. He sat in the chair, sulking before the door of death like any child.

"Open his eyes, God," he whispered once, "and let him answer me."

But the prayer did not rise even out of his heart, but stayed there and swelled through the whole day, through the time when the coffin went in and out again and the wagon crept to

the graveyard before the long procession—sheets of dust drifting westward in the breeze—and the preacher stood talking
in the church. When they raised the lid for the family, he knew
it was his last hope, and he saw the lid go down again. The
brilliant stiff home-grown August flowers—the marigolds and
zinnias and big fern—lay over the box and moved with it to
the yard, and after that the dirt grew swiftly upward. So he
never knew.

13

"A family is a funny thing," Amos told Arney when he returned. "They all wished ill to me."

"Aw, Amos, you know that aint so."

"I'll tell you exactly," said Amos. "Ephraim. He claimed to
want me to stay and help with the farm and store, that I was
welcome back, he said. Yet he knew if I stayed we would fuss
and there would be meanness said and done and everybody
aching with it all over the house. So if he really wanted me to
stay, it means he likes the fussing; he likes making me feel
wrong, so he can feel right. What he hopes is that I will go broke
over here and have to come home and beg to live there.

"Aunt Reesa and Aunt Fanny George. They done made it
up amongst them that I'm into something over here. That's
because I don't talk none about my business. But they done got
it all decided. They set around and say, Wouldn't it just kill
Mary to know? and they don't know themselves what they're
speaking of, but they hope Mary will find it out and take on, so
they can come hear all about it and make like they're sorry.

"Durley. He's swelled up to be doing what I ought to be doing, helping Ephraim make a dollar. Everytime he sees me he

grows another inch. Then he comes and asks me to take him back with me. He hones to find out whatall I really got, and he's got a sneaking suspicion I aint doing as bad as Ephraim hopes, and he thinks he might could make some cash money.

"Mama. She took up this notion that she wanted Ned home and she went at it crafty—"

"You oughtn't to talk so about your folks, Amos. The Dudleys are as good a set of folks as ever come down the pike."

"—so she laid in bed for two whole days and had us thinking her low sick, and me setting up with her late nights and listening to her talk. Last night she says, If I thought I could see Ned again, I'd lie easy. So I says, Mama, if I could fetch him to you, I would.

"Right then she bucked up in the bed and says, Oh, would you, Amos, would you? And before I could answer she spiels off this idea she's got that Ned is in the Texas panhandle where she's read about a new oil field being. She's got the squib clipped out and handy under the pillow for me to read. If he aint there she thinks he might be in upper California. I never got to her reasons for picking California instead of one of them other states out there. Maybe it's the only name that come to her. So when I get through looking in Texas, I'm supposed to go on to California. I tried to tell her how far it is to them two places and between them too, but she just never heard me. I asked her how she knew he was there, and she never heard that either. I asked her how come she didn't call on one of the others and then she said, But you have the means and the love. I thought it was love for her she was claiming, but she went on to say, You cared for Ned—only you and the girls—Ephraim's swayed Durley and the rest. The girls have the love but not the means.

"When I told her I couldn't go, she might as well not think

about it, she caught aholt of my arm fit to mash bone and she said, But I prayed you would. You aint really sick, I said, which was like Ephraim and a mean thing to do. You can't go finageling when you pray. I had to say it though, or I'd a-been gone to Texas. She most had me for a minute there. I didn't figure she'd admit to it, but she seen I was right and let me go, and the next morning she was up to cook breakfast same as always, with her eyes like two rocks in her head. I took one look and knew I couldn't stand no more, so I put out. I didn't care none about Ephraim and Durley and Aunt Reesa and Aunt Fanny George, but when you see a trap which your own mother has made, you'd sooner walk into it and catch yourself than admit she's made it, and I wasn't sure but what she wasn't just pretending to give up and waiting for me to go stick my head in the noose. It was right after breakfast that I put out. Lord to God! If I didn't hit that road!"

"You don't mean all that, Amos," Arney said anxiously. For Arney's serious thoughts were mournful and kindly, like a song. "If I thought you meant all that against your folks, I'd walk out of here this minute and never come back. But you don't mean it."

"I don't care if they want to act that way," said Amos. "I just don't aim to get trapped. They ever' last one tried to trap me and I don't aim to let them. It's what I say: you don't look for it from your own folks."

"They're crazy about you, Amos. Your mother sets a great store by you, and Ephraim, Amos, he's proud of you. You know how I know? One time last fall I seen him in the store and he said—"

"I don't want to hear it."

"Just let me tell you what Ephraim—"

"I don't want to hear about it."

The Indictment: Arney

I WAS friend to a fellow onct, but I couldn't never figger him. Oh, most fellows I can figger. Set me down in a poker hand like last night—never seen them boys before. But I knowed Rowley—that his name?—was one to play it straight for a spell and then pull a bluff when the pot grew, well, so big. You seen how I worked it. But this one I started out to speak of, he was no poker player.

He wouldn't scarcely know what to do with a deck of cards if you handed it to him. He was dumb about cards and he wasn't much of a one to figger folks, but some ways he was a heap smarter than me. I reckon, now that a right good many years has past, I can get a better bead on him, and I reckon the thing he was smart about was himself. He knowed how to work for himself and how to handle things for himself a damn sight better than me. I let the day come and the day go, but this fellow he figgered it. It was not one month to the next and how he was going to get the cash to pay the grocery bill, and it wasn't one year to the next, how he was going to borry the money to stock the commissary so the niggers could stock up through the winter on a credit. He took in those things too, but they were all like the separate little rows in the field, when what he had was ten fields. It was his whole life he had figgered—all of it! Like you seen a woman lay a pattern down on dress goods laid out

83

on the piano top and pinning the pattern down to the goods. Then the scissors crunching, laid to wood. He had it that complete in his head, and him hardly turned twenty. Now how would you be friends with a fellow like that, with him so busy figgering and so shut mouth about it, all the time you knowed him?

But him and me was friends. He was the best friend I ever had. When his daddy died, up in Yocona where we was born and raised, it was me they sent to tell him, not uncle or brother. He was near Cypress Landing on Quiver Bayou then—just south of the Sunflower, if you know the country in there, and forty, forty-five miles in from the boss river. I found him living in what folks around there said was one time a Indian trader's house, though if they told Amos Dudley that he never heard it, being too busy at the time with trying to lift a whole plantation out of the swamp.

When he come back from the funeral, he was in a peeve with his folks and said things against them. I was setting right there by him on the back steps of the house, pulling at the jug, but when he talked like that, I felt like an old mule shut off in the pasture somewhere ten miles from the tail end of nowhere. It do take the gut out of me to hear a man talk about his folks and the only way I could line it up was that Amos didn't mean it, him upset over his daddy and all. Just the same I went and got my hat and coat and said I best be getting along. He set for a good while after I said it, not saying nothing back, till I thought, Now he's done got hisself riled at me.

So I said, I don't care if you go to Texas or not (that was where his mama wanted him to go to seek out his brother that kilt a man over here at Greenville and left this part of the country, though his mama never knowed why). I aint said one blessed word to you except don't talk against your kin which is right and you know it.

So he answered me back real meek and low, Yes, it's right. But I told the truth, Arney, it was the way they done me. I seen it.

I don't care what you seen, I said. Where would you be without them? Just answer me that? You wouldn't be nowhere, I tell you. They'd lock me up, I tell you. You want to know why? Because I'd be standing here talking to something that aint even there.

I done spent my life, he said, like he was going on eighty, fighting back at Ephraim. Now I know it aint just Ephraim, it's all of them. Even the look on my father's face and him eating fish. (That's his words.) But Arney, he says, this aint no bad place to stay for a while. Is it, Arney?

I knowed it was me he meant, wanting me to stay. Well, I had places I could have gone and to tell the truth I never did shine up to this Delta. I done picked up a living from it here there and yonder, but I'm a hill man and next to that a river man—but the Delta. Well, it just do seem like the land's so set and same it makes the people skittish. Still, the way Amos said that, it called to mind our fishing days and picking days and how what your friend asks for is what you do.

So I says, It aint no bad place, and set down to the jug again.

Then he done a funny thing. He taken and put his hand in his pocket and pulled out a little paper sack and handed it to me. I bought that for m'self, he says, when I changed trains at Winona. But I aint got no use for it.

Now what you think was in that paper sack? A bow tie. With red polka dots on it. What in tarnation Amos Dudley ever thought he wanted with a bow tie, is one place where I aint never yet seen the light. Still, his way of handing it to me and maybe the red polka dots made me wonder if he didn't have it in mind all along to give it to me—knowing me for a sporty dresser in them days—but I never let on. Whichever way it was I didn't think no more of Amos's words against his folks. For he had showed hisself to be one of them.

It strikes me as odd now that I thought for one solid year the best thing I ever done was to stay there with Amos Dudley and Thelma Dubard and help him raise that place out of the swamp. I wish now I had walked down the back steps like I threatened and felt bad the rest of my life about leaving that pore boy to sweat out swamp, buckshot and malaria all by hisself.

For this is how he done.

I ought not to say all the way, This is how *he* done, because there was women in it and when you get women in it things do seem to get set antigartlin, whichever way you turn them. There was Thelma stayed there with him and cooked. I got no word against her. She taken me in with no more stir than putting an extry plate on the table, and she had no word against me. Not even after the night Amos was away and she had to knock me half acrost the room with a skillet. It's true I was drunk, but I had my reasons before I got drunk and I kept a pretty steady hold on them afterwards. Amos getting himself slicked up and heading for Greenville on business. Business, nothing! It was that other one—that Ary Morgan. But it was six months after it taken the skillet to keep me off'n her, which was a little over six months after I come to send Amos home to his daddy's funeral—over a year in all, then, and in September with Amos's cotton busting out'n the bolls so thick and light a nigger could just stand straight and walk along the rows trailing his fingers and leave the bolls slick as a whistle, and him standing over it all day and weighing in long past dark. Well, that was when she took to come.

In a buggy. With the black paint new and shiny and a black shiny nigger setting up front to drive. And a shiny bay horse floating along in front. I never laid eyes on her before, but I knowed who it was even with Greenville forty miles away and nobody with her. I was out on the front steps letting my dinner settle before I went to take Amos his'n. When she got out of the buggy I thought, Lordamercy, she'll be in the house if I don't mind and Thelma will see her. So I got up off my tail and come down the steps to meet her.

I had to walk straight into her to stop her. You know how that is? Usually it's just the way you sit there and look, much as to say, Well, who are you? Or if that won't do it, coming down the steps looking, much as to say, What can I do for you? will stop anything, human or not. But not her. I was scared of that woman. There aint many women I can say that of. She was all woman, but there was something extry about her that had to do with her coming there in the first place. It's the extry something about women that can buffalo me, one way or the other. It's the thing you never asked for, never looked for, never wanted. Then you get so far along and you run smack up against it, and what do they do? They blame you with it. That's what they do. There was this school teacher up in Yocona—but no, this extry that Ary Morgan had wasn't nothing like that school teacher. Or if it was, if you could carve it out and fish it up and hold it in daylight and call it exactly the same thing—that didn't make no difference. The symptoms of it was shore different. And the dealing with it was more than a little different. You could walk off and leave that school teacher and feel like a sonofabitch maybe for two weeks, but with this one you was a sonofabitch to start with, far as anything you wanted to say about her. And if this extry something which they want to call love had got aholt of her, she was up to matching it, card for card, and the devil take the hindmost, which is you. Or in this case, Amos. At least, I reckoned so.

Hearing about her one time before from Amos, I wondered and kept on wondering up till she came, What would a lady like her, out of some high-steppin' Delta outfit, want to look twice at Amos Dudley for? At the time I thought to myself she never had looked twice. But after she came in the buggy, I never wondered that no more, nor thought about it so much as to ask myself why I never wondered it no more. I can see that too, now—taking a bead down the barrel to a long time ago—and I can see how her coming there and getting out and having to be stopped from walking right in, wasn't like anybody else I'd ever known except Amos Dudley. It was so like him, I wonder sometimes if she ever said a word about what they want to call love. Or if Amos did either, for that matter.

She said, straight out, Does Amos Dudley live here?

And me all set to lie. Yes, ma'am, I said, he does, but he aint here now. You ride back to the tip of the bayou and cross around and he's in that first cotton house when you strike the road running this way. If he aint there—

I raised a sweat, whirling around on the end of my arm, pointing.

Well, she went on off.

It aint none of mine, I says to myself, going in. Then I recollected Thelma. I went inside and she warn't there in the big room, nor back in the kitchen. The dishes was setting in the sink. not touched. Praise God, she was at the privy, I thought, and swung out the back door to look and nearbout stepped on top of her. She was setting on the back steps right in the sun and it the middle of September.

Aint you feeling good, I asked her.

She sat there with the sweat rolling out from under her hair. Then she opened her hand. It's a conjure bag, she said. It was, for a fact. Little old greasy tobacco sack she had untied so the insides was sticking out in her hand, piece of yellow hair to match hers, and a snip of dress. That's the fourth one I done found since I been here, she said.

Aw, Thelma, aint nothing to it. You'd a-been underground and rotted was there anything to it.

Take it, then, she said and shoved it towards my hand.

I don't want it, I said and drawed back from it.

She laughed. You see, you see. Nothing to it.

Throw it out, I said. Burn it. That's it, burn it. Fire can kill them.

That's just what I done with the other three. But I think I mizewell swing on to this one. Oh, it aint no difference whether I keep it, whether I don't, whether hit was ever made or not, whether anybody ever feared me to make it against me.

She helt it all in her hand, like a grown person holding a little kid's set of jacks, then she filled the sack up again and tied it, and helt it till it shamed me to a-said I was scared to fool with it.

Then you don't think there's nothing to it, I said.

She sat there quiet until I started to ask her again; then she got up. I just happened to look at her and when I did I almost fell off the steps. Because she was all twisted up out of shape like—well, like a big old hill way off you can see and say That looks like a woman, but you know it aint and it would scare the fool out of you if it turned out to be one. She was hard as bed rock in the hands and wrists and around the eyes. If she'd had a gun in her hand, she'd a-shot me, but all she had was the conjure bag which she threw in my face, but it wasn't me she was mad at. Or it wasn't just me she was mad at, but everything in creation, and getting mad at everything has reason to it a whole lots of times, only there aint noway to hurt everything. You got to blast away at the nearest critter.

Nothing to it! I say, nothing to it. Nothing to it, same as there's nothing to everything else I cross the path of. Say it's the reason, say it aint the reason. What use I got for a reason?

Then she come out with a string of words it was cold for me to hear her say. For me and her and Amos had always had a peaceable time together, not counting the skillet, which didn't do no harm and made things more peaceable even, because if Amos had his secrets, we had our'n too. I set and heard her and tried not to look at her, but it turned the whole year into something like when you done et too fast and can't nap for belching. Then she went in and after while I heard the dishes clanking. I went on past her like nothing had happened.

Arney, she said, Amos was aiming to be in the upper field by dinner time. You tole that lady wrong.

It didn't make no difference then, not if she had flung hog slop in my face and cussed all evening.

He aint going to do nothing wrong about you, I said. I know Amos, Thelma. I've knowed Amos Anderson a long time, and his folks before him. When it comes to a show down, they'll go down the line for you.

Don't talk to me, she said. (She didn't even so much as look at me.) You been knowing this a long time and never talked to me.

Whatever he even starts to think he might do against you, I can show him. I can argue him into seeing it right. Ever'time.

She laughed somewhere off in her head, but it never showed on her face.

You might as well argue with a conjure bag, she said. It's all the same thing.

I went to the field to look for Amos, but the niggers giggled and said he done rid off in a buggy, so I come on back to the house and set with her and formed my speech which was going to put us back on keel again.

I was figgering all the time, see, on holding us together. We latched up together nice enough. Amos bossing the place—he had come by it through nothing but luck, so it wasn't as if he had done no sweating for it because one man's luck might as well be another man's luck too. And Thelma for him—him giving her a place to stay and all, and to tell the truth I thought Amos might go on ahead and marry her sometime. And me—well, nothing really for me except liking to be there with them since Thelma taken the skillet and aimed to keep on taking it, and I was handy to be called on and the fishing was good. Everything set together in a sort of circle in my head: the place and Amos, Amos and Thelma, Thelma and the skillet, me and Amos, me and fishing and whatever else. A circle is a good way to live because you can keep on going around it and don't never wind up nowheres else.

The only thing besides Ary Morgan that didn't set right was the way Amos had lowrated his folks. Don't ask me how I know Ary Morgan was connected up with that. She just was, that's all I know. One thing like that you forget about, two and you're unsettled.

When Amos finally come in that night, he acted like a man in a strange house, not knowing the dish pan from the wash bowl, and I knowed he was unsettled for exactly the same reason I was. That's the funny thing: he knowed it himself.

Well, you can't tell a man about something he already knows and so long as he knew it I was counting on the Amos which brought me the bow tie and asked me to stay and the Amos which took Thelma in pregnant with the baby she lost falling down the steps so that the doctor said her organs had got snatched so crooked she couldn't never have another one. But what really put the quietus on me that night was Thelma.

You wouldn't a-thought that. Not that she said anything. She had put on a dress I had never seen her wear before, a soft silky flowerdy dress, and she had done put her hair up different. She cleared the table and come and set down in a rocking chair by the lamp and she rocked slow and easy and let the light slide up and down her and looked off at the corner and never said a form thing. Amos and me set and listened to the rocking chair squeak and squeak and we never said nothing either. But while we set there, it seemed like the room turned into Thelma. Amos finally got up like he was dragging hisself up a rope hand over fist and pulled the jug down off the shelf. We set on the back steps together and Amos tried to talk about farming, but it trailed off; then he started on the niggers, but that went the same way. He even tried to pronounce on the government and after that we set there and pulled at the jug and you could hear the rocking chair squeak, and Amos couldn't think of nothing to drown it.

It was me that wore down first. But then I didn't have no fine gal from Greenville over to pay respects to me that evening. Hell fire, Amos, I said. I got to go into Cypress.

I got up and walked down the back steps and turned around and looked back at him. He was all drawed up close to the railing and holding the jug by the neck like he was drownding.

If you just going to set there, I said, I'll go in and keep Thelma company my own self.

Be damn if that's so, he said.

I think that's what he said; you couldn't hear him very good.

You aint got room for three in that bed, have you, Amos? I said.

Three hell, he said, and was up and in the house like you'd turned loose of a spring.

Well, that went on for five nights straight. Five nights. I seen it happen. Him coming in the house not wanting it—or wanting it different, in a ordinary way he probably wouldn't no more remember the next morning than going to the privy—and her setting in the rocker with her hair always a little bit changed and the silky dress on and making it rise in him. Maybe she was hexed; I don't know.

Amos commenced to get right peaked and pale before it was over with. The sixth night I had to go out after dark and find him. He was sleeping in a cotton house and I nearbout shook his teeth out before he woke up.

I aint going back in that house, he said.

He hadn't shaved in a week and his face was little and somewhere way off behind his whiskers.

I think it'll be all right, I said. She's back in a old dress and her hair aint been combed since last night. Added to that, she's barefooted.

He ventured after me then. I don't know what got into her, he said.

I told him about her seeing Ary Morgan.

She never said nothing about it, he said.

Maybe she's waiting for you to say.

And I bought her that God damn flowerdy dress length myself, he said. Out of my Yocona silver.

So we both thought she had been out to hold him and took that way instead of talking. It did look like to me that she'd won.

I'm looking for the time when folks wind up at the place I think the sights are set for. I aint never seen it yet. For me and Amos together couldn't read Thelma, and Lord knows I never read Amos, though I reckon Thelma said the truth when she said, You might as well argue with a tobey sack.

It was a little more than six weeks later, Amos finished taking his cotton to the gin and paid his niggers off and come in and said, I'm aiming to start my house tomorrow.

And Thelma answered back, I'm going to have a baby, and there we three set at the supper table, like any other night, and I said, Pass the peas, and it didn't seem like no unusual thing to say right then because none of it made sense anyway.

Amos thought a minute and he said, I'm a good mind to shoot that God damn doctor. Well, he says to her, what you think you going to make me do?

I pulled Amos up by the collar and taken him out on the back porch and knocked him down the steps. I didn't care if it killed him. He come back up blinking and thinking.

Arney, he says, you set there and seen it and she knows it for a fact that she done it for and as good as by herself and it looks like to me you're thinking about two other people instead of her and me.

Thelma was standing right behind me. You crazy, she says to me, Amos is right, and wipes the blood off his head with her apron like he was her child and she had ten others she liked better. We walked through the door into the kitchen where she had set the light. I don't expect you to do nothing, she said, and laid both hands on top her hair and settled it down like she was preening with a hat. Nothing you aint already done, she says. And I'm here to tell you, with all the trouble she had done had already and the more trouble she knowed sure as fate she was going to have, that there woman was as proud of herself right

then as Miss Ary Morgan ever was when she rid them fine horses
Amos said she had. And Amos knowed it. It outdone him.

We went on back in the main room with her fetching up behind with the lamp, and she set it down on the table by the
rocking chair and smoothed her dress out over her knees in the
rocking chair, and I set in the other chair. Amos set over in the
shadows on the bed and dabbed at the blood and licked it off
his fingers. He sure was outdone. The more she wouldn't say
nothing, the more outdone he got.

Say one thing you want me to do, Thelma, he says.

I don't know if she even heard him. She set there and rocked
and it would of reminded me of them nights she made Amos
bust out of his britches except she was all poured up inside herself now and like she was listening to herself grow.

I didn't understand it all, but I set there and never said no
more. I didn't want to set there but there didn't seem no other
place to go. It come over me that somebody had done stamped
out the circle we had been treading around. I didn't know who
had done it, but I knowed it was gone.

Thelma, said Amos, I done come down here and took you in
and give you a home. You never asked me what I was here for
and I never said because I didn't know if I would get what I
wanted or not, and the saying is a bad thing when there aint no
guarantee. I never said stay, but you stayed and I let you. Now
just when I get ready to take what I want, what I'm here for,
you go and cheat me. You done it with malice aforethought.
You seen her come in the buggy that day.

Them niggers worked like the dogs was on them because I
was here, she said. You wouldn't be ready to build no house
hadn't been for me.

All right! he said, and got up and bucked around the room.
That aint nothing you done—it aint nothing you decided on and

done. The niggers think you got a hex. You can't say you give it to me, the power of the hex they think you got to make them work for me because they think you got it.

She didn't say nothing.

That aint no argument atall, he said. If you'd left me alone last month we'd a-come out of it even. Even and clear.

You and me's even, Amos, she says. I come with a baby and I'm leaving with a baby.

Leaving? he said, and then it dawned on him. He was right by the bed and his knees give under him and he dropped back down on it, same as before, and the room was quiet and she never rocked once.

I set and smiled to myself, thinking how smart she was to take a woman's way instead of driving for what she wanted, to make him see by showing him the only way he couldn't let her do. I seen how it would latch up together again, me and Amos and Thelma with the baby where the skillet was, and the circle come in my head again, faint as a ghost, which was what it was. For Amos never got up off that bed.

It was Thelma finally got up and went to gathering up her clothes from where they was hanging on a nail behind the bureau.

If you leave, Amos said, while she was folding up the clothes into a cloth, you done cheated me just the same. You'll rise up on me in the night till the day I die.

She whipped a big safety pin out of her dress somewhere and fastened the bundle together. Then she commenced to take down the coffee pot and a couple of boilers and the skillet.

I don't care what you call it, she said. All I want to do is go back to Arkansas and have my baby.

It don't make no difference you not caring what I call it, when what I'm calling it is right. How come you to cheat me?

I never did set no store by what doctors say.

Never anything but good to you, and you cheat.

They must have gone on like that for two hours, but she didn't know he never heard a word she said because she had quit listening to him and he had quit being surprised she either couldn't or wouldn't answer him.

I didn't put in no word.

I heard Thelma leave before day and I cut across the field and met her in the road and when I come back Amos was coming out the front door with the shot gun.

Come on, Arney, he says, we got to catch her. She done took all my cash money out of the chimney.

Oh, set down and shut up, I says. It was me took hit.

He set down and shut up.

I tried to get her to let me go with her, I said, then when she wouldn't do that, I tried to give her money, but she wouldn't take that. She said she didn't want to have to fool with no more men and she said the money would be nice, but you would come and get it back from her.

I give her enough to get her to Arkansas, said Amos.

That's what she said.

Where's my money then? he says, like I was a nigger stealing chickens.

Amos, I says, I never tried to do nothing belonged to me to do; only what belonged to you to do when I seen you wasn't going to do it.

Where's my money? he says again.

You're going to get your money, I says, but not before I tell you one thing. I done seen you grow up and I done thought plenty of times, Amos is wrong about this or that, but never before last night did I ever think: Amos Dudley is a evil man.

If you think that, he says, setting on the steps and looking boned, the way you feel when you puke, you better give me my money and go.

I taken the sugar sack out'n my pocket and threw it up on the steps to him. He didn't pick it up or look at it.

That money's for starting my house, he says. Did you know that when you took it, Arney?

I knowed it, I says.

It aint much to have left maybe, he says, out of all you and her has ganged up on me and taken, but it's all I got.

Well then keep it, I says.

He leaned down, weak as the new born, and touched the sack. Where's my other money? he asked. Where's my little sack?

What little sack?

My silver dollar sack, he says. Twenty-eight dollars left where once there was $96.84. You know the sack I mean, Arney. It was in the chimney too. It was in the chimney when Thelma left.

Then it's still in the chimney, I says.

Against Ephraim I earned it, he says, starting out low. Against Tabernacle, against Yocona and the name of Dudley. Arney! You wouldn't take it, Arney! Arney!

His voice got louder as he went along, and shook him, but he couldn't move, no more than a dog that sits howling at a train whistle, pained in the ear. I couldn't stand to look at him.

I went on in the house and got my hat and coat and what little stuff I had and went on out the back door and through the end of the bayou to the road. I had been better friends with Amos Dudley than with any man in the world, but I just didn't want to have to pass by him and look at him again.

It was him passed by me. I hadn't got out of the swamp road into open field before I heard him hollering for me to come back. Then the hollering stopped and there was a thrashing in the brush. I stepped back out of the road and watched him pass. I wasn't hid nor nothing, but he was looking so hard for me and going so fast to find me, he never even seen me. It was early morning still, with fog rising out of the cane, and where the road ran into the cane from across the cotton patch I saw him go waist deep in fog, running, but you couldn't see feet nor legs nor nothing, just head and elbows pumping, like somebody marking time. Then the cane got him. That was the last I saw of him. I heard him hollering for me to come back, and quartering ground for me, but I went on through the cane in there where the mosquitoes and varmints and every kind of critter is worse than I ever seen, and when I got in the open, headed for Cypress Landing and the railroad, he was still back in the cane, hollering for me, time and time. I could hear him a long way up the road.

The Indictment: Dolly

W<small>HEN</small> my aunt, Ary Morgan, married Amos Dudley from the hills, he took her to live in his new house over on his new place near Cypress Landing. My aunt Sara lived in Cypress too and so did my father and so in a sense did I, but from the time of my mother's death I became a frequent visitor with relatives, in this respect almost as bad from early childhood as a seventy-year-old maiden aunt. My favorite place of all was Uncle Amos's.

His house to me as a child was a heart of happiness. If there is a wonder childhood possesses which makes it forever superior to what shall come after, it is the happy and uncritical love of whatever is happy, place or person, it does not matter which. At least, it was so to me. My mother was the happiest person I ever knew. When she died—so young; I was four and the only child—there came a great wonder in the Morgan family which has never gone away. After so many suitors, after a marriage so improbable that no Morgan ever got it through their head that Louise was not joking, it seemed more incredible than ever that death should be the one irrevocably to claim her. They had expected this to be done some day, but by some other. Though I was only four, they had succeeded in communicating to me that air of dismissal, altogether pleasant and altogether vague, with which they viewed my father. A mild-spoken minister, small, turning gray as his suit as early as his wedding day, what had he to do with the Morgans, least of all Louise? He had the audacity to take her out of the Delta to Isola, a forlorn hill town where he preached, and there in the hills to beget a child which he even went so far as to let her give birth to in the Isola manse, having let himself get cut off by floods even from the Grenada hospital, to say nothing of Lake Washington and Greenville, where she should have been. It is true that two years later he accepted a call to Cypress Landing in the Delta, but everyone knew that it was Louise's happiness at the prospect of returning to the land of the living (or near it) that made him accept. And very shortly afterwards, on a soft spring morning, she was dead in the Cypress Landing manse, not at Lake Washington where she ought to have been. So for years, they said of me, looking at me, but speaking to some dark knowledge which had to do unfavorably with my father: "Poor Dolly. Poor little thing."

It was at Dellwood they would say this, that big house where cousins and aunts and uncles were forever advised to come and make themselves at home and were forever taking the advice. I would feel uncomfortable when they said Poor little thing; not that I wished to defend my father, so much as I wished to act in some way that would justify the inordinately long stares of some two or three great-aunts. I once under such provocation proceeded to do magnificent backward somersaults which I had learned from my cousins, Davy and Patrick, and again when they said this on the front porch, I ran out in the yard and climbed a tree. But these things were not right for when I finished they were talking hard at something else entirely, and were unaware of my existence.

But at Uncle Amos's house, I was never called a poor little thing.

The house itself was less formidable than Dellwood. It was one-story, like the manse in Cypress, and was set high off the ground for the floods, with green lattice-work, tall as my head, running all the way around it to close the underside from view and keep the chickens out. From a distance it seemed that two houses sat there side by side, for there were two separate roofs, each with a crown and slope; but I learned that the small one on the right had been built first, three rooms one back of the other, and that Uncle Amos had planned to build three other rooms opposite these and connect the two sections with an open hall, like the house he was born in. But Aunt Ary (my name for her was 'Tary) had planned the second side instead. There was a porch, screened off toward the left with a swing and couches in the screened area and a waxed, gleaming floor. Inside was a low hall, furnished on either side like the hall at Dellwood, with a sofa and easy chairs at the end where the light came in through three broad windows. The hall continued to the left, opening on to the bedrooms in the wing, and here where little light came was a bare, unfurnished stretch of floor, with a gun rack, a rough shell box, a pile of tanned hides thrown down carelessly in the corner, and a crate of stuff I was never drawn to play with, for its contents were associated in my mind with the guns and shells and hides as being rough, business-like things, resentful of levity.

But on the whole the house was small enough to seem bright throughout when the sun was shining, and unlike the manse, big enough not to crowd us. I say us, for I was part of the family then. Even the baby, Elinor, I thought of as partly my own and helped to tend daily with a sober inward knowledge of my family task. I would wonder, away from her, if certain ministrations in which I was most adept were being properly performed.

On Sunday Father and I would go there for dinner and when it was time to leave along about four-thirty, 'Tary would say, "Let Dolly stay all night with us, Nathan." Two or three weeks later (or in the summer, months later) he would succeed in getting me home for a few miserable days in the dark-panelled rooms of the manse, or some relative would drag me away to Dellwood.

There my great-aunts speculated openly on whether or not I would "fill out" when I grew older, tried to fluff my straight hair into curl but gave up with a sigh, and thought aloud on Louise's dimples laid over by the cold ground. My uncle, the one we called Uncle Brother, who was handsome and funny, returned from Europe, saw me and cried, "You mean to tell me that's Louise's child?"

It is only against all this that I can set up the great kindness of Uncle Amos. For Uncle Amos, in all the hours that I spent with him, did me the favor of not even noticing my appearance, much less comparing me to anybody more attractive. I do not think that he ever paid attention to the looks of any of us. He had a certain conglomerate of features and action and attributes attached to a name, and the name to him was inclusive of all he meant by us. "Dolly doesn't want to do that," he would say, as though anyone should understand that Dolly, being Dolly, did not want to have a new pink dress and be a flower girl in Cousin Edna Lawrence's wedding. As surely as I knew that he never thought of my looks, I also knew that he sensed my heart. He understood those highly important physical things which most adults are annoyed to have to deal with in a child: being tired or hungry or sleepy or wanting to go to the toilet, or simply being bored. And once when I cut my foot on the blade of a hoe and ran to him with the blood welling marvellously between my toes and clotting the dust, he carried me running to the well and when the water gushed into the blood we watched it together, and he held me tight, turning my ankle this way and that for better cleansing. I felt him shudder to the bone. I was closer to him then, I think, than to any other human being in the world; perhaps I was never to be so close to anyone again.

But if my love for Uncle Amos was always in the foreground, my affection for 'Tary was a quieter force with a reality of its own. I used to wonder who they thought they were talking about when they spoke of her at Dellwood, for she could avoid comparison with Louise no more than I, and in this comparison her looks were judged a poor second. It is true that she was not flirtatious. She had an open, direct manner of speech. Bending to some irksome little job she was apt to frown as though she disliked to waste her time so. In repose her face was a little sharp-edged for beauty; her mouth was too small. Yet I always thought of her as beautiful, perhaps because save for a few times, I see her always in motion, a quick small body moving fast, as though in flight like a bird's. They said that she rode horses a great deal as a girl.

They said other things about her during the long weary afternoons at Dellwood. They said that she was always cold and haughty, so different from Louise, whose affection flowed at the smallest thing; and I sat and thought how this was not true, for though 'Tary never lavished kisses on me as my great-aunts did, her eyes loved me often and she held me warmly to rock me to sleep. So I gave up believing any of the things the Morgans said about their own; it was as though they talked about another family with similar names. I did not take them seriously enough to let them trouble me any more, and indeed the Morgans hardly seemed serious themselves. They would throw off the direst accusations on their kin with a round of light laughter, or a casual side-remark, like Grandmother saying of Uncle Brother whom they all adored: "Selfish to the bone, always was." Or the time that 'Tary was taking me out to the buggy to go home and Grandmother stuck her head out the window without getting up from her nap and called pleasantly: "Don't worry about Negro trouble, Ary. I've always said Amos Dudley is a ruthless man."

Therefore, when I told Uncle Amos what Aunt Sara had said about him, I thought no more of telling it than if I had been recounting a dream. We were walking back from the barn when I told him. "Aunt Sara says you're just a hill-billy come down here and got yourself a plantation by mysterious means."

I liked the sound of "mysterious means," but Uncle Amos did not like the sound of it. He backed me up to the fence and looked straight through me.

"I'm going to tell you one thing," he said. "You're old enough to listen to lies and you're old enough to know the truth."

"Yes, sir," I said.

"The Morgans are all right," he said. "Your mother's grandfather came down here before the Civil War and got himself some land at a time any fool could get land by holding out his hand to the government for a deed and he had plenty of niggers to help him clean it up and it paid off as it was bound to do if you had one eye half-way open to watch it. So he made himself a lot of money and built himself the kind of house which his own father probably never dreamed anybody by the name of Morgan would ever set on the front porch of and call his own. During the war, the Yankees some how or other just didn't pass by Dellwood or if they did they weren't in a burning mood or it wouldn't be standing there. After the war, they claim to have had a mighty hard time, with eight thousand acres of land to raise vegetables and wheat on and niggers flocking in to turn out the cotton. They saw the cotton come up again out of the ground it's always come up out of and they thought, first new dresses and suits they could buy to strut through the Gayoso again, The Morgans must be some folks; we were here before the war and we are here after the war.

"They see new folks move into the Delta whose own fathers fought the war, like mine did, and they never ask about the war because being from the hills they never figger you've heard of the war, and when you settle thirty miles from them in what is swamp and cane brake and sweat like a nigger to clear land and bust it and plant cotton on it and build a house, they come over and take one look and say: A hill-billy. What right's he got in the Delta?

"For the Delta is theirs, you understand. They've misplaced the deed and other folks have misplaced the memory, but all the Morgans think they once saw the deed, so they hold on to the memory which says: The whole Delta belongs to us. What do you know about your Aunt Sara's husband?"

"He was a gambler, and handsome. He bought her a car and married her for her money, but they eloped in the night with Grandfather close behind. Just when everybody got to liking him all right, he ran away, nobody knew why."

"A cheap river-boat gambler he was, and smelled like barber shop perfume. Nobody knows why he ran away—six thousand dollars of your grandfather's money is good enough reason for a man like him to run. He had a face like a turtle. He was nothing but a cheap crook."

"Uncle Amos," I said earnestly, "his picture does look something like a turtle."

He put his arm around me going home. "You have to see things the way they are," he said kindly, "not the way the Morgans want to tell you about them. But they're over yonder;

we're over here. We got nothing against them."

I was so glad when Uncle Amos said "we," that I would have gladly given up anything to him for it. Though I had done considerable thinking about the dashing qualities of Jack McGillister, standing before the portrait that Aunt Sara had got painted from a photograph. He had on a bowler hat that the painter had tried several times to remove, but she had never been satisfied, so he painted it back on and left it so. But one thing still worried me. It was 'Tary who had told me, Nobody knew why he left. For this reason I brought the story up at the supper table.

"There was some mystery about it," 'Tary insisted. "Sara always hinted there were things we didn't understand."

"Of course, *she'd* say that," Uncle Amos said. "You know she would, Ary. Sara? Of course."

"I suppose so," 'Tary said, and I took that for an admission that Uncle Amos was right, and we were all agreed. My mind, like sand, was smoothed out again.

It was at the party at Dellwood that I had my romance with Uncle Brother. The reality of it extended through three hours, the dreams of it through one night; but no other word but romance will do, even though the party was given for the guests come to Uncle Brother's wedding. I was standing near the wall in my lavender flowered batiste dress with the lavender organdy sash and my hair was slipping out of the lavender organdy ribbon in pieces stubby as weeds and my tough feet swelled miserably in the patent leather shoes. Other little girls were standing near me; I had drawn close to them because of their measurements alone. It did not occur to me that they were fourteen like me, for they sat with ease in their flowered dresses and were of another order which had nothing to do with their being cousins and playmates at other times.

Then Uncle Brother came, out of the lighted rooms where the laughter was, into the lighted hall with the orchestra, the children, and the dancers who seemed to notice nothing but their partners in the proud kingdom of those who dance. He came to us. I looked away so as to escape the little pain of having him see me and know me and search beyond me (for I was born with the true instinct of a wallflower), but he said: "I am looking for Dolly," and even then I thought he must mean another Dolly, until he stretched out his hand, smiling with a gay radiance which even the Morgans lavished only on the most extraordinary. He taught me to dance that night, or tried gallantly to; he brought me punch and sandwiches and led me around the room; and he most completely won my heart.

For half the night after I was sent to bed I reviewed the evening; for the other half I planned the morning, the next day, the months ahead, leaving a tiresome space of two weeks for Uncle Brother's honeymoon. Of all this, the morning was most important. By the time the room was light, I was running down the stairs. I wandered about the empty, disordered rooms for an hour; then I went to sleep on the sofa with my head sliding uncomfortably against a spangled handkerchief. Uncle Amos and 'Tary woke me and laughed.

"Too much party, darling?" 'Tary asked.

I pulled the handkerchief painfully off my cheek, one spangle at the time, and said: "I'm waiting for Uncle Brother. We're going riding."

"Riding? Why, baby, Uncle Brother's got to get married today."

"He'll go with me," I said, but I could make it no more than a whisper.

Uncle Amos picked me up. "Now, honey. Uncle Brother

wanted to show you a good time last night, but he won't be noticing you today. He wanted to be especially nice to you on account of your mother—he missed her so."

"Oh, Amos!" It was not until 'Tary cried out that I knew the arrow was indeed in my heart.

I struggled free from him and went to her and cried. I looked up only once at Uncle Amos, in some unvoiced appeal for him to take it back, but he stood distressed and adamant, as pitiable in his way as I. "I didn't know—" he began, but he could not finish that because it was not true; he had known; and as he turned away Uncle Brother himself walked into the room.

My tears were gone; I stood apart. Half-way through the room, he saw me and smiled. He kissed my cheek. "How's my sweetheart?" Then he was gone.

I felt that I owned the high rich room that I stood in and faced Uncle Amos who was right.

"He did notice me," I said, and held my hour of brilliance in my heart defiant, for he could not see how one could love a thing and yet disbelieve in it.

The day of the big quarrel was a quiet, uncomfortable day, a Sunday when 'Tary had the Morgans to dinner, a dry sunny fall day, still hot, so that my most vivid memory of it comes with the wry taste in my mouth of a long talkative dinner and an eternity of talkative afternoon, the fidgets of my Sunday dress, petticoat and shoes.

Tanky Phillips, a cousin from Memphis, was there, being a visitor at Dellwood. Tanky was not her name—I forget what it was—but they called her that because when she was little she said "tanky" instead of Thank you. She had on a grown-up sort of dress: a dark green skirt with light green panels and a matching green bolero jacket over a white lace blouse. I stared at this costume until it is a wonder it did not dissolve, but I was not at all covetous, because it had never occurred to me that I would ever be eligible for anything but little girl clothes. Grandmother told me to take Tanky in the yard and show her around, but she did not want to play at the well for fear of getting wet, she thought it was too far to walk to the bayou, she gave only one glance at the barns, and she finally stepped in some chicken stuff and suggested we go back inside. She made the whole outdoors seem very dirty and distasteful.

"How old are you, Tanky?" Grandfather asked when we walked into the hall.

"Fifteen," said Tanky.

"I'm fourteen," I said, marvelling.

They all looked at me. "Are you trying to tell me," said Grandmother to 'Tary who hadn't said anything, "that that child is the same age as Tanky?"

"A year younger," said 'Tary.

"Come here to me," said Grandmother and inspected me, prodding, as though I were a horse. "Louise's child," she mourned at last. "Ary, what on earth are you thinking about?"

I went back and sat down. "Cover your mouth when you yawn," said Grandmother.

Uncle Amos held me next to him under one arm, but there I seemed monstrous, even to myself.

"What would the good Lord have us do?" Grandmother asked Aunt Sara and Uncle Brother and Aunt May, Uncle Brother's wife. There was that little casual exasperated charm in her aging voice, the way it always was when she called on the Lord. I suspected Grandmother of something; she knew perfectly well how old I was.

"Let her alone, for one thing," Uncle Amos said sharply, but nobody paid him the slightest attention.

Aunt Sara applied herself to the problem. "I know," she said brilliantly. "Send her to finishing school with Tanky."

"I've already got a roommate," Tanky said quickly, and looked away.

"She wouldn't have to room with you, of course," said Aunt Sara. "Don't be so snooty, Tanky."

Whereupon I thought that Tanky was going to cry and fascinated with this discovery about the limitations of green taffeta, I stared at her a long time while they went on discussing me. I was surprised when I started listening again, that they were still on the same subject. This was quite unlike them. Usually they could not pursue one thought to the end of a sentence. I listened closely until I caught on that while they were addressing all their remarks about me to 'Tary (it is perhaps unimportant to recall that my father, poor man, was not present), they were in reality not talking for her benefit at all. They were not even particularly interested in me. What they were doing was criticizing Uncle Amos. They were taking a hand in something that had been badly done, though of course since 'Tary was a Morgan she was not responsible. Also they were going through another rite of affection for Louise.

"Come here, Dolly," Uncle Brother said, and took my hand. "Wouldn't you like to go to finishing school and meet the boys? Wear pretty clothes like Tanky and learn to dance?" (He did not remember. My look said he had betrayed me; but he did not notice.)

Grandfather absently patted my head, while Aunt Sara, a magazine on her knees composed a letter about me to the finishing school in Nashville. She was the only one who would take it that far. No Morgan but Aunt Sara would have pursued a Morgan commentary into the reality of a postage stamp. It was she who had actually married her flirtation.

In writing the letter, she established for Uncle Amos a point of attack that was sound and real, a thing which could be asked for and taken and torn in two pieces, which is what he did to the letter. And I knew as he sat there, bent slightly forward, with the pieces of the letter one in each hand, convicted in every eye of unforgiveable rudeness, that the Morgans had won a small victory because they had thought this all along about Amos, but that Uncle Amos who had known all along he was rude had won a larger victory: he would never again have to pretend to be bothered with the Morgans.

When they had all gone home it was dusk, and 'Tary stood by the lamp in the bedroom crying with a sound like a child's cry so that I thought the baby was hurt or feared the dark. Uncle Amos's voice surprised her coming out of the closet where he was finding his work shoes. He came butting out from the hanging clothes in his sock feet, his hair mussed.

"What on earth, Ary?"

She turned her face away into the lamp, and I saw her eyes dark as lamp smoke, and the strange downward turning of her mouth. "You cannot say you did it because you love her," she said.

"That's right," he said, "but unless you stop them, Ary, they have you lock, stock and barrel, sign on the dotted line."

"There is no other reason," she said and her voice was clear without a tremor though the dark tears splotched her eyes into her face like ink— "There is no other reason to take and tear and trample down except love."

"If you don't clear them out once in a while, there aint any space to love anybody in."

"But you did not do it for Dolly, Amos? Tell me, Amos. You did not do it for love?"

"That's right," he said easily and came closer to her. "I did it for myself."

There was fear in her turning to face him. "Then I don't want to talk about it any more," she said. "I don't want to have to think about it."

"All right, Ary." Then he dropped the shoes. "But come here, Ary. Let me just tell you—Ary, please!"

She turned and darted from the room, and I sped soundlessly ahead of her, for I had taken off my shoes the minute the Morgans left and they had not heard me at all.

I knew then about 'Tary's happiness. I knew that it was a flight from terror. She was like a planet, forever hurtling and forever bound, and Uncle Amos was lonely and bright and powerful, like the sun.

For a week I roved the barns and the bayou as I had always done, but the old sights wearied me and the world seemed as dry and dirty as ever it had to Tanky. For all things that had seemed one now stood separate: trees from water, barns from house, cabins from field, Negroes from master, 'Tary from Uncle Amos, I from all else. In separation many became weak, and many became meaningless. I was both, and so I did not wait for the day which should fling us facing on the field; I went ahead of time to surrender.

I came from the well to where he stood talking off the side porch to three field hands. It was after lunch, his nap was just done, soon he would mount and ride into the fields.

When the Negroes left I was there, standing in the place where they came day and night to call for him and say request or grievance up to where he stood, one hand on an unpainted post worn smooth from his grasp, a foot propped on a rail muddy from his shoe.

"What little nigger gal is this?" he asked me.

"Uncle Amos," I said, "can you send me home today?"

He knew at once that I meant more than going home for a visit. "Come up here, Dolly," he said. But I stood in the place of not-crying. Then he said: "Is it 'Tary?"

"No."

"Is it the other children?"

"No."

He thought a minute, and it came to me with surprise that it was hard for him to think about himself and his mind when he did so went slow as a rusty bolt. "Me then?" I did not answer. "Why, Dolly?"

I had to answer him. I knew that the same as I knew that I could not go away without coming to him, or tell him through 'Tary, and I knew that my answer had to be the truth. I looked up at him and adored him and said:

"Because I am afraid of you."

He shuddered at the words, and I remembered the day when my foot was hurt, the blood and the bright water washing.

"What have I ever done to you?" he demanded. "I told you the truth once or twice—" he, at least, remembered the dance— "but you needed to know the truth. I won't have you made a fool of, sent to fancy schools for prissy old maids to show you how to hold a tea cup. Was it that? You wanted to toady along behind your cousin, and wear fancy clothes? I'll buy you—"

"No!" I cried. "Not that, Uncle Amos. You know—"

I could not finish. I could not say, You know the way I am better than anybody; they know that I will never be Louise's daughter, but you know that I will never try. I could not bear the thought of the clothes Uncle Amos would buy for me.

He waited a long time for me to go on, but the tears choked me, and my hands were awkward and rough, and my body, bigger already than 'Tary's, would have stretched all my mother's grace thin to cover it. When I looked up again, I knew why the veils of security that Uncle Amos had covered me with by saying "Dolly" and not noticing, had fallen from me, for his pride had shut him from me, and the eyes that regarded me were clear as sunlight. I stood there naked to his gaze, miserable and ugly and crying, wishing to go back to all the things I renounced when I came to him—silence and understanding and endearment, to say what I wanted his heart to say, I am only a child.

But he gave no quarter. He spoke to me on equal ground, kindly and direct. "I have kept you and fed you and given you everything I would give to my own child. But you are free. You are free to go home and you are free to come back whenever you will. We will always be glad to have you. I'll see that you get home today."

I saw him walk away from me down the porch, through the screened section and down the front steps, out to where his horse stood hitched by the fence, and he mounted and rode away. He did not look back once, and no one at all could have said: This day is different for him from any other.

I went into the house hunting 'Tary, but she was gone with the children, I couldn't remember where. I lay on the sofa in the empty hall and watched for a ghost.

The Indictment: Ary

POOR DOLLY! She was Louise's fault, I suppose, the same as I was Louise's fault. Louise living had a ghost with her. Louise dead left the ghost behind. The ghost was what they thought she was; and though I knew what she really was, I still contended with a ghost.

She was the one they compared me to. Sara was older with the energy of a horsefly, the inquiring walk of a chicken, and the martyred, dictatorial goodness of a mule—she does not invite human comparison. But Louise. How should what they thought of her drive me to acting differently from what they thought of her, when they were wrong in the first place? I knew she was pretty. They said beautiful, and that was right too, sometimes: and she had luck: the times she could whistle up beauty happened to be the times people wanted to look up and see it. She became the girl every man who knew her will see when bald, fat, fifty, and slightly drunk, he sings the old songs. All the Morgans see her too, when they speak on family things; for she was what Morgan men meant by Morgan women, but before she happened, they were never quite sure they weren't lying.

Yet all of us had exactly what Louise had: manners, family attitudes, many stories, a few secrets, and good humor that shot up like a child's temperature when company came. One thing she had in excess of us all, and that was life: she was alive as life would have her be: she was abend with it, tree with wind. This was her great talent, and it took energy to feed. The same energy that I found in myself to feed strength with, for if Louise is the pretty one, I said, they will call me the strong one.

Horses were a way—I rode them, the wilder the better, calm outside because inside I had to keep the fear small, and when I walked the ground again with no bone shattered, I felt clean. Men were another way—they never flocked to me, still I was never alone. Good ones came with the serious look all ready to grow; I let it grow, thinking, Maybe and Maybe; then suddenly I would know the truth and that truth is cold. And after they had gone I would feel the cleanness again, whetting the bright blade of strength. I remember thinking that it would be a man I chose, not a husband; the difference, I told myself, between a good horse and one that will get you to town.

We were playing with Aunt Grace Linley's children just before Duane Stevens came along. We played the same old singing games with them my children like to play, children being forever the same: Chickamy, chickamy, craney crow, went to the well to wash my toe, and Hickamy, hickamy, horney cup, how many fingers do I hold up. Louise had a new one, the one about John Brown's baby had a cold upon its chest, and you go through it over and over with gestures for words until you finally aren't saying much of anything. You rock your arms in a cradle for Baby.

"Do it again, Louise!" the children cried.

They turned to me. "Ary do it, too!"

I swung my arms for them.

"Heavens sake, Ary," Louise said, "you'll make John Brown's baby cry, rocking him like that. You look like you've no idea about a baby."

"Why should I have?" I asked.

"I'll have three," Louise said. "Two girls and a boy. That's what I want."

"Then you can die among the diapers," I said.

"What's this?" Aunt Grace Linley called from down the porch. They were pretending to talk, but big pitchers also have big ears. "You don't want *children*, Ary?"

Mother just laughed, but Aunt Frank, who lived with us, said in a low tone you could have heard to the levee: "Way she's going she might as well not want," and they all looked away, quick. I knew then I had them worried. I was nearly twenty-two.

I got up. "Has it ever occurred to you," I flung toward the grown end of the porch, "that having children is one thing Morgans and trash do exactly the same way. That and going to the privy." Louise giggled. "And dying," I said. I ran upstairs, fast, every step, going nowhere, and ran through the upper gallery and plunged down the servant's stairs, my skirts scooped up to my knees. I swung round the bannister and there he was—Amos Dudley. I had forgotten about him, though he was usually my way, when church was over, of remembering it was Sunday. It was mid-afternoon; the servants were all gone to meeting; the kitchen and all the back of the house was still, except for Brother out near the cistern trying out a new casting rod. I guess Amos Dudley had been out there too. So many Morgans swamped him. You could hear the zing of the line playing out and the clickclick of the rewind.

Amos Dudley stood with his head raised to me and his mouth slightly open, so that anybody else would have looked like a moron; but he had too bright a face for anything to make him look dumb. All that summer long, he wore to Dellwood a gray wool suit with the high white collars of the day coming up tight under his chin. The suit was a little small for him, though he was not large, and made him look like certain old family pictures we had of small stronglooking men in rough-textured clothes, their faces slightly startled and perhaps slightly outraged at the idea of a picture or maybe at the fool who took it. There was a good deal of laughter in the family at Amos Dudley's expense, and a friend once brought the gleeful news that her husband had seen him ride into Greenville at dawn, wearing overalls, straddling a mule, and carrying a valise like a doctor's bag. He left the mule at the livery stable, put on the gray suit in an empty stall, and rented a horse to ride to Dellwood. The story irritated me. I asked her what her husband was doing out so late, and the subject died a natural death.

I could believe the overalls while he stood looking up at me on the stairway, but I could believe the suit too, and its likeness to the old pictures, so that in the long moment before I spoke, I had the distinct impression that one of the old photographs had come to life to move, vigorous and doubtful, among us.

I dropped my skirts and laughed. "Well," I said, "you look like I caught you stealing."

"It makes me proud to see you," he said, and tried to catch himself, but it was too late. Somebody must have told him once that a straight line is the shortest distance between two points; then whoever told him that lost the book. "Usually I know when I'm going to see you, and I can draw myself up to meet it; but coming on you sudden, I had no time to plan. It made me say I'm proud."

Before I can answer a word, he was gone. I went reflectively into the kitchen and ate a tomato. I was proud, too, proud of myself. When he said that, the pride came back. That night Mark Sandefur came to see Louise and Duane Stevens came with him.

There was a great deal to say against Duane Stevens. He drank and gambled too much. He was the only man I ever knew who disliked Louise intensely. He saw past the surface charm of her, just far enough to think her wily. He rode a tall strong horse that clove ahead wherever you rode with him, and had always to be reined in tight. He had come into a plantation down below Rolling Fork. Before that he had lived in Memphis. He had come to the Delta when the old lady—a half-sister of his mother's, enraged at her own family for moving off to Texas and striking oil without, she said, saying Pea-turkey to her— left him the place and he had come with a certain set of ideas about how a planter ought to act. It was not so much then that he liked to drink and gamble, but that he thought a planter ought to drink and gamble. He had that sort of fascination for himself that I had too, only being a man with money and property gave him leeway that dizzied me.

I arrived quite coolly at this analysis of his faults, but I was a few days late with it. The heart will not be commanded; it forgave the moment the mind accused. Not forgave, no; the heart would not listen. It knew where it was happy, and curled up there, contented as a cat to blink and purr and betray.

For three weeks I behaved with him as I had with all the others, but there was a difference. He knew it, and I knew it, but nobody else did. Then one night everyone sang for a long time, Louise at the piano frilling the old tunes like crepe paper for a party. There were three men for her and none quite sure (least of all Louise) whose she was that evening. It was late, after the singing, when those three left; but Duane was later. He was the last of all. I was alone downstairs, locking the door, and at the sudden strike of hooves on the drive I ran out, down the steps.

The polite chatter was gone from us, knocked out of us as a

fall will knock out the breath. Our words came sharp and rude like hurled rocks.

"Tomorrow night?" "Yes." "By the gate?" "Yes, when?" "After dark." "Horseback?" "No, the buggy. Stand by the oak." "I will. By the oak." "Here. Ride with me."

The tall horse shied violently as he drew me up, but I was off the ground then, clamped between his arm and knee, and we rode kissing, while the horse reared and danced all the long way to the gate, and when he set me down my twenty-two years of Morgan raising were nothing the smallest breeze could not have carried all the way to the river. I was Ary and I would stand by the oak tree the next night.

I walked about the next day in wonder. I did not any longer have to say that I was strong, or tell myself that I was not afraid. The wonder took care of me, and night fell slowly about me. They say that gods have sometimes come to women when they felt as I felt then, and sometimes brutes and fools; I think it just depends on whoever sees her first—feeling that way, how can she know a god from a swan? They're both absurd, once you think about it. Almost as absurd as a man. Mine is an old story, too: I stood by the oak tree and nobody came.

Duane Stevens had discovered his new buggy horse had a lame foot, so rather than hitch up a mule he had put the tall horse between the shafts. It wasn't trained for that. Still, he might have made it if one wheel hadn't jammed with a limb along a stretch of corduroy road just before you get to the levee coming from his place to mine. He got out to free the wheel and about that time a mule (the one he wouldn't hitch up, for all I know) came up on the dump and a white-face heifer jumped up on the other side, out of nowhere. The horse reared and bolted straight up the levee, leaving Duane sprawled out on the corduroy stretch with a broken knee.

That is what happened, but my heart would never hear a word of it. "He would have come if he had wanted to come," my heart said, a bitter waning mutter, bereft of wonder. I did not try to make it listen. I did not answer his notes and when four Negroes carried him to the front door on a mattress like the man in the Bible, I wouldn't even come downstairs. Louise, distressed at the sight of true love below, wasting visibly away (I think she believed the thought of me had snapped the bone), kept shuttling between us. "All right," I finally said. "All right." "But Ary—not like that. Your dress." "Is it a party then?" I said and went down as I was. I knew what she meant though. She was a little bit like Sara there. Sara wouldn't have taken anything for marrying an adventurer who spent all her money and then ran off with a good deal that was Father's. That two years they were together she got to make all kinds of speeches to him, demure or wounded or tempestuous, a costume for each part. She even went all the way to Africa a few years ago, thinking he was there we all decided, though why she thought so we never knew—a dowager; but there were the speeches she never got to say. I had no speech to make. I've never believed in speeches. All I knew was that I had been a fool once and that I wouldn't be a fool again. No matter how sweet the wonder was when I slipped away through the side yard walking the wet grass to the oak tree. I was stronger even than before; I could laugh at the tears in Louise's sweet eyes, going down the long stair.

Then Louise married. Nathan Marshall. A preacher. We had never been so shocked. She told me about it on the back steps after I had been nervous for two days with the threat of it hanging all over the house—not a room you could go in but what you found it, and everybody thinking: Surely not!

Then she told me. It was like waiting so long for a shot that when you hear it you jump worse than ever. And when I jumped the words fell out: "That sweet little man! Oh, Louise, don't be so ridiculous!"

Then I said I was sorry, but she never forgave me entirely. I would never have forgiven her if she had.

"I wish there was something else to do besides get married," I confided, trying to make it up to her.

"I'm glad there isn't anything else," she said, trying too. "I'd be awful at it, whatever it was."

"I'd be good at it," I said.

"I know it."

Then she said, honestly, because she was still trying to forgive me: "I'm afraid of there being nobody to love me a great deal. Nathan loves me more than anybody else except you all."

"I wouldn't be afraid of that," I said.

"Another thing I would be afraid not to do is have children."

I didn't say anything to that. Children! It thudded you to earth, the distortion and the pain, the released muscles sagging into fat, the tired hot afternoons, and age, looking back at you out of the mirror. Louise and I would be old.

"You don't want children, Ary?"

"If you have them you don't have anything else."

"What else do you want?"

"I don't know, but something— OH, it's all too horrible!"

"I know it, Ary," Louise said sweetly, but I didn't believe her.

Nathan Marshall took her away, from me, from the Morgans, from all the broken-hearted boys who stood through the wedding gallant and stiff as West Pointers, from the Delta. Miss Louise Morgan was a preacher's wife in the hills! Miss Ary Morgan was at home with her parents, Mr. and Mrs. Ross Morgan of Dellwood Plantation, Lake Washington, Mississippi . . . recently returned from Memphis . . . entertained Mr. and Mrs.

Gavin Morgan of Holly Plantation and their three children, Margaret, Davy, and Lisa . . . are visiting in New Orleans with their relatives, Mr. and Mrs. Francis Dumaine. . . . What can you do with strength?

Then somebody told me something. It was young Tad Elmore from over at Cypress Landing. I was spending a few days with Sara who was trying to start something called The Planters Ball and thought for some reason that having me in tow would bolster her prestige.

"Planters!" Tad Elmore confided in me. "Now what's a planter? I ask you. Over at Greenville, around where you all come from, Miss Sara saw it different—the Morgans have been there for some time, a few folks like that. But over here! Why, thirty years ago everything you see was woods that didn't know the Indians had left. Then the lumber people came and raided and the cane grew up—a jungle—and the red-necks poured out of the hills with a little cash money to lay down for a lot of cheap land. You go over here a little way, there's a man still clearing land. Still clearing land. A planter. Working like a fiend in overalls and busted shoes and a straw hat. Got six nigger families at it from daylight to dark. I tell you the stumps are still smoking on that man's first field. Right in the cotton. Yes, sir, tell your sister she's got to issue Amos Dudley an invitation to that Planter's Ball."

"Who?" I said, and "Where?" I said.

I went there that afternoon in Sara's buggy, the one the colored man drove sitting up front. It was no twin rows of oak and elm that I drove through, but a twisting rutted buckshot road piled high on one side with black rank earth dug out of the bayou bed to level it. At the tip of the bayou we ran into forest where a wild gloom lingered from the first days and sudden there before me was the house high up, and the slumped hook-nose man in faded overalls coming out, and the woman's face at the window, the eyes that claimed when I asked for Amos Dudley.

I found him out in the open, standing before a little shambly shack that he already had the nerve to call the commissary, weighing sacks of cotton in with the iron weights lying about his feet and the book laid out on a rickety stand.

"Not to the cotton house!" he called. "On the wagon, the wagon! I got a bale to gin this night. Where you think the cash is coming from to pay you? Go to the gin and sit with it. Tell Mr. Eason I'll be along. Dudley. Mr. A.A. Dudley's cotton, you tell him."

"Mr. Dudley," Sara's colored man said for the third time.

He wheeled. "I heard you," he said. "Just give me—"

Then he saw me. He stood in overalls and busted shoes and a straw hat. He stood on his own land, weighing in his own cotton. He came to the buggy without hesitance or apology. He leaned on the buggy step and wiped the sweat from his eyes, and waved his hand out over the stretch of field that broke, dividing at the bayou, and spread away on either side.

"Well, Ary," he said, "how do you like it?"

I looked on every hand, the chunky fields yielding cotton with a jungle-like eagerness of growth, the ragged stand of trees around the bayou and at its far end where the house stood— that stretch that was wilderness yet, like a beast in chains. My heart beat faster. "I like it very much," I said.

"It's yours," he said. "Yours if you want it."

He thought he meant it: he said it to be believed, and I believed him. My strength flared up again in bright relief against him, the wilderness, the raw fields. I heard the words within me: I have come home. Speech of the heart, the old

betraying heart, answering the lie he thought he meant with
the strength I thought I had.

2

I suppose my trouble in those long ago days was merely an
excess of the Morgan complaint. I was romantic, like them; but
I craved a hardier kind of romance than they seemed to offer.
And maybe the thing that I cried out against that day when
Louise and I spoke of children was not age, or loss of beauty,
but the loss of that romance which had so long homed in me
as to make dislodgment slow and painful. Yet, oddly, it was
from my own children—the first two, at least—that I gained
reprieve, for no mother ever looked on two more dashing off-
spring than Elinor and Winston.

They came of age in the Delta of the 'twenties, with plenty of
money to spend and clever, rich, fagless people to run with.
They nearly drove Amos out of his mind. It was useless, I felt,
to dream of ruling them; one could only sit tight and hope for
the best. I could wish for the slower pace of my own day,
which had seemed breathless enough; but I could not help it
if the new Delta infected them, with its speed and spaces.

Elinor loved horses, my sleek daughter—all black and white
she was, black straight-pulled-back hair and black habit with
the white stock. I see the pound of the narrow, shining legs
and the fling of hooves out in the big ring with floodlights
slipping down the night air, the band playing softly, and the
loudspeaker calling gaits out to where the horseflesh heaved in
a silken pack and the dirt flew; then out of the pack she comes,
sturdy and skilled, in black and white, a small neat mast steady

against the wind. Ah, she would be like me, she thought; but though I did not tell her, she was never like me, for she would dirty herself in the stables to care for them and the knowledge and skill she was at pains for to set herself apart were common things in my day and no more thought of than table manners. But times had changed; she loved inordinately the horses Amos could afford to give her, and when she rode, especially when she won, a beauty came over her that I did not see again after Amos sold the horses in Louisville, Kentucky, and she fled home alone riding day coaches in a dusty habit, the white stock staining, mile by mile, with soot. There floated in her wake during the succeeding weeks a dozen or so two and three dollar checks, cashed in out-of-the-way places by I do not know what method of young and purposeful despair.

Then Winston, so prodigal with time from birth that when Amos says he slept for sixteen years I can find no defense for him except to see him stretched out in the glider blonde and brown, one finger making little pushes against the wall, lashes thick and lowered against a face so careless, it seems to me as I recall it, now that he is dead, that he foresaw death at nineteen and to the look that I remember is added the incredible insolence that says: Yes, I know it; but name something better to do than sleep in the glider on the front porch with a breeze in the oaks.

Yet at sixteen he did wake up, let himself be taken to the University, Ole Miss, that school the gods created to be a haven for young Winston Dudleys, and from the hour that he saw that green place of self-amused and indolent frenzy, he awoke and to nobody's knowledge ever slept again at any time, save one.

I could not have named one particular thing that Winston loved until some friends of his borrowed his car to go to the bootlegger, a place or a man named Whispering Willie, dodged first a one-eyed car which was dodging a mule, then rammed into a telephone pole where the motor parted from the hood. Nobody was hurt, but the mechanic took one look and called the junk dealer.

When Amos refused to buy Winston another car, he went back to school with the blonde, drawn, disbelieving face of a man who rides home from the hospital where he has left an arm or leg. I had not realized myself before how car-centered a life can get. I saw him then as he saw himself, as no doubt he was too many times for those who knew him ever to forget, a blonde, laughing, forever unjaded face alive and talking at the wheel with the night wind rushing past and the rustle of evening dresses in the car with the glow of a cigarette or two, and perfume, lazy in the heart of speed like a slow unwondering fly by daylight.

"Let him do the borrowing for a change," Amos said, more than half-amused that anything (to him) so small could cause such woe, and Winston did just that four months later and wrecked, coming down from the hills into the Delta at night when the flat road leaps up like a loose ribbon off the careless sleeping surface of the land. Measure for measure, in a way, but to whom is the measure made? For Winston's luck was bad; there was a truck off a sideroad instead of a telephone pole, and four hours later, in the Clarksdale hospital, he was dead. And the pained, blonde astonishment from off the white pillow was greater perhaps but still of the same ilk as the day when Amos said: "No, you certainly cannot have another car. You're up there to get an education; now go back and get it."

But Elinor's way was different, for she was not careless in happiness nor disbelieving at loss. The beauty that sat on her when the horse drew prancing with arched neck before the judging stand and the ribbon went between her teeth and the silver cup in her free hand was born out of long discipline, the hours poured into the work uncounted in the search for perfection. Therefore she was perhaps as a person more valuable than Winston. But again, to whom is the value stated? Winston, less like me, was more my own. What is there to do when you don't have a car except to borrow a car?

But Elinor girded herself for the hard world that had called her attention to its existence, went out and got herself a husband, divorced him six years later, and went on to something else, a good job with a Memphis clothing firm and all the accoutrements that draw a circle around so many people: an apartment, a kitchen, a liquor closet, and a handful of friends. I do not worry about her, for she cannot despair of herself, and if one thing fails there will be something else which she knows may possibly fail too. It is the way of the world she has discovered (and possibly the moment of discovery was the moment when Amos said: "I just sold your horses") not ever to despair and so to admit by the very strength of the denial, the total despair of its being. I have not seen her beautiful these fifteen years.

Well, so they were both gone. It was 1925, the year that Amos sold the horses, the year that Winston died. Amos was forty-one. He sold the horses because he came on Elinor swinging a bridle with force and fury into the face of the trainer, a white boy named Tommy something who had given a five-gaited mare new lease on life and a blue ribbon by barbing the throat latch and pouring a box of red pepper under her tail. She hit him in the mouth with the bloody bits. Amos said that no piece of damned horse flesh in creation was worth making his daughter think she could lord it over a boy like Tommy—what was his name? Everett? Amos took a liking to him—who was his friend.

She pranced back with the blue ribbon and turned it in to the judges with a pronouncement of what had happened; whereupon Amos said she had disgraced him and promptly sold the whole string of horses to one of those Eastern horse women with a Florida tan and a whisky cough and more money than she knew where to throw away. He made a good clean profit, he said, even counting all the time and outlay thrown into the training and carting them around. But when he went to look for Elinor he found she had already lit out for home; and when he went to look for Tommy Everett, he found it was more than the horses the Connecticut woman had bought. So he limped home, driving the station wagon, with the two Negroes, one old and one young, slammed from one side to the other over the curving road and hugging together for fear he drove so fast and silent. They all thought he was hanted anyway.

It hurt him the way Tommy Everett did. He was restless until he could refuse Winston the car; then, as though he had waited for just that event, he pronounced to me: "We are going to start living like white folks."

My eyebrows went up; I said I was not under the impression that we lived like anything else. I wondered if he felt bad about being rich. But I decided not, and further decided that, to turn the old saying around, it was not the money he disliked, but the things the money bought him. He had not felt right with a string of fine horseflesh, with his son driving a Cadillac, with the cases of Scotch and bourbon and champagne. I didn't care. In common with any Delta girl, I had floated in parties and weekends and balls from the time I could walk; society is generally worshipped, I've found, by the ones who can't quite make it. I had cultivated the extravagant, loud, and practically illiterate planter parvenu around Cypress because Amos urged it; I had not found them either unattractive or boring, but giv-

ing them up was no matter for tears. Besides, any number of
them had fallen into the time-honored Delta habit of living on
next year's crop which might at any moment turn into year-
after-next's crop, mortgages, and ruin. Amos had more than
tripled his holdings through just such failures, and they all
knew it. This made things rather embarrassing at times.

So we laid aside the blueprints for a guest house on the
lawn, and dismissed the idea, which had appealed to me, of a
brick paved terrace for summer parties. But Delta money cries
to be spent. Amos replaced his barbed wire with white fences;
his barns had running water in every stall, a spray system
cleaned the concrete floors. He invested in fine stock: poland
china hogs, housed with respect to the winds, and white-faced
Hereford beef cattle. He planted three hundred-acre tracts in
forage, and many a patch was beautiful with grain and hay. It
all turned to money. You couldn't stop him there. I doubt if he
could stop himself. He was bright about it; he never listened to
a soul; he cared no more for what farmers had always done than
he cared how the Egyptians built the pyramids. He saw as
many spooks as a half-witted Negro, but he called any ref-
erence to the color of the moon rank ignorance and went about
his business. He said he wasn't going to study about the moon
till he saw it turn to blood. At that time, he said, he was going to
head for Yocona like a bat out of hell and he hoped the Lord
would give him time to make it.

Dudley was very beautiful the spring after Winston's death.
You came to it out of Cypress Landing heading east along the
new hard surface road that ran through the place, crooked
around the house with its sweeping shady grounds and white
fences cast out to circle the big barns, a pleasant sight to rest the
eyes on before you righted with the highway into the glittering
Delta monotony of cotton, concrete and tin. The railroad ran

for a little way beside the highway and on the station stop you saw DUDLEY: Amos was a town now. A gravel cut-off across the tracks led to the commissary with Amos's office attached; the same road branched down to the gin.

Spring came early and bloomed in a wicked riot. Roses climbed the white fences overnight, flowering as they went, and a gigantic yucca plant stood white as moonlight in a damp corner of the yard.

I went back to Dellwood for a while. I was pregnant at forty-two.

It was after Winston's death that he decided we should have another son. I tried to argue with him, to tell him I was too old, to say that even if I should conceive, we were both too old to rear a small child. We already had a third child, a daughter about five then, named at the time Mary Louise—that was before Amos changed it—and I tried to show him that even she had been born later than I would prefer.

"We'll be so old they'll think we're their grandparents," I said, "and be convinced they're illegitimate."

But he would pick his point to argue on and ignore all the others. "If you just don't pay any attention to what doctors say, it don't have to cut any ice."

"Amos," I said, "doctors did not invent change of life."

"Maybe not," he said, "but they don't figure rightly how everybody's got a different life to change."

I saw he had his head set, so I agreed after a number of these almost formalized arguments (which lent to the act of sex a kind of ridiculous pomposity) to cooperate in the enterprise. The truth was that I was too lonely to care a great deal, one way or the other. I would not, in any event, have another Winston.

"All right, then," I said in conclusion, "but it's not going to do a bit of good." I said that a good many times, enough, I suspect, to become very irritating.

Soon after I became pregnant, I grew more lonely than ever, and that was why I went home. I took my daughter Mary Louise with me. My family called her "the afterthought" and driving through the rich soft sunlight toward Dellwood with the very weight of the air lightening at every mile, I saw their faces at hearing my latest news and laughed aloud.

The child beside me laughed too; I gave her a startled look. She was not laughing with me; if anything she was laughing at me. What do I know about her? I asked myself in a panic. I had never once thought that about Elinor and Winston. She had pale eyes and hair that clashed with her solid country strength of limb. It seemed at the instant of her laughter that she was not mine, nor anybody's for that matter.

I suspected then what I later had to realize fully: that I could go back to Dellwood if I wanted to, but this new loneliness was not a mood of sorrow; it was a new condition. There was no longer a Dudley among the Morgans; but I, a Morgan, was among the Dudleys. It was in the empty mimicry of her laugh that I knew this first; and from that moment the sheen dimmed on the day.

3

Mother had broken her hip the year before; she lived downstairs in a wheel chair by day, in her padded rocker upstairs from twilight till bedtime. Then night and morning we'd all have to leave her when Tee-Nincie, the little colored girl she fancied, and Ed Hoskins, the house boy, came in to lift her into bed and out of it. The door stayed shut throughout; no one of the white race ever looked upon this ceremony. Downstairs, in other rooms, we acted as if nothing were happening, knowing this was what she wanted, though she never said. Then a door shut softly, feet passed down the servants' stair, were gone; then the tinkle of her little silver bell, rung gently, audible for a mile. She was ready for us. Company had thinned out of late; the dinner table was down to only three extra leaves and sometimes we didn't extend past the centerpiece.

"What's happened to us?" I asked Father one night while the ritual went on upstairs behind the closed door. I spoke softly in a house where once you had to shout to be heard. I expected him to launch out on his piece, the one he used to declaim with a glass in one hand, pacing porch or parlor and waving his arms while nobody listened. I listened one night and found I had heard it before. The gist of it was that high-class Southern people cannot stand the climate, that it eats away at their energy and will, and that is why fine families decay, the men take to liquor and dope and the women are fractious and choosey about husbands, don't marry or think they're above the men they do marry, are weakened out of reason by child-birth because they think they're better than the men who the world knows topped them, at least once for each child. It all goes back to the heat, he would say; as my children's seventh grade geography book states: "The Southern region of the United States has a humid, hot climate which extends from March to November." They had to learn that and write it down on paper. Father was as sleek and unworried a specimen as you can find anywhere; he could deal in blubber among the Eskimos and trace their troubles to the cold. Sara waxes in social energy and sets up an investigation that would put the FBI to shame every time a new family moves to the Delta. Brother is rolling around Atlanta selling insurance like hotcakes, and belongs to the Rotary Club. You can't step in the Delta and Memphis for Morgan cousins—one turns up every week or so on the front page society section of the *Commercial Appeal.* Now how will he work this around to decay, I wondered when I asked him that: "What's happened to us?"

He hitched up closer to the fire and spat and answered me one word: "Scattered." He scratched his ear and said in a hesitant tone, as though this were a confidence we must let go no farther: "Run to women. Not so before my time. But in my time—all women." Then the silver bell cut between us and we went upstairs.

Sara coasted over in her Cadillac with the Negro chauffeur at the helm, and we lighted a fire in Mother's room, for it was cool for June and the damp gathered in her bones. Louise was very much with us the hours we sat and talked; she used to sit cross-legged with her back to the blaze, in loose nightclothes that tied at the throat and brush her long hair that turned red where the fire came through. She would make us tell over the times we used to go on trips to New Orleans, Memphis, and the coast, with Aunt Alabama to chaperone us and how I slipped off from Sara and Aunt Alabama once at Biloxi and rode all the way to Ship Island with a British sea captain—and the rest of the story we would tell if Sara was not there; how my safe return put adventure into Sara's head and gave Aunt Alabama a migraine on the boat from New Orleans home, so that while I took my turn with the cold compresses, Sara went up on deck and met Jack McGillister who ran off with her first, then with her money. And here Louise would bend limber from the waist and lay her head on her knees while her hair spilled over the floor and cry: "Oh, I missed everything! Mother, why didn't you have me sooner?" Now my late-born daughter sat where Louise was, but the talk went merrily those nights and I would almost have stayed without thought of going home, except for hearing, in odd moments, the emptiness of all the rooms that father's single cough from the library now and again made plain.

The next afternoon was fine and warm and Mother was outside with us on the porch. I chanced to see through the curtained windows of the parlor, a chair that rocked on a stand, and recalled how once as a baby, my hand had fallen down from Mother's lap and caught under the rocker painfully. But Sara said, "Oh, Ary, you were too little to remember that!" And Mother said, "You couldn't remember it, Ary. It didn't happen to you. It happened to Louise." And I, who had felt the stab and swell of the pain in all the personal exactitude of remembered experience, knew that she was right, it had been Louise; and I knew a wild grief of heart.

I waited until Sara drove away home, then till dusk when Father went into town to a Delta Council dinner, and while the servants were bearing Mother upstairs, levelling her like a full punch bowl, I laid my book aside, placing carefully the leather marker, and walked into the hall through a strip of late sunlight in which the dust moats floated timelessly. I peered into the parlor at the platform rocker, which assumed the crafty innocence of any object about to be stolen. I picked up the chair and hurried around the porch and down the sidesteps by the cistern, out to where my car stood under the walnut tree.

It was when I leaned back to close the door that I heard something which I thought at first was a footstep behind me, and as I turned my hair was suddenly drenched with sweat and I leaned gasping against the door. From far within me I felt the long, dark, bottomless drop begin, the loosening and soft warm rush of blood.

Mother said later with an irritated laziness, lacing her small fingers through the afghan holes, that she would have been glad to give me the chair; that was after they knew I would be all right. Amos said with an irritated energy that he could have bought me twenty chairs just like it; whereupon Mother said it was an antique and she doubted it. I did not care, being in such total disrepute. Alone with me, Amos said that I had done it on purpose, that I had never wanted the boy (he had not only seen it born the right sex, but had half-raised it already in his mind), and I could not summon enough energy to believe that he meant it. I just went to sleep.

I slept until he took me home that day and at home I slept throughout the warm green June, day after day eating and sinking into sleep, and I thought sometimes of Louise who died on a bright morning like yesterday and today and tomorrow and thought that it would be now for me too and that I did not care. But the day came when sleep ran out like water drained with a suck from a full tub, and Amos stood in the room at the foot of the bed.

I had never seen anybody so alive. His hair, which was short cut and thinning evenly all over, was touched with red like sunned fruit. His belt indented a slab of belly; the skin of his bare forearms and face was tough with health, and caked mud spilled unheeded from his boots.

"Come here, Mary Louise, darling. Come give me a kiss."

She had run to the door, barefoot, and brown as he, with eyes all the more pale so that it seemed the sun would have blinded her. She was unspeakably dirty with grass-stain and mud and smelled of the colored children she played with. Amos caught her up to the ceiling.

"Tell Mother your name, big girl."

She looked down at me. "My name is Dinah Lee Dudley," she said, as though replying to a stranger.

"I changed it," Amos said. "She liked Dinah Lee best."

"You don't do any such thing!" I cried. "She was named for—"

"I know who she was named for. Just like Winston was named for your uncle, and Elinor for your mother. But this one's going to have her own name, not anybody else's. I would have asked you, but you were asleep."

"Well," I said, and laughed.

"You can go back to sleep now," he said.

It was then when he seemed so alive that I recalled in detail the day that I thought he was dead. He had been out cutting sorghum in a patch between the garden and the barns when a twister came and ripped up the front fence. I had called him twice to come in, but he wouldn't; and I saw him out there swinging the long knife along with the Negroes, who fell running in all directions when they saw what was on the way, stopping to point first and cry: "Whoo-ee! Whoo-ee!"

Then in the still and oven-hot weather in which the coiling black pillar of wind tacked and played out beyond the highway near and far and near again, he was left alone and small and working, the knife blade rising and falling against the cane. He had yet to hear anything unusual.

Elinor and Winston and the servants and I stood in a quiet little group on the front porch and watched it cross the highway. When the white board fence out by the cattle gap clattered suddenly and vanished, I ran out toward the sorghum field. He did not even see it until I reached him, and then it was gone, dissipating in open field. The wind, rushing inward upon us in its wake, tore the hair from our scalps and thrust the sorghum every which way while the oak leaves in the yard whipped, screaming. All he said was, "Well, I swan," and looked at me with a sudden tender gratitude. He followed me back into the house like a child.

Inside, he broke into a terrible sweat which he could not explain and fell suddenly in work clothes and dusty shoes down on the floor where he began to cry out aloud until his eyes closed and his breathing filled the house. His face was a white-green, and his beard seemed to spring out in an unsightly stubble. I helped him to lie on the couch. The sweat had soaked every stitch of his clothes and his dusty shoes sprawled over the fresh green-striped covering. He was not pretty. Whatever held him erect and constantly on the move was loosed like a broken buckle and he fell in all directions.

Elinor and Winston stood in the door. I said: "Call the doctor at once." But he opened his eyes and said, "No."

They did not move to do anything; they only looked at him and through lowered lids out of whatever profound torture had come on him, he looked back at them. I saw how beautiful they were, how straight and clean and swift, and I dropped his hand and circled his head suddenly with both arms, blotting him from them. But he pushed me aside to finish out the look with which he replied to them before his eyes searched for the child, the little one, sitting on the floor where he had lain. She had run in from outside when the storm began to brew and though I had sent her out clean in body-waist and pants and dress, she had left the dress somewhere and the pants too. She sat cross-legged, unconscious of nakedness as she was of the dirt that streaked her or of her tangled blonde hair and crusted nose. For a moment more we heard the suck and heave of his breath; then he whispered to the child, "Come here," and she ran to climb and fall on him and shut him from their sight. I ran at the door. "Get out of here," I said, and shook my apron before me. "Go somewhere, anywhere, just out." When I turned back he was sitting up; he rubbed his eyes with one hand and the child was on his knee.

"I saw a ball of fire," he whispered, "turning slow and blazing bright. And in it were the faces that I knew once, a long time ago. But they suffered, Ary, oh, they suffered so."

It was from that time that Mary Louise Dinah Lee Dudley was his, but in the Delta rush of excitement and disaster I forgot, perhaps we both forgot. But he remembered first and changed her name while I slept. From that event the attention of the Morgans turned elsewhere (as perhaps he had known it would when he stripped her of Louise's name). She grew a tomboy whose sensitive eyes and delicate hair could not manage so much as to belie her dangerous activities, but held on for dear life like helpless things in a stormy boat. I fought with dirt and never won; she was a patchwork of scratches and dirty adhesive tape and not a day passed I did not see her go out on the place with Amos without wondering what state she would come home in. I had dreaded adolescence for Winston and Elinor: for Dinah I entreated it to hurry. Something was bound to happen then, and it did: she became very clean. Instead of khaki shorts and middy blouse soaked in watermelon juice, she now wore jeans, soft, laundered, and faded, like an old Negro man's on Sunday, but rolled neatly to the calf; a clean white boy's shirt rolled high and tight on a fine length of arm; worn leather barefoot sandals in warm weather, and a cheap bright gold locket from the store. Her room—small, the last on the wing—was neat as barracks, the dressing table with no beauty aids but a dozen lipsticks and a brush which kept her long hair silky. The walls were all but papered in pictures cut from movie and fashion magazines, incredibly handsome stars in sumptuous dress, the models reclined in velvety languor, their eyes looking everywhere. I wondered for a long time that she did not imitate what she studied with the patient care of an astronomer, but it came over me once when I had business in there alone that in her own secret way she had imitated, that her jeans, shirt, sandals, locket and long hair formed an ensemble as calculated as ever lamé and cigarette holder were. Calculated to place her in Dudley as Dinah, known at great distances from one end of the place to the other, known about the store where fine dress would have hobbled the free ease with which she sat crosslegged on the dressgoods counter and talked with any and all, known to Amos who thought that all unconsciously she had fitted to the mold of his mind. And perhaps she had. It is natural for women to suspect each other.

But purposely or not, she had turned up a blind street, I feared. Junior Wavell, at the store, was crazy about her, but she had pushed him out of trees as a child and still beat him unmercifully at cards and dollar pitchings in the shade back of the store. Nothing would happen there, I thought, but I stayed alert for signs. I didn't want any Wavells in the family, good people, of course, but. No, she would have to stray, and sometime soon she would want to; then I would be ready and Sara could be mustered and Morgans everywhere could turn again.

4

I waited and while I waited she turned sixteen and winter came, the winter of 1937, very cold. Elinor, childless after six years of marriage, had gotten a divorce a few months previously, which was to Amos a fact as cold as death and perhaps made the winter seem even colder than it was.

The water pipes froze and burst. The servants' hands cracked and turned ashy when they bore in water. The well, in spite of sawdust, trickled thinly down a splintered tube of ice. By mid-morning the heater roared red hot in the hall and a wood fire blazed in every room and yet there were the chill places where I hugged my sweater around me and fled as if from drawn steel. I who have a gift for coolness in summer can do nothing with the cold but hate it. It turns my hair so dry it clings crackling to the brush. If I touch iron after silk the shock bites me. My rings slip on dry fingers that no lotion will soften, and I bend and run from fire to fire. There is an hour or so of the afternoon, however, after the house is put away that the hall grows warm from beam to crevice and then I can curl on the couch and breathe the steady breath of human weather, and read or think in peace. It is the hour before the low sky will lose its metallic glint and grow loose and dull, before Amos's step will descend upon the porch and he will stand in the open door while the cold springs past him upon me and cry: "Good God, woman! It's too hot in here."

It was during that still hour or two that winter it dawned on me one day there was someone around the house who had no business to be there.

I had seen him first, I think, from the unsheltered side porch that ran the length of the house and gave the wind a fine free stretch. Tools hung on the porch wall and I was out for pliars and hammer. I ran, my fingers clenched against the touch of the cold metal; the wind knifed tears into my eyes and through their haze and the sound of the wind and the dread of the iron touch, I saw him standing languid by the gate to the well, a five-gallon galvanized bucket in one hand. He wore a scarred leather jacket and denim work pants and the top buttons of his shirt were open on a bare brown throat. He stood with one hand at rest on the iron gate and watched my flight curiously, as though he looked out of some past summer day. Back by the stove I forgot him; the heat wiped him out of my mind. Afterwards, at various other places and times of day I had seen him: once bringing wood into the kitchen, again at the kitchen door; then crossing the yard to hunt between Amos bundled in brown and a Negro in blue he stopped lightly in the same jacket and open-throated shirt and the hand on the shouldered gun was bare. But each of these times I could remember the sight of him only for a moment, never long enough to see where he had come from or where he was going. It was as though he had passed these several times (and others, until there was no place in the yard or among the outhouses that I could not recall him) a window in my mind.

That very day I had invited Sara and two visiting Memphis ladies to luncheon and bridge. Amos, who had had no appetite for social life since 1925, had his dinner at Wavell's house. We had adjourned from the table into the hall, and I excused myself to look for a score pad in my bedroom. My step across the threshhold broke the fascination of the perfume flagon. I discovered him bent far over it, his elbows spraddled on the dresser top to bring his nose down close. The exact reverse of a tiptoeing child, he gave the same meddlesome impression.

I shut the door. He replaced the thick stopper, watching me closely from the mirror, so that the leaning figure, back toward me, was of the same glimpsed nature as the times I had seen him distantly here and there, but the face that came out of the mirror at me seemed infinitely nearer and belonging to another, invisible but reflected. I was confronted in the same moment with the mystery of distance and the shock of nearness. It was an ordinary face, with no sharp feature, dark blonde under dark blonde hair which lay boyishly soft. His slightly heavy lips were parted, though not smiling and the blot of a missing front tooth added to his boyishness. But his eyes overrode the rest. They were noticing eyes; immensely aware of attractiveness and signs of money, but more curious than covetous; they retained their knowledge of his self-approved dignity.

I have known for a long time that the first person to speak in any situation is almost sure to lose, and I knew that he was in no position to delay. It must be said for him that he did not continue to wait for me, but turned, saying: "I come to chunk up the fire."

"I have servants to do that when I need it," I said. I pointed to the opposite door which opened into the back bedroom and so out to the side porch. I obviously could not send him out through the hall. "You can go that way. And close the door tight."

I played such an efficient game of bridge, I took high score from my guests which was hardly polite.

"Who is he?" I asked Amos that night. "I found him in the bedroom today."

"He said you turned him out."

"I should say I did. Meddlesome thing."

"Doing what, Ary?"

"Smelling my perfume. Down like this, smelling."

He went to the dresser, unstoppered the bottle and smelled it himself. "I reckon he never knew anybody could have such a big bottle of per-fume. How much did that cost, Ary?"

"That's neither here nor there."

"No. How much does a bottle like this cost?"

"Oh, thirty or forty dollars. It lasts for years."

"Lordy! Let's hope he didn't spill any."

"But who is he, Amos?"

"Joe Ferguson by name. Wavell took him on at the gin last fall. No good at all on a steady job, but fine for this and that. It's me he likes to do for. Anything at all. A good shot too."

"But where's he from?"

"I don't know as I ever asked him."

"I don't want him around the house."

"Why not? He's a good boy. I know him well."

"I just don't want him around, coming and going like he owned the place."

Amos held the heavy bottle between himself and the lamplight. "There was a time," he said, "when I'd stand in front of the jew store windows in Leland and wish the eyes out of my head for such as this to give you. Not just to give you either. Wondering on the like of folks who'd have little enough use for any manner of thing to put cash money out on what didn't matter. If I could have got through the window glass I'd have had to smell it because I would stand and think, Suppose it don't even smell good? Now wouldn't that touch it off? Oh, many's the time," he finished dolefully, "I stood coming back from the store in the cold, and stared at such as this."

"I did my share of window gazing, too," I said crisply, "but I'd certainly never have gone into anybody's house to meddle. And you wouldn't have either."

"In Dellwood I meddled," he said. "That was my courting days. I just saw that I never got caught. Oh, come off it, Ary. You see Joe Ferguson tomorrow and tell him you're sorry."

"*I'm* sorry?"

"Sure sorry. You ought to be sorry. You think he hasn't got feelings like anybody else."

"I doubt if he has more than anybody else," I said.

And the next morning I found, wrapped in a piece of newspaper and stuck in the wastebasket in the back bedroom one of my hand-painted china plates from Dellwood, broken beyond repair.

There came one fair warm day to make me care if I lived or not. I puttered around the winter ruin of the garden, mostly looking, thinking nothing at all. I went in for coffee finally, stopping on the front steps to admire Dinah. She sat at the far west end of the porch. One leg dangled toward the ground, the other was propped up. She was eating a biscuit and jelly sandwich. Her clean shirt—an old one of Winston's—was rolled almost to the shoulder, revealing a fine length of arm and wrist, nowhere near delicate, but strong like her broad long hand and curving fingers. Her jeans, rolled half to the knee, fitted smoothly over her thigh. From out her open collar, that grimey locket she fancied swung shining in the sun. I saw then why she was not looking at me.

Joe Ferguson was crossing the side yard with a closed molasses bucket in his hand. The leather jacket was slung over his shoulder and his arms were also bare to the warm day. "Bucket's leaking," she said. "Crazy as you look," he answered; and she dropped from the side of the porch like a stone. I saw as she went to him, her head tilting up as though she climbed to meet him, that tall as she was, he was taller, and that his hair was the same dry silken texture of her own. I saw this in great detail but as though at a far remove, like surveying some large vista backward through a telescope, or seeing Lookout Mountain prismed in the pearl-size glass of a souvenir paper knife. I felt the smallness and outrage of one who is tricked, and I closed the distance between us to stand over them at the edge of the porch. But what, after all, could I say?

"Where did you get that molasses?" I asked him.

"Mr. A.A. told me to take some."

"Then where did you get the pantry key?"

He waited, and I saw him wait.

"I got it for him," Dinah said.

I stopped her in the hall when she came in. "You didn't give him the key," I said. "It was not with the others and you can't ever find anything. He found it himself."

She handed me the key which was tied by a rawhide strip to a cedar board marked Pantry. The pantry was an outhouse, and I was particular about my outhouse keys.

"He's just as good as we are," she said. That would have taken us right into it, but I wasn't going to be that easy.

"That's neither here nor there," I said. "The King of England has got no right to walk in and get my pantry key."

"I got it for him," she said.

"Where did you find it?"

"On the dresser."

"No," I said. "Wrong guess."

She was ashamed. "You have no cause to lie to me," I said gently. "About anything."

"No'm."

"Have you?"

"No'm." She made no excuse, and for this I kissed her forehead.

"I'm going into Greenville today," I said. "Wouldn't you like to go and buy some new clothes?"

"We're going fishing," she said, and stood on her toes, happy to have the lie business over. "Daddy and Joe and me. Right after dinner."

"Oh." I wandered into the dining room to let more sunlight in. There I said "Oh" again, but so differently that I brought her in after me. I knelt over my Meissen compote from Dellwood which lay shattered on the rug before the buffet. Which one of the three?

"Dinah, who could have done it?"

But she hardly cared enough to notice, much less to have broken it. "Mother," she cried in a happy burst, "you come go too."

"Go where?"

"Fishing. With me and Joe and Daddy."

I got to my feet. I had never liked to fish. "All right. I'll go too."

It was while we stood out front after dinner with Amos and Joe loading the bait can, roach trap, and tackle box, and strapping the poles to the car windows that a sleek Studebaker rumbled across the cattle gap with my cousin Julia Morgan, her brother Broderick and that rich widow who chased him for years. They were upon us.

"Let's all go!" Julia cried. "It's fine weather to fish."

"Oh, let's!" the widow echoed. She wanted it to be thought that she was still good for anything. Broderick groaned.

I knew at once what the trip would turn out to be: a kind of prank, with many jokes and much helplessness, hooks to be baited and interminable lines hung in the brush. Joe was interested, Dinah was stricken, and Amos gave me a little warning sidelong glance.

"Dont be silly, Julia Morgan," I said. "Do you know what these people fish with? Red worms and roaches, live, with legs! You've rescued me and I love you for it. Come let me get into something decent while Bobo fixes us a drink."

"That's more like it," Broderick said.

I herded them to the gate. "Isn't it fine martini weather, Broderick?"

He threw his arm about me. "Fine martini weather. Cousin Ary, gal, I love you. I come all the way over here to pick a bone with you. You don't mix enough any more. Years since—"

I turned back from the gate to wave them off, but Amos was busy backing and Dinah sat aggrieved with lowered eyes. Joe Ferguson answered me gaily.

Dinah worried me at later times to go with them, but I never agreed again. It would not have done, I knew; I could not compete where I had no skill or liking.

There was rain that night and a heavy wind and the next day the ground was hard with frost and the cold sun glared.

5

I told Amos Joe Ferguson was stealing us out of house and home, and I had a chest made for my keys. I wore the chest key around my neck.

Ornaments from Dellwood with which I had dressed my house and table kept breaking with the nerve-wracking irregularity of lightning. It was true I had simply made off with most of them; since Mother had been unable to visit we had all quarried out of Dellwood and could only shudder at the things another had beaten us to, each too far gone in crime to accuse. During one afternoon I found a Dresden teapot, one of a set, marred with a long crack and shoved into the corner of the cabinet behind some goblets, while a French china inkwell Senator Percy had given Father awaited me lying in scattered pieces over the hall desk.

"I simply will not," I announced to Amos, "put up with it any longer."

"Well, get rid of her then," he said.

"Get rid of who?"

"Eula, of course. Who else?"

I had not once thought of Eula. She had come to Dudley from Dellwood with her mother, Old Rheba, whom Mother gave me as cook when I married. When Old Rheba died three years before, I found Eula in the kitchen cooking and she had been there ever since. She was a stout black Negro with a thin nose and a steady quietude. She had been sad the day after Old Rheba died, and had stayed sad ever since. But it was a comfortable sort of sadness. We held long conversations in monotone with ten minute pauses or more between statements, so that at work in the kitchen together it was not very clear whether one of us was speaking or not. She lived fully three miles from the house, beyond the bayou down near the Sunflower on what we still called the "new place," though Amos had bought it out from under Tad Elmore fully fifteen years ago. She resisted all suggestions that she move into servants quarters by simply not hearing them. Her husband, Tonky, a reliable, hard-working wage hand, had a second legal wife and children living near the house. Nellie, the second wife, sometimes came to the kitchen for buttermilk. She was a lithe, light Negro with quick eyes. She and Eula would always converse briefly with a grave courtesy. Eula never mentioned her. She criticized Tonky with the freedom of a woman who has not a single doubt. I don't suppose she did have any doubts at that. It must be a comfort of a kind to see the other half of your husband's life walk away with a fruit jar of buttermilk like anybody else. I sometimes felt motherly toward Eula and sometimes daughterly, depending on which of us had the more to fret on.

"Why would she do it," I asked Amos, "and not tell me?"

"She's from over where you live," Amos said. "You ought to understand her better than me. Why don't you ask her?"

I asked her.

"No'm," she said, slushing for spoons in the dish water. "I aint broke nothing."

"You've seen things broken?"

"Yes'm. Seen 'em lay. Yes'm."

"But you didn't tell me."

"No'm. Aint said a word."

"Then you must know who did it. Tell me, Eula. I'll never say you told me. Tell me, Eula. Who?"

Her glance, lowered, came at me sidelong, fixed for an instant near the hem of my skirt; then she turned and lifted her hands for the dishtowel. The suds slid down her wrists as over black metal.

"I don't know no more'n you, Miss Ary."

It was I, she left me feeling, who had been presumptuous.

"Very well. But if I ever find you responsible, you will have to go."

That night at supper we heard the crash from the kitchen. "Well," said Amos, for I went on eating, "there you are. Loose-handed, just like I thought."

"A plate, I guess."

"You don't want to catch her." He got up. I was through the door ahead of him. A wedgewood vase lay split neatly in half on the white enamel surface of the sink. Eula's hands hung above it and drops of water fell trembling from her fingers.

"I suppose," Amos said, "you didn't break that either."

"I retched up to get it," she returned. "I aint never touched it yet."

"I can mend it," I said.

"It jumped off the shelf, you mean to say?" Amos pursued.

"I mean to say I'se standing here and hit fell, Mr. A.A.," Eula returned. "I aint knowing who done it."

They eyed each other, for a long space. I had the distinct feeling that in that moment Eula and Amos were on common ground. Then he laughed. "Go to grass," he said, and went back to his supper.

The kitchen door shut far later than usual that night.

"She's late leaving," Amos said. He threw his paper aside

and unbuttoned his shirt to scratch, his nails crackling the stiff hair.

"She was waiting for me." I jumped up. But if she heard me call out the back she did not answer. I was lonely for a moment, standing in the cold dark doorway, and what I was lonely for was whatever meant for me that Eula had taken away with her into the dark. She had waited an hour, while I had seen Dinah to bed, turned down our covers, lighted our fire, thumbed a woman's magazine. Then she gave up and carried whatever was meant for me off into the night, and it was lost from me now, for good.

I came back into the warm hall.

"I don't feel right about it," I said. "I don't believe she did it. Any of it."

He laughed.

"I think she told the truth about the vase."

"All right, honey. It jumped off the shelf."

"I made her nervous this morning, fussing at her. Whatever you're afraid of will happen."

"Any way you want it."

"But she won't be back now. You hurt her pride."

"*I* hurt her pride."

"She thinks she's mine. Like Old Rheba did."

"It's high time somebody told me that."

"You knew the way they were."

"When it gets to the place a man can't boss the servants in his own house, it's high time they got moving."

"I could drive down there to her tomorrow—"

"You'll do no such thing. She needs a comeuppance. Her and her pride. Now, Ary, honey, I'll get you a new cook tomorrow, three of them. I'll bring them here and you can see which one you like."

"Breaking in a new cook," I said.

"What about it?"

"It's hell," I said.

He laughed.

6

Mother died in March. It was not unexpected, and many people will gather to tell you that even so it is always a great shock. I agreed, though I never grasped quite what they meant. To die in sleep seemed such a sensible thing, involving no final fruitless task for courage. She left me her fine set of French Empire silver and on the way home from spending a few days with Father, I stopped in Greenville and bought Dinah a really pretty and very expensive dress.

Amos greeted me with the news that Joe Ferguson was sick. "Down there in that old house by himself," he said.

"The weather's warm now. He went around half-naked all winter. Are you sure he's really sick?"

"Sick and down there alone."

"Then I'll send Bobo to stay with him. He can take his meals down."

"You won't get a nigger on the whole place to stay down there in that bayou at night, Ary. Why I don't know. But they won't."

"You do know," I said. "It comes back on you. They thought that woman was a witch."

"Thirty years ago."

"Once a witch, always a witch. Well, what do you want to do?"

"Bring him here. He can stay in Winston's room."

"Apparently it's all decided. What made you wait till I got home, Amos?"

"Now Ary. You've gone and wore yourself out. Let's just set here awhile and drink some whisky."

He brought Joe Ferguson in after supper. His approach across the yard, up the steps and into the house was an obvious triumph of will over weakness. Two little Negroes trotted behind, carrying stacks of pulp magazines and an old-timey crank victrola. Amos scurried about for pajamas, towels and the like. The little Negroes made another trip for his records. One nearly slid off the top; Joe Ferguson caught it, scolded, leaned panting against the wall from where, noticing me, he smiled gravely, and blackness came out of the snaggle tooth.

I caught Amos in passage. "We don't know what's the matter with him. It might be dangerous. I've arranged for Dinah to stay in Cypress with Sara."

"You don't want her near him. You don't want to say you don't want her near him. Call her."

"What do you want to say to her?"

"That she can stay where she likes. That her home is her own."

"You're making an issue."

"I won't throw off on you. Call her."

"You're speaking to me like a servant."

"All right then. I'll find her myself."

I gathered a quilt up out of the cedar chest. It smelt cleanly of moth balls, cedar and good order. "She's gone already," I said.

Not at once turning, I started at the little sound behind me, but he was only knocking his pipe and finally he laughed. "Tell me, Ary. How'd you manage it?"

"I can manage," I said, "when I want to. Dinah and I understand each other pretty well."

"At least, you foxed her into thinking so."

"What kind of deceitful thing do you take me for, Amos?"

He gave me a slap across the backside, going. "You'll fox me if you can, Ary Morgan; you'll fox me if you can. But it aint easy, Ary Morgan; it aint a bit easy."

He turned and laughed from the doorway and I, smiling in spite of myself, said, "Get out of my way," and went by him with the quilts.

7

What was wrong with Joe Ferguson I never knew. He ran a fever that started daily in the late afternoons and climbed until, by night, sweat drenched him and his face grew red as if from stain. In the mornings his skin was the normal outdoor brown, darker than his hair, and he would luxuriate in bed, propped on my best satin pillow reading pulp magazines, his long big toe prodding the sheet in time to whatever tune whanged out of the victrola. In the mornings I would convince myself he had invented the whole thing out of sheer laziness; at night when his head drooped low in the pillows and his eyes floated hot and bright in his head and his voice came quick, I would feel sorry for him and wonder with a kind of inexplicable personal guilt if he would die. The doctor, after his first visit, came daily. Every malaria test he gave showed negative. He swung between anger and curiosity for a time and then deserted, leaving a drug store size jar of colored aspirin.

In the late afternoons when the two of us were alone in the house together, I would hear the victrola switched off and silence from the wing would grow upon me until I would take up my crocheting and go sit with him.

The amenities past, there seemed at first to be nothing to say. I had sized him up pretty well, I thought, and I waited for the subservient compliments which should have been his opening trial. But nothing came. Whenever I looked up, he was watching me with eyes that grew progressively brighter as the afternoon wore down to dark and the red touched his cheekbones like a spreading stain. The sheet lay lightly over him from the armpits down; fresh linen on his bed looked crumpled and dingy within an hour and smelled of fevered skin. The length of him, which I remembered as rather compact, sprawled loosely downward. If I had expected him to compliment me, I expected too some effort at a deceitfully rustic charm, but all he did was lie silent in his body and look out of it at me, or rather at the twist and return of my fingers leading thread on the wooden crochet needle. Sometimes I almost forgot him and once when I looked up to rest my eyes and stretch, pressing my fingers into my waist, I caught his eye in passing and we both smiled.

"How on earth," I burst out, "did you lose that tooth?"

"Kicked out," he returned at once, "by an old black mule."

"That's not true," I said.

"No'm."

I picked up my work.

"Miss Ary, ma'am?"

"Yes?"

But he had no idea of what he wanted to say. His eyes showed only surprise that he had spoken at all. The tooth saved him. He touched one finger to the gap. "When I looked in the mirror, it was hanging by a little old white piece of root."

"Really," I said.

When I switched on the light he had limped his body for the daily onslaught of fever; only his eyes lived, quick as fire, in his head.

Between the spring furnish, income tax returns, and a spell of poker (which delicate game he played as clumsily as he threaded a needle, never understanding why he lost), Amos was gone much at night, and while back in the kitchen Olamay, my new cook, dozed through to his arrival, or entertained the gentleman callers she attracted like a cat, I, who must have conversation of an evening, would take a little brandy back to Joe Ferguson. I went back to pour a little for myself, and finally brought in the bottle. He pointed out to me a picture in the magazine on his bed. Drawn in black and white on the coarse paper appeared a stretch of what I suppose they call "the mesa," with a number of ranked cowboys galloping in at the corner.

"I been there," he said. "I seen it. Just that away."

"You may have seen it," I said. "But not that way. In your head maybe, but not really."

He let the pages fall closed. "No'm," he said, "not really."

And for a while, as after the episode of the tooth, he seemed to give up, to let the truth take him as unresisting as to the fever.

But he could not stand silence any more than I could. It was he who always broke first: "Miss Ary, ma'am?" "Yes?" The moment he grew glib I called his hand; he spoke largely then in halting statements, his quickened voice jerking unpredictably upon the words like a needle on a bad record. He talked of nothing but himself, and on that, his total subject, he told me the truth because I demanded it.

8

He came down, like Amos Dudley before him, from the hills. He was born there, in a town named Sheila up north of Holly Springs toward the Tennessee border, a dead town on any day but Saturday. The gullies surround it, any road you take in; they eat up to the houses and after a hard rain the streets may fall in two. In summer the cudzu covers the trees and the dust covers the cudzu and all you can hear on the dead square is the click of ivory from the pool hall. That was where you would find him. Playing pool. Day in, day out.

If anybody had remarked to him on the pity of it, he would have agreed wholeheartedly for different reasons. He lived uptown by day and the better part of the night, but just the same he had to go home to sleep and get up to leave. At home was the fantastically sick woman who was his mother. He never went to bed or left in the morning without having to listen to her. She circled the fringes of every day he lived; a great pity, he would have agreed: he couldn't play pool in peace. She was a patchwork of gaudy illnessses, head to toe. Yet she never took to bed. The doctor had always been to see her in the afternoon: a crisis to hear her tell it. The preacher had called too, the one who prayed such a sweet prayer; and sundry neighbors. If he didn't get a job he would be the death of her. It seemed to him that one of two things was true. Either she really was sick and just thought it would make her feel better if he got a job, in which case his getting a job would destroy her last hope of getting well. Or there was nothing wrong with her at all, in which case there was no need of getting a job to prove it to her.

His father was dead and gone—or gone and dead—he was never sure of the order. Her own father had left her a place out from town. The small rents came in regularly; she doled out a share to him, labelling the amount every time: "That's what ought to go on new linoleum" or to fix the back steps, the front gate. But he knew if he gave it back the doctor would get it.

Uptown in the café for a nickel and anytime over the pool hall radio, he could hear cowboys make mention of their mothers and he would feel as sad as they sounded, over a mother far away. They sang about girls too, and he heard them out with tenderness that had nothing to do with any girl from Sheila. When a girl had a visitor, "Who is that?" he would see her ask, out in the car. "Joe Ferguson. He's awful. Nobody will date him." But the truth of it was—as he knew—he could have dated them all if he'd wanted to. He was not interested in them, that was all; he thus became more interesting to them, and this he enjoyed.

He went to the picture show everytime it changed. Sometimes when the action was thunderous across the screen, soldiers or cattle or a hero battling many evil men, he would lean back, unaccountably bereft of that familiar tension, not caring what happened, abandoned to the smell of popcorn and human breath and darkness and the same old voices of children asking: "What they trying to do now, Daddy?" Then he would slip out and hurry to the pool hall or the drug store, or if it was past closing time, he would walk the dark streets, alert for any living thing who could divert him from this strange occurrence. He had lost interest in a picture show, a good show, too, plenty of action. What was the matter with him? Then, as some subtle modulation of quietness made him know the late hour, he would find his answer by what he had to do: go home to her. It wasn't enough that she had the fringes of his day;

now she was creeping in on his pleasures. He began to wonder if she would never die.

Before long she had got into the Western magazines; they all seemed like the same story told over and again. She took the pool hall next; he was too good for anybody to make a game interesting. He had a set-to with a stranger whom he caught cheating, moved a cue ball, a little man, too little to hit, but he did it anyway, egged on, and felt bad afterwards.

What would she take next? He had just walked out of the pool hall going toward the drug store when Dr. Benny Thompson came down the steps from his office. "I was just going up to your house again, Joe," he said. Here goes another two dollars, he thought. "I just come from there," Joe said. "She says you needn't come. She's feeling a whole lot better."

That was the day she took to die. A heart attack, clean and hard, one punch and out; Dr. Thompson couldn't have done a thing if he'd been there. It happened right after she called the doctor, before he could possibly have got there. But to Joe Ferguson it was as if she had been sitting up beside the sun spot on the water tower watching him, had seen the moment of his betrayal and died for spite.

But the house was his now. He rattled about in it; stacked his Western magazines wherever he wanted to, bought a loud victrola and a stack of cowboy records, and ate contentedly out of cans. He stayed at home a good bit, reading or learning the words to songs, mainly savoring the quiet. He had a liking for Negroes, had always fished and hunted and shot craps with them. They were the only people he felt any way privileged to be around; he also felt they were the only people who knew how to live—in Sheila, he qualified.

Then within a month, his two sisters husbands both died. One of them must have already made up her mind what she would do; it took the other one a couple of weeks. They converged on him the same afternoon. He had left the first one, Pearl, sitting in the parlor while he went upstairs to think. That was when the second one, Beryl, walked in the door with a suitcase. He heard them from the stairs. They hugged and cried and told over the deaths. Then Pearl said: "I came home to look after Joe."

Beryl, right back, said: "I came home to look after Joe, too."

"Anyway," Pearl said, "it's as much my house as his."

"That's exactly what I said," Beryl echoed. "It's my house as much as it is his."

"Besides," Pearl said, "he just can't stay here by himself."

Beryl was getting mad because Pearl was beating her to everything she had planned to say.

"Where *is* he?" she asked. She called softly, "Joe. Oh, Joe."

He went into the bathroom and locked the door. Now they were both calling him. "I'm in the bathroom," he yelled. He leaned out the window and looked down on the weed-grown yard.

"Christ," he said aloud. "Jee-sus Christ."

In a week he was gone. He sold the sisters his share of the house and farm, made them pay cash out of what he knew their husbands had left them. They didn't want to do it; but he swore at them. They hadn't thought he would do that and were frightened. He bought a '28 Chevrolet coupe with the money, packed up his records and magazines and left. He went to New Orleans first. He worked there at everything from stevedore to hospital attendant. He had thought he would go to sea, but after work one night loading a freighter, two Portuguese sailors he had been sweating cheerfully side by side with all day rolled him just as cheerfully for his wages. Two days later he must have said the wrong thing to a French sailor, for it set off a melee of jabbering and handwaving with ten of them around him, his back to the cotton bales. None of them would hit him and he didn't know what they were saying. Passengers leaned over the rail and laughed. That night he watched the freighter pass lighted down the slow big river toward the gulf and he sighed, but he had learned a grave distrust for people whose language he could not understand. It was then he decided to go west.

He never said what brought him back to Mississippi. Perhaps that was the place the cowboy songs had sounded real, the place where the Western magazines dragged him on from page to page. He had seen the West, after all; the white filling stations thrown down beside the highway like dried bones, the empty stretches going on and on. Once he had seen it, he could picture the thundering herd better from a distance with no voided sun-shot spaces to give him the lie. And if it was the frontier he sought, maybe he realized, walking the squared, neon-lighted, super-modern streets of Western towns, that a man pulled out a gun quicker in Mississippi than most anywhere he had come across yet. He was in Arkansas a while, trapping along the river with a big well-oiled grizzly-haired Negro man. They had no license; there was a race with the law and a shot fired. Joe was driving, he gripped the wheel and shoved the accelerator to the floor, his eyes plunged on with the headlights through the cold dust. He heard the shot; a strange glory crept over him, chilled him first, then warmed him. Beside him the black hand pointed. He took the side road, ripping gravel, crossed over to a state highway, and slowed. He looked at the Negro. He had taken off his hat when the shot came and settled down low with his head on his chest. Now he was fanning; the dust was thick.

"That was close," Joe said.

"They aint want us," the Negro said.

"Didn't want us! They shot at us."

"Laks to see us run," the Negro said. "Cain' do nothing with river folks. River b'longs to any man. They knows it. Ever'body knows it." They were going down West Memphis, a honky-tonk midway frantic with lights. Harahan Bridge hung solemnly black ahead. "Where 'bouts you going to nex'?" the Negro asked.

"I don't know," Joe said. "Miss'ippi maybe."

"What part of Miss'ippi?"

"I don't know. The Delta maybe."

"Then I'm riding wid you. Hit's my home."

The Negro's name was Willie Bryant. It was to Amos Dudley's place that Joe brought him.

"I think I'll lay up here a while," Joe said. "Maybe get a job. I need a place to sleep though."

"You scared of hants?" Willie asked him.

"Hants?" Joe said. "Crazy nigger."

"I aint aiming to show it to you," Willie said. "But hit's a house."

"Take me piece the way," Joe said.

"I rather jes' set here and p'int out the road," Willie said.

That night Joe drove the car along the back side of the bayou and banked it off the plantation road along the heavily weed-grown lip of a dredge ditch. It was a short walk from there to the house. He moved in his records and the victrola and his stacks of magazines, the roll of bedding, the box of left-over canned goods, and the rope-tied suitcase. He put all these things on the porch; then he walked to the edge of the bayou facing east and took a long look across the fields toward the dark green blob of shade and ease where the house showed through, a patch of white here, a patch there, and the fences ran whitely

out on either side, circling the big barns, their tin roofs soft
as cream in the twilight.

Then he walked back to the house in the bayou and forced the
door open and took possession of what he had seen through
the window, the big room cool from the old clay chinking, the
bed and stove and chairs and shelves all ready for use.

"It was when Mr. Wavell give me a job at the gin that I
thought to ask, Who owns this gin? Who owns that-there fine
house and all the barns and land?"

"No," I said. "You'd already found that out, from Willie
Bryant."

"Yes'm. What I said was, If Mr. A.A. Dudley comes by, show
him to me. And Mr. Wavell pointed and said, Yon's Mr. A.A.
now. Then Mr. A.A. comes up to me and says, You looking for
me? And I says, I just always like a look at the fellow I'm working for—the high boss, you might say. And he says, Well, look,
son, 'cause that's me. Then he says, What's your name, son?
And I told him, Joe Ferguson, which is what it is, Joe Ferguson.
And he says, Soon's I check up on how much I ought to be
ginning today and aint, let's you and me skin old Wavell here
on a hand of five-up. I ain't felt so good as that in a hundred
years. He's a fine man, Mr. A.A., I thought, and one to make
you feel at home. He didn't talk like no rich man, nor dress like
one, nor make a fellow feel bad not to be one. It was all through
the game I kept watching him close."

"Yes," I said. "Was Dinah with him then?"

"No'm, not then." The lamplight cut across the bridge of his
nose. His eyes were two blots against the pillow. "She's like
that too. Like Mr. A.A. is. Now you—"

"I'm so completely different," I said, "I do not even want myself discussed."

"You're different," he said, "for a fact. Different from them.

You're more like me."

He could not have startled me more if he had slapped me. I could not see him well for the dark, but I felt despite all his long telling of himself, he would have remained shadowy without the dark—a façade shielding a mind coolly at work—planning or chancing, who could know?

"Why are you here?" I asked him. "Why are you really here?"

"Why, Miss Ary, ma'am, I just told you. Wasn't you listening?"

"You told me how, not why."

"Mr. A.A.," he murmured, "he's mighty good."

I laid aside my work. "Your fever's gone."

"Yes'm."

"Then you can go home this week."

"Home?"

"Back to the bayou."

"Yes'm."

9

Eula took morning to come. I found her sitting at the kitchen table on one of the long hewn benches. The wage hands had eaten and gone, and when I came in she was thoughtfully sopping sorghum with cornbread, but I did not need to see her empty plate to know that she had been there for some time. Her air of injured patience was enough. She did not look up at once, but continued to bend so low to her plate that her limp breasts were under the table with her knees.

"Well, Eula," I said. "I haven't seen you in a long time."

"No'm, Miss Ary. Hit's a fur piece."

"It's good you're here," I said. "We could never find that

batch of shrimp recipes we had out just before you left."

"You look outdoors in the pantry, Miss Ary? In that ole coffee jar?"

"You put them there?"

"I aint said I put 'em there. All I says is look there."

She talked a little batty, but the recipes were where she said and since she was making Olamay jumpy, looking through her as though she did not exist, I asked her inside and sat her in a straight chair in the hall.

"Miss Ary," she said, "hit's dat white man."

"What white man, Eula?"

"Mr. A.A.'s white man. Live down yonder in the bayou."

"Joe Ferguson."

"Him. You know down yonder on the new place? I lives acrost from Kaydee Jonas, me and Tonky does. Kaydee got this here light-colored gal. Folks study 'bout saying she light-colored all time. She no-colored, that what she is. Her and that pinky hair."

"Albino?"

"Albino, yes'm. They calls her Patty. You seen her, Miss Ary. She done switched her bottom round every man in this Delta."

"Now she's after Tonky?"

Eula got up and went out the front porch and spat into the yard. Then she came back and sat down again. "Tonky aint pay her no mind, Miss Ary. Hit's that bayou man got Kaydee worried. She aint took no rest in nigh onto a mont', dwelling on that bayou man."

"Joe Ferguson."

"That what they call him. Hit's what he calls hisself."

"What do you mean, calls himself? That's not his name?"

"Kaydee say there was dishere white woman lived down at the bayou one time. I aint never seen her, Miss Ary. I aint saying hit's so or aint so. Hit's jes' what Kaydee say."

"It's true," I said. "Mr. A.A. told me so himself."

"Hit was this same white woman birthed Kaydee's light-colored gal. Kaydee say that there chile was coming out head-foamus and black-headed as air colored chile is due to be. And that white woman turn and throwed water out the back and turn again and holler out the front: Make this chile albino! And Kaydee say that chile's daddy was watching the birth and hit look to him like somebody done throwed sweet milk on the head and he hit the floor on both knees calling, Gawd, Gawd! But hit was too late. That chile was devil-born and devil-marked, Miss Ary. And that same white woman went out of that bayou 'fore day one mawning, and I'm setting here to tell you, Miss Ary, Kaydee say she was toting a chile. And Kaydee say she aint going to have none of that bayou man hanging round ever' turning in the road and calling out'n the dredge ditches at dusk dark long as Patty so hot after men anyway can't one look sideways at her be-hind she don't fall down in the weeds a-moaning. She say she aint going to have him, she don't care who he is, even if he—"

"Even if he's what?"

"I aint come here out of no onkind feeling, Miss Ary."

"Eula," I said, "I appreciate your coming. I appreciate your thinking about me enough to come."

"I done seen him with Miss Dinah Lee a time or two, fer a fact, and I says, Miss Ary don't like none of this. Then Kaydee she come whimpering day or night, hit don't make her no difference. Knocking on my window glass, saying, Miss Eula? Oh, Miss Eula. I know Mr. A.A. sets a store by him. But he try to trot wid the colored and rack wid the white, Miss Ary, and it don't set right. I just keep on saying over to myself, Miss Ary she don't know hit. Hit don't set right. I mean to say."

"No," I said. "It don't set right with me either, Eula. Come

I'll drive you home. We'll go see Kaydee."

We came to Eula's cabin through a series of jerky roads, where the axle of my heavy car scraped more than once, and dust puffed up under the slow wheels. She lived in a shot-gun house painted that chalky red that you sometimes see on rail-road houses; it is a kind of paint said to preserve the wood, though I have begged Amos to change it to white and he has largely done so. The front yard was fenced with irregular palings that looked like old sticks of firewood and may have been. Every blade of grass was scraped from the yard and the two round flower plots where zinnias and prince feathers grew were outlined in brown Garrett snuff bottles. Eula went to get Kaydee. She was within hollering distance, there outside her own cabin which was set at an angle from Eula's house and the levee, the three making a kind of running triangle; still Eula did not call, but hurried plop, plop in the slow road dust until she came within a hundred feet of Kaydee where she slowed and approached with casual decorum to apprise Kaydee at great length of what she already knew. Kaydee propped the hoe (she was working her garden) against the side of the house and followed Eula at a little distance so that they did not have to talk or not talk along the way.

I sat in a wired-together rocking chair Eula had drawn out for me and looked down from the porch at them like a patriarch. It surprised me, as I looked beyond them, that I could not see my house from here—for in the Delta it is unthinkable that one should lose sight of any point—and moreover that I was not quite sure in what direction it lay. At that moment I became uncertain as to my judgment in coming at all. The two black faces turned up to mine—Kaydee's grinning with pretended innocence, Eula's a mask of sober respect—made me wonder if I were not the victim of some hoax. But I changed my mind on the ground of what they would not dare.

"Sit down," I said, pointing to the steps. "For heavens sake, sit down."

Eula obeyed, but Kaydee stood shuffling her feet inside a pair of man's rubber boots, sliced up beyond all usefulness into an intricate floral pattern over the toes. She was a small thin woman, breastless as a child, with prominent hipbones and legs like broken sticks.

"Where did you come from," I asked her, "before you came here?"

She pointed toward a far-off tangle of swamp and low brush, the fringes of a nebulous area that constantly changed owners, a partially cleared, low, stubborn section that gave down toward the Sunflower River.

"Out in yonder," she said.

"When?" I asked.

"Us come out wid the flood," she said brightly, having no more idea how long ago that was than any calf that bellowed for its mother in flood time from the top of an Indian mound.

"So it was down in yonder a long time ago the white woman came to help birth your child?"

Her face relaxed on the instant. It became sorrowful and secret. "Yes'm. Long time ago. Sho was, Miss Ary. It was her talked wid the spirits. Some says her skin was black up under her clothes. Some says time she's at the sawmill she'd lay out side the road in the sage brush mumbling for air man pass by. It was her marked Patty. I done take Patty to church from suck on, Miss Ary, but she aint never heard no word air Christian said. White woman go off, enter unto the bayou. I done hid under that bayou house day and night, scratching up any little stuff fit for tobey sacks."

"What good are tobey sacks?" I asked.

"I'o'no'm. Weren't so long twell she lef'."

"Well, she left, and she's never come back. I can't help it if Patty can't stay away from men. You ought to lock her up at night."

"I done had more'n my share out'n that bayou, Miss Ary."

I shook my head. "It's not the bayou, Kaydee. Mr. Joe Ferguson has got nothing to do with the white woman."

"He live down there," Kaydee said. "He gwine make my chile think she onloosed from the color she bawn. How come he head out of the bayou to my chile?"

"He just happened to that house, Kaydee. It was an accident."

"Nome," Kaydee said. "He that white lady name."

"*What?*" I strained forward squinting across the strong sunlight toward her long sober face that squinted earnestly back, the eyes socketed in sweat, there in the Negro smell, the open privy smell, the rankness of thrown-out dishwater and buttermilk which ran like white veins over the bare damp earth at the back under the single cottonwood tree. "He's her *what?*"

"He her name."

"Eula, what's she saying? What does that mean?"

Eula had her back to me. She was chewing a snuff stick. "Hit's just what they say, Miss Ary."

"But what is it?" I turned back to Kaydee, but she no longer strove across heat and sun, race and language to me. She had leaned back, as though into a pillow, and with a gesture precisely feminine brought the two ends of her collar together over her breast-bone. "Hit's jes' what they say."

I got up and shook my skirt. "Well, I came down here to see what I could do to help you, Kaydee. But you won't say anything I can understand, much less do anything about."

Kaydee caught my skirt. "Do pray, Miss Ary. Patty done been my stay. I aint want no white man knocking on my door, Miss

Ary. No ma'am, I don' want hit. Hit aint fittin', Miss Ary. Fo' Gawd, hit aint."

"All right," I said, and laid my hand on hers. "All right. I'll speak to Mr. Amos. We'll put a stop to it." But she was lying to me now, or rather saying the things that I expected to hear, the way a Negro will do for a lifetime, only to break out once maybe with an assertion of searing honesty, just as a mule will plough for you thirty years, they say, to get to kick you just one time.

Kaydee turned back to her house and garden and hoe. But Eula followed me out to the car and leaned her arms through the window, still chewing on the snuff stick.

"What did she mean, Eula?" I asked.

She spat in the dust. "Kaydee aint got good sense," Eula said scornfully. "Swamp nigger. Aint you sporting a new car, Miss Ary?"

"Since spring," I said, and looking into her absent face where earlier I had read friendship and loyalty to me, I felt that as far as she was concerned we had come to the end of whatever had prompted her into a long hot journey, but as to the meaning of the whole affair I was left baffled and angry. I was also hot. When I at last trailed down the tortuous little roads to a sight of the house, I longed for nothing so much as to strip off every damp, crawling garment on me and lie in a cool tub with a glass of lemonade beside me on the floor.

But I had no sooner entered the yard than I heard the sound of laughter and shouts from the side porch and I hurried around the corner to discover Joe and Dinah sitting on the edge with swinging feet, while out in the yard stood two young Negro men and a woman named Velda.

"Trouble is," Joe Ferguson was crying to one of the men,

"that woman there's too old for you, Dynamite. Aint nothing but fat."

The two men bent with laughter. "You right, Mist' Joe. You right. I done tole Velda aint no snake."

"It is! It is!" Dinah broke in, beating her fist against the post with delight. "Velda and me, we know it's a snake. You swallowed him little, didn't you, Velda? How big around is he, Velda?"

"Yeah, Velda," Joe Ferguson said. "How big around?"

Velda smiled with a cautious inward-looking pride and ran a thumb gently across her stomach. Then she made a circle with her fingers. "So big."

"Lord have mercy, Velda. When you going to birth him?"

"Aint no way to birth him, Mist' Joe. I'd-a sho done done hit 'fore now."

"You can feel it," Dinah cried. "Feel it. Pull your dress tight, Velda. Can you see it, too?"

"Ask Dynamite," Joe Ferguson said. "Can you see it with her clothes off, Dynamite?"

" 'Fore Gawd, Mist' Joe—"

Dinah dropped to the ground. "Can I feel it, Velda? Can I? Oh, a snake in your stomach, Velda. Just think. Oh, I can—"

That was when they all saw me at once.

"Dinah," I said, "you go right straight in the house. I'll tend to you later. Go on now. Go on, all of you. Lazy as you can live. No such thing as having a live snake in your stomach. I'm tired of hearing about that snake. You might think once how dead you'd be if it was really in there, then you'd quit trying to make yourself out to be so special. I don't want to see you hanging around this yard again. And you," I said, turning to Joe Ferguson, for we were suddenly the only two on the scene,

"I did not like any of that. I do not like to see people laughed at. I do not like those who do it."

"Dinah—" he began.

"I said I'd tend to Dinah. Right now I'm tending to you."

He climbed slowly to his feet and stood looking down at me. "Miss Ary, ma'am. My trouble is a whole lots of the time I don't know how to do. I'm willing to follow along on whatever you say."

"There's no need to stand up," I said, "for a lie like that."

As though I had been shot from a bow and had to keep moving I was through the door after Dinah, but with me went the look on his face as my words fell, the hurt accusation of injustice, as though he who had only the most rudimentary instinct for truth in himself, could not only be hypersensitive toward any faltering of my honesty but also be qualified to condemn me for it. Was I to admit to *him* then that the real reason for my anger was finding him and Dinah together again, as I did eternally find them whenever I stepped out of the house to so much as go for the mail?

I bolted the side door behind me without thinking about it, but the act so satisfied me that I bolted the front door as well, and bathed in a carefully locked bathroom. There in the clear water which lapped shining in its white basin, I tried to wash myself clean of that negroid quality which had come with me from Eula's, which I had found stridently awaiting me in my own yard, and which retired, would not be vanquished but seeped and sucked at steps and door like flood water. It had been grained into the broad common blonde head of the woman I had seen staring out at me from the window of the bayou house that long ago day I came looking for Amos Dudley. It was no less a part of Joe Ferguson who had dared to dare me at my very door.

10

When Father died, it was Sara and I who found him. From the drive we could see him sitting low in his chair by the second pillar. Sara gave him a token peck on the cheek and went back to the kitchen to change everything the cook was planning for supper.

But I bent to him and knew—broad-limbed man pushed down in his old white linen suit yellowed and wrinkled, big head toppled forward, man whose quiet planter's doings could never match up with his noble brow. I didn't want to have to cope with Sara just yet, so I wandered into the house. Father was always a terror when he couldn't find something. He could rifle a room in the time most people would spend shuffling through one drawer, and when he captured the run-away thing, he would slam the door grandly on a scene of plunder loose soldiers would have shamed to own. But today it was every room upstairs and down—drawers ripped out and dumped, beds torn up, old letters opened and flung down, stacks of books thumbed and scattered open, their old pages broken like thinnest wood, and pictures, snapshots and daguerreotypes lined singly across the rugs, and even clocks turned to the wall with gaping backs. I looked into the little office room where the plantation records stayed, and here was the worst of all: I could not pass the door. I went back to him, and ran through his pockets with quick fingers. There was nothing, nothing in his hands. They hung open by the sides of his chair, palms turned outward—a gesture of despair.

What was he looking for? "Poor Father," Sara wailed. "He was out of his head. Delirious." I don't believe that. Father's brain cells worked as slow as Christmas; he never went out of his head in his life.

Much later on the front porch at Dudley, I asked Nathan Marshall the same question: "What was he looking for?" (One thing about Nathan's being a preacher: he is always available for a long afternoon of semi-gossip.)

Nathan didn't know. "What will happen to Dellwood?" I asked. "You can't just saw it up forty different ways."

"Sara," Nathan said. He lives right across the street from her, but she never tells him anything. She is still mad at him because Louise died. But he hears things uptown in Cypress Landing. "She will buy out the heirs."

"Oh, my Lord," I said, "it will be the same thing as having it pass to strangers, probably worse."

"It will still be in the family."

"Technically, yes," I said; "but think what Sara will do to it. Club meetings, house parties, the young Delta set for dances. Why, Nathan, she might go so far as to charge a quarter for people to look at it."

"I'd hate the thought of strangers owning it," Nathan said.

"So would I, Nathan. The heirs are rioting. But as Amos says, If they care so much about it, why don't they go live in it?"

"Well, take me," Nathan said. (Though he was not an heir; Dolly was.) "Memories are painful to me there. I never liked to go back after Louise died. To look at the cistern was a thing too painful to indulge. She said she would marry me there. She went running out from all the company one day and I followed her. It was unbelievable, but we were alone. I caught up with her feeling as if I had run a long way to find her, for months and months just running to find her alone. It was a chance I couldn't miss. I might never catch her alone again. She stopped by the cistern and before I had stopped beside her I asked her. She circled the cistern quickly to put it between us, exactly as if we were playing tag, but I saw her hand trailing past on the bricks, that it trembled. I thought, ready to give up then and there, Bless her anyway, that her hand trembled. Then she said, Of course, Nathan, of course. And before I could take it in she had laughed, not at me or at herself or at anything that I could name, just laughed. It was, Ary, a hard laugh, the kind I had dreaded more than anything else when I knew I would ask her to marry me. And it came *after* she consented. I could never understand it. Louise was never hard. After she laughed that way she put her head down to the opening of the cistern, the way it feels good to do on hot days so that the cool comes up on your face, and she went through it again: Of course, Nathan, of course, and laughed again. I heard the sound go jarring down the cistern, all the way to the water line— Course, Nathan, course—and the laugh like something spilled into the water that would make it unfit to drink. Though I never understood it, still I cherished that hour. More, I think, than if she had behaved in some tender way. I had touched on something puzzling about her and it endeared her to me the more."

I could hear it, see it all as plainly as if I had been standing by the cistern, and I thought with pity of Nathan: She brought him back from the hills where his people were, where he wanted to be, back to where he is damned as the man who married Louise Morgan; and she knew it.

"I do not think," I said, with swift biting truth, "that Louise was entirely above knowing how she could make us feel about her, or using it either for that matter."

"What woman ever is?" Nathan said quickly. I saw then that he knew it too, had known it long, but loved her anyway, continuing to preach patiently and unremarkably where she had dropped him, her very death like a repetition of that hard laugh.

What was Father looking for? Some written record of fraud

or default or shining integrity—some proof to name to him why with four generations behind him he should be left alone and wifeless in a house that had sheltered his fathers, but no child wanted for his own? It must be nice to find a paper—the secreted will, the forged check, the stolen deed. The confession that would dim the pass with blood to polish this day's Morgan honor in.

Proof, that was what Father wanted. Proof of us, of the Morgans, of himself. Instead, nothing. He found nothing.

11

Thunderheads climbed daily in the August sky, spiralling one out of the other, black centers charged round with silky light. Every day they reached higher and made the sky seem higher still. Far below the cotton poison drifted, sullying the bright heat waves. The dusting plane moved through cloud and out again. On the afternoon of the highest thunderhead I ever saw (which mounting incredibly still discovered nothing but more sky), Joe Ferguson and all his possessions including victrola, records, magazines, the junky car, and a good many odds and ends not his own, disappeared from the bayou and from Dudley, nobody knew where.

Amos and Dinah would not be addressed on the subject, and even the store people refused to speculate. The Negroes walked with a studied innocence, afraid somebody would think they knew, afraid nobody would think they knew.

The next afternoon I sat on the porch in the sun-spotted shade and swung myself gently with the heel of my white summer sandal. I saw Amos drive his pick-up from his office to the back of the dredge ditch which drained the bayou. He entered the trees at a hurried stumbling walk; his thought went ahead of him and he had to keep up. A moment later I marked the bobbing yellow head among the cotton—she was so tender-eyed one stroke of sun should burn her blind. Then she too passed into the trees. So they would meet there, which was something I knew and they did not—meet, each driven homesick by a stranger.

I simply waited. I knew they would come home to me when they got hungry.

But at supper, Dinah pulled the skeleton out of a fried perch, baring each bone with a slow meditative motion; then her pale blue eyes regarded me across the light. "You told Joe to leave, didn't you, Mother?"

Amos was looking at me too. They had hatched this between them.

"I did not," I said calmly. "And furthermore I will be very glad when this insanity is over." With that I went on eating.

Abruptly, Dinah left the table.

Amos said: "Did you, Ary?"

"No, Amos."

In a moment I followed Dinah. Her door was locked. I did not call. Amos waited for me in the hallway. We stood quietly, regarding each other and struggling to determine accurately what the other thought and how strongly he thought it. There could well be, I knew, a terrible quarrel now. I knew that I had a slight advantage: Joe Ferguson *was* gone. I had never before, I suddenly realized, had such a fine advantage; for once the facts were on my side.

I plunged right in. "Amos," I said, "in my opinion, you have let that boy make an utter fool of you. You have done worse than that. You have encouraged Dinah to make a fool of herself over him."

But I couldn't jump him. He stood stolidly and after a while he reached into his back pocket and drew out a letter curved to the outline of his body and warm from it. It was addressed to the City Marshal, Sheila, Miss.; the handwriting was my own. It was stamped in red: No Such Post Office.

"There seems to be somebody else he's made a fool of," Amos remarked.

I finally laughed. It was what I got for dabbling in facts in the first place. But Amos did not dabble with facts; he lived by them.

He said: "If you had asked me, I could have told you where he's really from. Ary, why didn't you ask me?"

I did not ask him then. I did not throw away the letter, but stuck it in my dresser drawer under the velvet-lined box which held Mother's little pearl-handled pistol. Then I went back to Dinah, but the door still stood locked. So I went to bed alone.

At midnight I was still alone. I heard the clock strike and I sat up listening and what I was listening for went beyond Amos's return to the house from wherever he was. I wondered exactly what I did listen for. What happened at midnight? Roosters crow, for one thing. But the roosters were late, or lazy. What else happened at midnight? Dances used to break up then. But I wasn't at a dance. Then what else? Nothing, I said. Forever nothing. Nothing at all.

12

I awoke the next morning with such a sensation of lightness and good humor it was as though I had not known myself for a long time. The curtains stood out in the room, swelled by the early breeze, and the sunlight, as yet only pleasurably warm, streamed from southward down the porch outside. Two bird dogs romping on the porch had wakened me. I called them and we talked through the window; they clawed the screen and panted and grinned adoringly. I heard laughter from the kitchen, and thought how I had missed that sound without realizing it. What children they were, I thought, when two days of absence could turn him into forgotten past.

For Joe Ferguson had had a curious effect on the Negroes. With what degree of deliberation I do not know, he had encouraged their superstitions. Their intensity in such matters had mounted like a chant. Before he left they would sit until midnight in the kitchen, close around the dead fireplace on the hottest night with their knees drawn up close and their faces poking out of the dark. Velda, the one who thought she had a snake in her stomach, would have entered at some time with no reason except to moan where they could hear her. Night after night I had to drive them out for home and when I would enter the kitchen in the dark the air would be so thick from the room full of them, I would instinctively protect my face with my hands, as though I had entered a cave of bats. I would get them out the back door and there in the yard they would huddle again, for Velda would have let out some kind of wail and cried: "Hit a turning liver-wise." Then I'd have to fuss them out of the yard.

And that was not all. They made an uncommon show of their rabbits' feet and the punched dimes the women wore around their knees, and paid great respect to the crazy ones they used to laugh at, like old Aunt Fanny Osmond who locked the house up tight when the spirits got in and beat them around the ceiling with a broom like a bat in the house and blew on an old car horn you could hear all the way to Cypress Landing. Olamay herself grew so bold as to claim magic powers; they caught her using her foot to make the table walk, however, and she lost her prestige.

I could have sworn the drums sounded faster than I could remember them, and once they rang the All Saints' Well church bell when nobody had died.

I told Amos that same bell would ring for Velda if he didn't send her to the hospital. I did not argue that there was nothing wrong with her. Amos himself did not question but what she might have a live snake in her. He just said it wasn't hurting anything and he wanted to wait through cotton picking before he sent any of them to the hospital. But I got her there anyway —it happened to be about the time Joe Ferguson left; probably already her career was at an end.

So much seemed to be over and done, a whole house burned over night. I drew a long breath and decided to give a party. A big party with lots of people in we hadn't seen in years, barbecue with Sara's wonderful sauce, and fried fish, shrimp to start with in Arnaud's sauce, and mountains of green salad with roquefort dressing, a case of Scotch and two of bourbon, plenty of the young crowd in for Dinah, Sara would tell me whom to ask. It would take every Negro on the place in one way or the other, and we could all forget.

But where was Dinah? I drank coffee hurriedly and called the store. She was there and urged me with a shrill determined delight to come there immediately. I went eagerly through the shade, across the glittering highway. The interior of the store was cool and dim. It smelled of kerosene drippings on the concrete floor, of rice and flour and cottony piece goods, candy and tobacco and brown paper. Dinah squatted, as usual, on the piecegoods counter with a circle around her, Wavell and Junior Wavell and some nondescript white children in graduated sizes leaning near her, with Negroes ringed at an unusually timid distance. From above their heads, her pale eyes fixed on me. It was as if my own met a too bright glare. The circle fell aside for me. On the counter at her knees stood a large fruit jar, and coiled thickly in it, the folds pressed tight on one another was a large snake with a misshapen head like that of a human embryo and the dead white color of a maggot turned up from under a log. I drew back, repelled.

"Came out of Velda's stomach," Dinah said. "Just like she kept telling everybody. Only you wouldn't believe it, you didn't think it was true, did you, Mother?"

"Take it away somewhere," I said. "It's awful."

Junior Wavell reached immediately for the jar, but Dinah struck him aside, beating his unclosed submissive hand with hard slaps that reddened the skin. "No, you don't," she said. "Don't, don't."

I caught her wrist. "Stop that," I said. "You're acting like a baby. Come to the house with me."

"Don't you want to hear about Velda? She died. She was doing all right, but she got scared in the night in the hospital and tried to get out of bed and leave, and the stitches broke loose and she died. But they got out what you didn't believe was in there, and you see how wrong you were, Mother, look at it, just look."

She slid smoothly to the floor and thrust the unsightly thing close to my face, but this time I did not flinch. She turned away, set the jar on the counter, and walked out of the store. I did not leave at once. "Get back to work," I said to the Negroes, and "Get back to work," I said in a different tone to the Wavells, who immediately began to wait on the children. I would not have them all standing there and knowing it was Joe Ferguson and the hurt of his going that made her crow over the snake and sport at Junior and me, in our devotion.

13

I walked home slowly, head down, until I reached the inner gate beyond the drive. I looked up when I opened the gate and there on the front steps sat Joe Ferguson.

I came near and sat down on the concrete bannister, beside a fern. "Why did you come back?" I asked him.

"I was driving down along the coast last night, Miss Ary, ma'am, having it in mind to head for Florida. There was lights going off and on everywhere I looked, speaking of places with folks eating and drinking inside, with crap tables too, I reckon, and a slough of cars coming and going. It come over me then what Florida would be like, how I knowed it already, and didn't have to go to find out. But the only place that I didn't know and couldn't know what would be apt to happen once I got there was Dudley, so I turned around right in the middle of the road with a Cadillac breaking and cussing on one side and a truck on the other and headed back home."

I questioned the last word and pointed out to him that if he hadn't come back probably nothing at all would happen. He gleamed at this admission of his importance to us until I asked him why he left in the first place.

He stammered, feeling his way this way and that, but none of them seemed to suit me, so he said at last: "I was afraid."

He dropped his eyes and his hands dangled between slack knees. His face blanched to the hairline and he sat very still, as though any move would throw him into trembling. There was no doubt but what I had the truth. His fear communicated.

"Afraid of what?" I half-whispered.

"Where are they?" he asked me.

"Out there."

We sat silently studying the vast expanse of sun and growth. A wagon passed down the road which circled the bayou, stirring spurts of dust. Cars flicked past on the highway. Far up a buzzard tilted, as if asleep on the air. And that was all.

"Just supposing," Joe Ferguson said, "in place of something else to suppose and for nothing else, that you and me was ever put to running things together anywhere, we might do all right at it, don't you reckon?"

"Just exactly how could this ever happen?"

"Well, saying for instance if you owned a tourist court and I owned one right next to it, so that we were both splitting the business of the other one and we decided to get together under one name and have twice as nice a place with four pinball machines instead of two, I think maybe we'd do all right, don't you?"

We both got amused at the idea of my owning a tourist court. Then I told him: "I am more involved in my own people than you think. You can't say what I would do without them, because you wouldn't be saying anything about me, but about somebody else instead."

"Your own people? The Morgans you mean?"

"Well, partly. But the ones that belong to me, too: Amos and Dinah."

"Belong to you. You think that?"

"Well, I belong to them then. Either way. It doesn't matter."

"But suppose you found out that they didn't belong to you or you didn't belong to them so much as somebody else did?"

"Who, for instance?"

He did not answer.

"You?"

He was watchful.

"If you have told Amos Dudley lies," I said, "he will find out and you will answer for it."

"Not lies. I aint said enough of anything to him to make out a lie."

"If you have led him to believe a lie, then, or if you have led her to believe a lie, he will know it and God help you—I don't blame you for being afraid."

It was then I saw with a shudder that he might be caught between two lies, and caught, moreover, between two passionate and single-minded people who had each believed him and that every step was leading him nearer to the certain moment of their catching him at it.

"Get away," I begged suddenly. "I will give you money to go, any amount you name. Only get away."

He was indignant. "To set me so low as that," he said, and I pitied him, that he had to believe in some honor in himself.

"I don't want you hurt," I said. "Why I can't say, except that I would hate to see anyone hurt in ignorance of the full danger of what they tamper with. You do not know him."

"I know him pretty good. I might know him better than you."

"I dare you to prove that."

"I can't see him being wrong. I can't see him saying to himself or to anybody else, I was wrong."

I stared for a moment in angry defeat at the slowly broadening smile below the quick blue eyes.

"But you don't know," I said with authority, taking a long guess, "exactly where you stand with him. Negroes can talk all they please—but he has never said."

"Never said what?"

"I asked you a moment ago, Afraid of what?"

"There aint either one of us going to say it, are we?"

I said: "You've come a long way from Sheila, Mississippi, Joe Ferguson."

His recovery was immediate. "Sheila?" he grinned. "There aint no such place as that, Miss Ary. I just made that up to pass the time, seeing you was so nice to bring me back some likker. No'm, I was born over in Arkansas at a little crossroads. It was my aunt, Miss Mamie Ferguson, raised me. She lived on the outskirts of Little Rock, but her and Uncle Murray are long dead and gone now."

We were back on the tight rope again, but engrossed in his story, he seemed now to be enjoying it.

"I imagine they are dead and gone long, long ago," I said drily. "They make far less trouble that way."

He took that blandly, without reply, and told me a story or two about his trip south and back.

It was pleasant for me to be in his company. It seemed that we were, of all on Dudley, the only two who were entirely sane.

But I had to see Amos.

"He's at the gin," Joe Ferguson said immediately, at the moment of my rising. On that advice I was halfway down the drive before I looked back, doubting why he had been so helpful. The steps were empty and no one was in sight.

14

The gin at first seemed empty also. They were cleaning and checking before the first bales began to roll in; that would be a day or so yet. I climbed the steep narrow steps beside the suction pipes. It was hot up there with the gin stands and presses, in the huge room, but airy, and silent as a junk yard. I moved among the big machines, circling and calling softly.

Then I stopped calling and hunted, looking even behind the stacks of baling and under the huge elbow of the seed pipe. I do not know why I thought he was hiding from me. I went out the back on the open landing past the presses, and down the steps to the second landing where the bound bales would leap, falling. I stared out toward the seed house and the crook of the highway; then I heard my name called from behind.

He stood in the double doorway, beside the scales. The wooden slide, polished from use, laid a road directly between us, though neither of us could have used it; I would have had to circle to the end of the platform to reach the steps and mount to him.

"He's back," I said, standing where I was.

"Happy day!" he said and lighted like a child. He sat down above me, dangling his feet between the slide boards and clicking his heels together. "Is he all right?"

"Yes. Do you know why he went away?"

"I can hit pretty close to his reason. He was scared of being stuck in one place, of having to stay there and nowhere else. So I didn't try to catch him; I let him go. When he knew he was free to go, he came back. I counted on that."

"He left because he's afraid, all right, but not of what you think." '   .

"What of, then?"

"Why of selling you a bill of goods, of course, and wondering if you wouldn't catch on."

"Nobody ever sold me a bill of goods, Ary, least of all Joe Ferguson. For one thing he couldn't; for another he wouldn't."

"You won't deny what you have been persuaded to believe about him?"

"He has made no claim."

"Not in so many words, maybe. He will leave you to make

the claim."

"That he is mine and Thelma's son?" (So it was he that said it; it was Amos Dudley that said it at last.) "No, I make no claim either."

"Now, nor ever?"

"Now, nor ever, and never to you. Belief is free. Whatever I believe is a free belief. It is a man's right. I have followed what I believe freely since I was sixteen years old, and never broken a time to set the way of it down to anybody else except to my father's dead face, which was a mistake. Talking is a ruination. The person that hears you talk is another ruination. If a dead man's face can change the words you say, a live face could wreck the words till you don't remember what you meant. Your face would wreck me, Ary, here and now."

"Your silence is no more my business, then, than your belief. All right. But what you believe about Joe Ferguson can't ever be just belief, Amos. Joe Ferguson is real and quick to move and unprincipled and clever. Well, say I'm wrong about him then. Say he's the finest boy that ever walked the earth. But wherever he is on this place right now, Dinah is with him. And if he is your son, she has no right with him."

"And if he is not my son? Does she have any right then?"

The shadow of the gin fell from me, receding toward noon. I shielded my eyes with my hand to look up at him, where he still sat in shadow.

"Devil! What are you trying to do to me?"

"Do to *you?*"

"To her then. That's the same as me, or worse. She has no thought but him. If she discovers what he pretends to—"

"She need not find out anything. There is nothing to find out. She will have a right to him if she wants him."

"But if she does not want him?"

"I know," he said, gravely acceptant, lighting his pipe, "that you will do all you can against him for her. In case you succeed, he will still have his place with me."

"As a son?"

"You might say, the same place as Winston could have had. If he'd wanted it. The place of going on from me. The same as he would have if Dinah chooses him."

"Choose! You've seen that she has no choice. You've tied her to you since—"

"Since you lost my second son, Ary, grabbling for a stick of goddamned antique furniture."

"Amos." I hurried to the steps and mounted them and he stood to meet me. "I know better how you feel than you may think. I know how you have to believe something, or nothing means anything. My belief is in a handful of people who meant much to me—Louise, Winston, Mother and Father—see: they are all dead now. Whatever you want to believe is all right, whether you tell me or not. I know too how much you want a son to leave in care of Dudley, and how it might conceivably be called my fault that you lost the two sons you might have had. Winston took to me, or maybe you could say I took Winston to myself; then the other—it was not myself I thought of when I stole the chair, but it was not you either. So I'll say I'm wrong and sorry, and say if you want to call this boy your son, you are free to say it out, and I will never say you're wrong, or let on to a soul the lie I think it is. Call him son, and leave him Dudley and have your peace of heart. We both of us owe a debt, it seems to me, to Thelma Dubard. You because you left her, and I because you left her for me. And with that we can both be square."

"A neat bargain," he said, "to leave you with Dinah free of him in trade for Dudley that you've never cared for anyway."

"I do care for Dudley!"

I stood blazing with anger at him and for a moment I thought he would anger too; but he said: "Poor Ary. Don't take on so. I won't tell you the things I know. There wouldn't be but one thing worse than you not believing them and that would be if you did believe them. I won't have you walking knee-deep in fire. I got scared way too young into seeing sights nobody else sees and following along a road nobody in his right mind would pick to walk on, but once you're in it there aint no turning around. And then the other business of how they will turn on you, Ary. Every one you take on for a while. Even Arney, my old friend Arney. You know what he did to me? There was two sacks of money in the chimney the day he took to leave, and it was the little one I cared for the most. It was the last of the first money I ever made. Twenty-eight silver dollars, made by honest means in honest trade. Arney knew it, and took it. So from then on I knew what I ought to have known long before for there was plenty to learn it from—that the road I had got shoved on to had to be walked by nobody but me, and them you give the chance to walk with you will cross you up, or kill themselves trying."

"Except Joe Ferguson?"

"He won't get the chance. But you know what, Ary? I commence to feel more and more like I'm getting on towards the end, the rounding off, the setting-down place. You won't have much longer to fret. When this I got in hand is settled, which-soever way the cat jumps, I promise to tell you, piece at the time, everything you might want to know. But until then—you won't get the chance to cross me either, Ary."

"You are shutting me out," I said, "at the very time that matters to me most."

"I can't help that."

He turned from me and stood looking up at the great, blue, empty sky. I followed his gaze. A shudder ran up me, the kind evoked by some unpleasant small sound, like a dog's teeth on dry wood or a rope squeaking on a swing. "What on earth are you looking at?" I asked him.

"Nothing," he said. "What are you looking at?"

"Nothing."

"But if there was something there that I saw and you didn't, I would be seeing the nothing that you saw and the something that I saw both, wouldn't I?"

The sun had crept to the toe of my shoe. It was silent back there and very hot now that the breeze had died. I listened for some evidence of somebody somewhere on Dudley, but I could hear nothing, and see nothing but the seed house, big as a plane hanger, the big seed pipes, the big distance to the ground, and the gigantic sky.

"Wouldn't I?" he asked me again. It was as if he asked a child if two wagons and two wagons did not make four wagons. I did not answer him. "Because," he added, "that would be what I would try to tell you about Joe Ferguson."

But the words sounded behind me; I was through the gin and out again. Before I had been worried, puzzled, annoyed by turns, sometimes more interested than anything else, sometimes even amused. But now I was afraid.

15

Sara poured more coffee from the silver spigot as the little gold-mounted clock on the parlor mantel went ping for 2:30. I had come from Amos directly to her.

"The thing that frightens me," I said, "is that he believes in

something and I don't know what. He has believed in it all
along, and I never knew it. Now that I know it, I'm just as infinitely far from knowing what it is."

I was talking unwisely, for as Amos said, all talking is unwise,
but talking because I had to talk.

Sara embroiled her scarlet-tipped fingers in her two long
strands of beads and gave her all to the problem.

"You can find out once and for all, of course, about the
Ferguson boy."

"How?"

"Go back to Arkansas and check on him. Hire a detective."

"It is not what Joe Ferguson is. I know perfectly well what
he is. The problem is what Amos Dudley is. In whatever world
Joe Ferguson exists for him, no detective operates."

"Is it some kind of religion, Ary?"

"Suppose it is? Then what?"

"Well, you just have to find out the name of it, then you could
look it up."

"Look it up where?"

"Oh, I don't know. In the Bible. Or maybe the encyclopedia. I
know. Ask Nathan. He ought to be good for something of a
religious nature. It's his business."

"You won't find it in Nathan's prayer book," I said. "That's
the last place Amos Dudley's religion is."

"I'm afraid for you to go back out there, Ary," Sara wailed,
as though Dudley were the jungle.

"What difference will it make to him if I come or stay? I'm
completely out of this. He made that plain. Thirty-one years of
being married to the man and what do I learn? That I'm completely useless to him."

At this point, we both looked up to where Jack McGillister
sat above the mantel, with his bowler hat almost cocked and

his mouth about to grin. "I was not completely useless to Jack," Sara sighed. "He wanted money and he got it." She bowed her head like a girl, humiliated afresh for having believed in him, more than if she had been the liar and the thief.

"Ah, we have been used," I smiled, "and badly used at that."

And so we giggled as we used to before boys turned into men, until Sara said: "Ary, is it God?"

"Is who God?"

"Is it God Amos believes in? Just like anybody else, only a little bit more. You might talk to him about something that simple."

I reflected. "I find, Sara, that about God I have practically nothing to say. Do you?"

"Nothing I can think of right now."

"But I think that if it is God, it is many other things beside, and no more God than, say, witches and conjure and miracles—that sort of thing."

"That sort of thing for Amos Dudley! Now really, Ary, you go entirely too far. So upset, poor thing. Why, Ary, *I* know Amos Dudley. He never believed in anything in his life he couldn't put to some use or other. Mark my word, Ary, whatever powers he's discovered, he's got them trotting in harness by now."

"I know that. I've thought that too. The use of it is plain enough. A son. He wants it. But I ask myself, Why now, of all times with Dinah coming on? And why Joe Ferguson of all people, the one I couldn't stand from the minute—"

"That's it," Sara said. "That's just it. *You* couldn't stand him. It's you he's after, Ary. Don't you think I remember the day he turned on me over Dolly? I tell you right now, Ary—"

"Tell me what?"

"To be perfectly frank, Ary, I'm afraid I'll hurt your feelings."

"Nothing could be less important right now than my feelings, Sara."

"I will tell you then," she said, and leaned close. "He is jealous of the Morgans. That's why he has to defeat you."

A good try, I thought, but not quite good enough. I could have put the arrow in the gold, but I did not want to, not to Sara. It would have to be someone else.

"Give me a drink," I asked, "good and stiff. A very little water, no ice."

Then I crossed the street to Nathan's, aimlessly.

The porch at Nathan's is enclosed with a brick ledge and short wooden posts hold up the roof. Ferns between the posts, great big ones; and the bay window juts out at the side. A dark, unwholesome house, smelling of damp and cold food and books. The front door was locked; no one came. I walked around to the back, picking my way through the tasseled weeds, the kind that stain, and sat down on the back steps. The house rose behind me, needing paint. The water pipes climbed the vineless walls. On the damp grassless earth by the steps, two hens paced quizzically near, then drank from an old stove lid. Their thick yellow clawed feet, heels striking earth with that minute thud. And eye, bright beneath the film, the pupil like a blue bee-bee, rolling back at me.

Above me a window shot up, loose and knocking in the frame, and a voice called down:

" 'Tary!"

It was Dolly, running downstairs now, through the room where Louise had lain in her coffin. I remembered the day. Two carloads of Nathan's old hill congregation showed up, heavy-footed and awkward, herded in the hallway. Nathan came into the parlor where we had sat waiting for the hearse to come and carry her back to Dellwood where she would be let down into the ground. He closed the hall door and stood, his hands behind him on the knob, facing us, the family.

"My people are here," he had said. We thought he meant his own family, until he told us. "I will open the coffin for them," he said. "They will never understand if I don't."

The shock fled through us, passing around the room. It was I who leaped up, running to the door which shut us from Louise. I had held the twin knobs that slid together, catching. "Not Louise!" I cried. "Oh, Nathan, not Louise."

Nathan's eyes, weary and certain, above the starched white-wing collar. "She will let me," he said, and turned to open the door for them. And still I stood, hands tight on the twin knobs until Amos came (how young he was then!) and took my hands away. "He is right, Ary. Come away."

And so we sat, a semi-circle of statues, watching them file through on heavy, muted feet, going sideways, one shoulder higher than the other, the way of country folk out of place and shy. Nathan pulled back the sliding doors. They ringed the coffin and the lid went up. There was a long silence. "Just like her own sweet self," a woman's voice said, breaking. "Ready to speak," said another, and they cried, the last to look upon her.

"Coffee, 'Tary?" Dolly asked me. We sat at the kitchen table. She poured out two cups.

"Why don't you ever come back to see us, Dolly?"

"I did, 'Tary. Only yesterday." That was true. I may have forgotten. Or did I mean, really come to us, as our child, as things once were?

"Dolly," I said, "there is something I have never understood. Why did Amos frighten you, when you were a child and ran away?"

I saw her face remembering what to her was past and gone; a peaceful face it is now, a homely patient peaceful face, that watches other women's little children nine months out of the year—nine months every year these ten or fifteen years since she went to finishing school and then to college, and still no child to call her own.

"I have not thought of it in a long time," she said.

"I know. But think now."

She had long pale fingers with nails the same color as the flesh, clipped very short with an unsavory whiteness beneath the tips like old chalk dust. She touched the objects on the table with her finger ends, a shrinking manner, as though she read life timidly like the blind.

"I remember that he had frightened me before, but I did not know to be afraid before. In fact, 'Tary, I took him as what I had to stand up against, big as Fate and not hearing me perhaps, but feeling me. I could, you might say, dent him."

"How?"

"By defying. But then I found out to be afraid."

"But why?"

"It was you."

"Me!"

"You made me afraid because you were afraid. I saw you run from him the night the Morgans left. I'll turn the question back to you. Why were you afraid, 'Tary?"

"I was afraid," I said and the words fell evenly, like a good horse walking, "because I know that he is death. He has to possess and what he possesses he has to destroy. To all that I love, hide it as he will, he is sudden and ruthless death. Elinor run from me to a bad marriage; my Dellwood china broken—oh, it was he! You, Dolly—my first child, in a sense—driven from us. And Winston dead. And why? For me—to move in closer, to destroy, my heart, myself, me. Me utterly. Oh, he is death!"

More I could have said then, but did not. About the woman that he drove from him and then the friend, Arney, who left. About Elinor, tears staining the black broadcloth riding coat, bereft in Louisville of all her horses. About Winston, driven to the borrowed car, crashing in his rebellion toward death. And Dolly who had pled foolishly against his sword. And now the last: Dinah. The last: Dudley. And what for them both? Joe Ferguson. Whatever was left of me then would, I suppose, be easy enough.

"Or you might say," I went on, steady again, "that he wants somebody who will think he's just as right as he thinks he is. All the time."

"Poor Uncle Amos," Dolly said.

"Poor Amos," I said.

I suddenly felt quite weak, and my hand fell limp across the table. I saw it lie there as though it were another's chopped away from the body—capable across the knuckles with clean graceful nails, the lines running backward toward the narrow flexible wrist, strong to rein a horse, or quiet a child, or lay control upon a household with key and gesture. The hand lay before us both and I could not move it at all.

"Call Dudley for me," I told Dolly. "Tell them to come for me. I must get there, at least to see. I don't feel up to driving though. Tell them to come. But not Amos. Call the store and tell them."

"Tell who then, 'Tary?"

"Joe Ferguson," I said. "Tell him."

16

He came in a passing truck and drove me home in my own car. We rode without saying a word. The house and lawns were quiet, laden already with dew and twilight. The doors stood open. I called for Dinah, but no one answered. The kitchen was scrubbed and empty. I came back into the hall.

He stood in the living room near the door. I crossed the threshhold and our eyes met.

"He licked you," Joe Ferguson said. "I knew it, but I hated to see it. I hate to see you licked."

He arranged cushions in the easy chair and cocked the floor fan to strike it. But I did not sit down.

"You are the finest lady I ever saw," he said. "I never thought I'd lay eyes on anything in all my life like you. There's nothing else that looks like you or walks like you."

"I wish you could have known my sister," I said. "She was much more what you mean than I."

"I seen her picture. She's all right, I reckon, but set her by you—she don't hold a candle, Miss Ary, ma'am, with all due respect."

He shut the glare out with the shade and fetched a glass of ice water from the kitchen. I reached my hand out eagerly, but he drew away and pointed to the chair. I smiled and gave in, drinking deeply, then sinking down into the cushions. A drowsiness came over me so that it seemed I must fall asleep in spite of myself.

I said to him: "Amos has made you safe in all that I can do to you now. But be sure that nothing happens to make you answerable to me."

He smiled, easy and assured in the doorway. "What will you do?" he asked.

I brushed my hand before my face. A cloud of sleep was settling fast. I do not think I ever answered him.

When I awoke I thought it was dawn. With effort I ordered myself by what the clock said. It was 5:30; I had slept for twenty minutes only, if it was not tomorrow. Outside Joe Ferguson leaned against the front gate, talking with Amos. They were both laughing. Amos spoke vigorously, waving his arms toward his land, pointing to this and that, far out there beyond gin and store. Pointing really to the future. He was a great one for the future, Amos was. The sun was thinly clouded over; dust rose thick from the fields, colored that strange redness one sees often in the fall.

Well, I thought lazily, why not? And as though they had heard me, they laughed again. But even Amos might have thought Joe forward just now, if he had heard what he said to me, if he had come into the hall and heard. But Joe took escape so casually, as though it were the ordinary way to live. How could I know where he had just come from when Dolly called? My mind was like water into which a small stone falls. Watching them, I backed through the house, room by room, calling softly. At the back steps I stood glancing behind and calling, but too softly. Then I ran.

The cloud had put the chickens to bed; they slept uneasily, afraid they might be wrong, and two talked when I went by. The path to the barn lay deep in dust and at the end of it, by the lot fence, two Negroes stood and talked.

"Have you seen Miss Dinah?" I asked.

"Aint seed Miss Dinah all day," one said and the other agreed: "Sho aint seed Miss Dinah."

By the second barn a Negro stood in a wagon bed and

watered his team. I asked him: "Is Eddie in the blacksmith shop?"

"Eddie? I'o'no'm."

He dragged on the lines and shouted the mules on. By the time I reached the shop, he was gone and the two Negroes by the first barn were gone too. Eddie was not there; he kept shop by fits and starts; if nobody came to talk to him, he went wherever they gathered. In the long low dim interior that smelled of iron dust, I at first saw nothing but the black forge and the black burned earth around the forge like a tattered rug. Great iron wheels leaned against the wall; a whole lame tractor crouched in the far corner; parts of a cultivator were scattered nearer the door, and along the dim walls hung plows of all sizes, dismembered and whole. Somewhere in the conglomerate, I remember seeing a child's tricycle and wondering what it did there. The charcoal in the fire-box was cold and black and against the twin doors opposite me that would open to let in the big machines, a Negro woman with dead white flesh half-sat and half-lay, her arm thrown across her face, her full limbs relaxed, sprawling and half-clothed, as though she were just awaking from sleep. Her negroid hair showed a dull pink through the thin stocking cap that bound her head, and with a darting gesture she lowered her arm to peer curiously out, and I saw that the mouth hung deranged and that blood welled scarlet on her cheek. Her arm leaped back, foiling the hard blow of the plowline and a length of blonde hair swung out, blotting her face from me.

"You're here after him and I know it, you hear me? And don't you ever, ever come back here again, you crazy white stinking nigger, I'll beat you to death if you go after him again!"

"Dinah!"

I screamed it, covering my eyes, not wanting to see her face turn to mine, for had I ever really seen her face before?

For a blind instant I did not know where I was and to save falling I threw out my hands to catch something. Dinah was bolting toward me; a second more and she would have been gone. I knew desperately that if she got by, she would be lost to me forever, and I jumped directly in her path. She was larger than I, taller and stronger too, so how I stopped her I do not know. The shock brought me to my knees, but I was up while she still struggled to gain balance and I looked down on her for an instant before I drew back my hand and struck her with all the force in my power across the china-fragile eyes. The blow hurt; her head snapped a full half-turn aside, and she gave down to her knees again. But she did not stay there. The life I found myself so suddenly compelled to destroy or quiet, bring to bay, roiled up in her, frantic for escape. She dived from her knees to go under my grasp, and I fell to stop and clutch her, fell deliberately down, and we rolled grappling together over the smutty floor.

The albino woman that Thelma Dubard had brought into the world crept past us on hands and knees with a silent calculation, and gaining the door cast one wild backward glance and shot away, crouching, swift as wild game.

We rolled over twice, hands beating, stood upright and fell again, but this time I was uppermost. A moment later we were up more weakly, but her back was to the tractor and I held her there pinned against the cleats of the tall wheel. I held her by the shoulders first; and the dust-clouded room enclosed our panting. My hands slid down her arm; she was quiet now. I held her wrists; she would not look at me. I took her hands lightly in my own, and risked a step backward. She stood, trying nothing.

Then she said, in a calm woman's voice: "I'm so sick of it, Mother. I'm sick and tired of it."

That was when she told me about it. She spared nothing to me, nor to herself.

She said, first off, that he had seemed to fit so well into all she knew and loved. She hit on the idea once, some months after he had come, that he was something Amos had given her, had waited until she needed somebody without knowing it really, and then had wished the right one for her, and there had been Joe Ferguson. When she thought this, one night before she went to sleep, she sat up straight in bed, drunk with the sweetness of what she had thought, believing it because it was sweet, because she had thought of it, and because it made her cry. She wanted to climb out the window then and run through the night and to the bayou, unafraid, and tell him about it.

But it took longer than that. It took many days and many false starts to get it out and she thought she never would until one day with Amos fishing just beyond the bend in the bayou, only one cypress frond to screen him from them, Joe had bent suddenly and kissed her. She told him then, whispering. She was, she said, a different person alone with him, not loud like the day with Velda, or laughing either, but actually kind of sad in an easy drifting way that had nothing to do with real sadness at all. But after she told him what she had thought that night in the bed, what had swelled up within her and turned to tears, she saw his eyes jump, a flicker that turned them a sharper blue. She remembered that later.

They used to tell us they were going to the show and she would read the plot of the show that was on and all about the actors and what the star wore, all set forth in the movie magazines. Later she would tell me all about it. They would go off down the highway toward Cypress and take a sideroad by the levee, circling back by intricate means, a long secret way to the bayou where they would sit and talk and kiss sometimes.

She did not want to tell me the truth; she sensed my dislike for Joe, and Amos had explained this neatly enough: he told her that I felt superior to most people. She did want to tell Amos, but Joe wouldn't let her. He told her that Amos would have them marry sooner or later. "Wait and see," he said. When she asked why not right away, he answered that you couldn't hurry Mr. A.A., he had to work it out for himself. She wanted to know what he had to work out, but he only kissed her and asked her for the first time to stay with him that night. She said no, quickly, trembling, and he began to whistle for a while, then they tried to talk of other things. She would not return to the bayou with him for a long time, and in that time she thought he was sorry or ashamed or had forgotten.

But the next time she went there with him, he told her a story he had had from a man he met in New Orleans at a water front bar, a tall gawky slow honest man, Arney Talliafero by name. But Dinah must never tell Amos that, or mention the name of Arney Talliafero, and especially she must not mention that Joe Ferguson had ever seen him, or anything that Joe Ferguson had learned from him. She promised eagerly, waiting for a good story about Amos, maybe when he was a little boy.

Then, in a voice coolly deliberate, he had told her about Thelma Dubard. (She never knew that Amos thought Joe might be his son; but I knew where Joe had got his first lead now, and what had brought him to Dudley.) They were sitting on the porch of the bayou house at the time. She got up and left him sitting there, and she said that he seemed as she left him to sit with a tenseness inside that his casual posture deliberately denied, but it was only afterwards she remembered that. At the time she thought only of the past. She wandered into the dark house, the one big room and the back room and looked down the long steps and returned to the front door.

"He didn't send her away. She wanted to go." She spoke to the silent shoulders. But Joe Ferguson sat looking off into the woods and never turned or said a word.

"He wouldn't do that," she said. But he did not answer or turn.

"You don't think he would, do you, Joe? Joe. Please tell me." Still he sat, unhearing.

Then she said at last: "Joe. Please. Come here." He heard that, and he came.

She said simply: "And that was how it happened, Mother."

After that, they were both afraid; he that she would tell what he knew; she that we would know what she had done. She said it seemed to her that I knew already, that in every step I made I cried it to her. They felt safe only together, where they could watch each other, and not be watched.

She ran to the bayou one day to find him and met the albino woman coming out. She said he did not seem to feel how deeply she was hurt. He was sheepish and off-hand at once. It was then she doubted him most. She said she could not understand him yet. "He knows the right thing to be, but he won't be that for long. I thought that a bad person wouldn't even know the right way to be." She shook her dusty yellow hair and sighed. I could not help her there. She had stated at last the thing that I had never been able to state about Joe Ferguson, the heart of his strange talent with us all.

But she did not falter there. She pushed straight on. She said he became steadily more afraid than she, and the more afraid he got, the more she lost fear, as though they had only so much between them. She loved him still, she said, but she could sit back, too, and watch him grow afraid. For one thing, he sensed his failure with her over the albino woman. For another, he was losing the Negroes. Eula was at work against him; two in one day passed guarding themselves from his eye. He thought the gatherings in my kitchen at night had to do with him. One day he came home to the bayou house and found a tobey sack laid casually beside a carton of hominy grits. He told her later that when he found it down there in the bayou alone, he wasn't sure what year it was, or if he walked out of there he would see the same people he had seen in the afternoon. He felt swung back from one time to another and forward into he could not know what, and he was so afraid that he left.

Late the morning of his return (and it seemed hard to believe that we were still living that same day) she went to the bayou. The albino woman was there again; for one thing, she supposed, he was afraid to be alone, but for another he had wanted her, the mumbling, smooth-skinned imbecile; and Dinah knew for the first time the sickening enormity of his greed. She told the albino to leave the place and never come back, but she doubted at the time if she understood and circled the grounds all day to find her. The albino woman had circled too, "in heat," Dinah said and winced. When she found the woman near the barns, crouched and peering around the corner, she dragged her into the empty shop.

"She was somebody to take it out on," she said. "I hated her for showing me what I was."

"What you aren't," I said. "What you never can be. Oh, Dinah, would it amaze you to know that I went to run away with a man one night, before I married Amos. He didn't come, but that was not my fault."

"You, Mother? You?"

"You will say to yourself what I said then. You have made a mistake, but you need not make a mistake again."

She regarded me humbly, and what I said may have helped, but it was no answer. A generation lay between us, and there was the Dudley in her. She did not even cry, but followed me out of the shop holding to my fingers. It was in the tightness of that grip alone that I had to know her, shield her, and take her home.

17

I took Dinah directly to Sara's that night and installed her in Sara's airy upstairs bedroom, the one that overlooks the back pasture and the shed she had built for the 1902 honeymoon car in which she had eloped with Jack McGillister.

Eating sandwiches with Sara downstairs, I remarked: "There is something wrong with all of us. We long for the dazzling moment and when it does not come we throw ourselves tooth and nail on little sordid things not worth the time."

"I never knew you had any such moments," Sara said, with a certain superiority.

I nodded. "Duane Stevens."

"Oh, Ary!" She giggled.

"Not that anything *happened*, Sara. But it would have been sordid just the same. Don't you breathe a word. Amos Dudley. He thinks anybody should not even give a second thought to his living for over two years with that Dubard woman, but if he knew anything of the sort ever entered my head— What do you suppose he would do, Sara? If it had all come to a head yesterday, say, and Duane Stevens was on hand?"

"Shoot him," said Sara without pause. Then she said: "Ary, what's the matter with Dinah?"

"Dinah? A touch of sun, I think. A little rest and quiet for two or three days—"

"Delighted," said Sara.

Amos was not in the house when I had left; I had written him a brief note. He drove into Cypress the next morning, put out with us for flying off. He was a man who liked to have his family about him. I met him at the front door and marched him straight back to the car. I sat in the car beside him and told him everything.

He turned from me as I finished and sat holding the wheel and staring through the glass absently. My voice hushed and we sat there together, as though nobody had said a word for a long time. I found myself studying him with detachment. He was not a large man, but he was tremendously compact with a compactness not of the delicate mechanism like a wrist-watch, but of the sturdy natural organism like a beaver that uses tail and tooth for work. Physically, belly, slight double chin and all, he was like a stout leather belt, well-worn. His face in repose was thoughtful, little-lined and more serene than anything else; it irritated me that he should appear so now as much as ever, and when I thought that he would never know the clear pain of Dinah's hurt as I had to know it, that placid thinking profile with firm lips drawn in a little, very nearly enraged me. In a minute he would decide his course, like the answer to a problem in long division, then things would begin to mend. All he needed was a little time.

"I was ready to give them everything I had," he said at last, "and still they went against me."

"Why won't you listen to the way it was? It was he who got her into it."

"She should have come to me. Why wouldn't she come to me? I'll see her right away."

I leaned, restraining his grasp from the door handle. "No. Please, Amos, no. It would kill her to think you know. She begged me not to tell you."

He let his hand be led away. "God knows," he said, "I don't

want to see her."

"I would never have told you except—"

"Except what?"

"Joe Ferguson. He must be dealt with."

"Him too. Yes, him too. You're right. It will be easier to see him than her. His eyes won't be quite as bad to look in. Well, I'll go to him now."

"Do not forget how he heard of you from Arney and he came, deliberate and shameless. Don't forget how he took her and shamed her with that filthy half-wit albino."

He shook his head. "The only thing I can't forget is that all this time I thought I had a little daughter, and to say it at the least, a true-hearted friend. Well, a man is a man, but is it so hard, Ary, for a girl to turn one down?"

"At times it may be very hard," I said. "Besides, it was you he used against her."

"She should have come to me. I could have told her—"

"Told her what?"

"How it was. Well. You can talk all day."

"Be careful," I begged and gripped his arm.

I alighted from the car and stood on the pavement, leaning in the window. "Be careful," I begged again.

"I doubt if it will take a shotgun," he said with a wry little twist of his mouth.

"Get away from the grounds," I said. "The rifles—"

He was observing me closely; then he laughed. "Now, Ary. Not even you could call it rape, for God's sake." He started the motor.

"Then what do you plan?" I cried.

"To have them marry, of course. At once."

The car, departing, almost dragged me forward onto the pavement.

It was late that afternoon at Sara's that the phone rang, a small buzz, as though it nudged for attention. I was there at once.

"What?" I said. "Can you speak louder?"

The low voice came again, but slower this time, pausing between words like a telegraph wire ticking off its code. A Negro woman's voice; I could not say whose.

"He—going—in—yo'—house. He—going—in—yo'—house —and—there—aint—nobody—home."

In a matter of minutes I was at Dudley.

It was the hour just after twilight, in first dark, when the summer singing of the insects had passed from bayou to bogue and risen along all the running ditches that bound the fields and meshed our yard and trees to the sound of all the Delta high above the immense lost stillness of the ancient sea-floor. The house, unlighted, seemed to float in the far-reaching current of sound; it was as though the flood had come again.

The house was shut up tight, but as I stood in the open front door a draught blew softly against me. I stepped immediately to the door of our room where the household cash was kept, and switched on the light. He shuddered in the strict glare for a moment like a moth on a pin before he righted. He had managed to close the wardrobe door in time, but not to make it to the window, if indeed he had wanted to. I decided later that he hadn't wanted to; it was a part of his "what-next" attitude of life to remain.

"I hoped you'd come," he said at once. "I wanted to see you before I left."

"Left?"

He smiled. "You'll never think good of me, spite of all I can do. So I asked, What would please her? And that's it: for me to leave. To give it all up. Though it fell in my lap, you understand, and I couldn't help it falling there."

I sickened suddenly, and turned back into the hall. He followed me. "You have seen Amos?" I asked.

"Mr. A.A.? Why, no, ma'am."

"You have seen him," I continued. "Or he has seen you. And you know now it won't be the bed of roses that you thought, belonging to a man who will tell you at every turn what you must and must not do. Having once betrayed him, you will never be allowed to run on a long rope again. He will never act as you want him to again. In fact, your wanting him to do anything will be reason enough to do the opposite. And all his goodness and his giving will be a favor, for you will belong to him and do only what he wants, being allowed to marry his daughter, with the inheritance held continually over your head, until he dies. He will live a long time, Amos Dudley will, and you know that too, and don't like it. For you have crossed him, and he looks at you with a different eye. What have you got in your pocket. A gun?"

"Yes. A gun."

"It's not a gun. Let me see it."

"It's not a gun, sure enough. It's why I came. I found it in the bayou chimney when I went to get my little cash money out. The chimney fell, or half of it did." He touched a fresh bruise on his forehead, and drew from his pocket a small sack that had once been white. It chinked with a dull brick-like sound. "He thought his friend stole it," he explained, "a long time ago. I came to bring it back." He set it on the table.

"No. You would have gone with it, if I had not seen it. You came to see me, as you said at first. You came for me to tell you that you were all right. Though why that is so important to you, I don't know."

"I don't know either," he cried eagerly. "I just know it is.

Oh, Miss Ary, ma'am, it is." He stepped closer to me. I leaned back against the wall. We had spoken slowly, almost lazily. "I'm sorry about Dinah," he said, "sorry for what it's put you to. But you understand a man, Miss Ary. She didn't know it maybe, but she put me in a spot where it was hard to do anything else. But you wouldn't like us getting married. That makes me right to go. Don't it make it right?"

"Provided it's what you don't want to do, maybe."

Our eyes met and he grinned. I saw the dark pink of his mouth through the missing tooth. I saw beyond the tooth to a blackness with depth. "She loved you," I said.

He took it as his due, without answering, and still I saw beyond the tooth, that dark point laid in a boyish face, as a hole the size of a peg shows black in the ground and by that blackness you know that the earth beneath your foot is rotten, eaten secretly away from within; and I had stared beyond the tooth until I gripped my hand to my face. "Wait here a minute," I told him and slipped past.

I went into the lighted bedroom and shut the door. I did not have to look but a moment. Father had looked so hard. Ah, but it was Joe Ferguson that he had needed, I knew that now, though Father had not known it. The gun lay pearl-handled in its plush-lined case, delicate as some odd piece of table service. Mother used to take it out and sleep with it by her bed, alone in the house with the children. And knowing of it, this tiny instrument to set against all that the river, land, and swamp and wilderness beyond could spawn to threaten us, how soundly we slept. How gently sound. Not a cartridge had ever been fired. To our shame.

I returned to the hall, leaving the door open to give me light.

It would be forever to his reproach, and mine, that he thought I intended to give him something.

18

I shut out the bedroom lights and switched on a single lamp in the hall. Gun still in hand, I wheeled out a chair and took my seat, facing both the crumpled body (which looked poor and harshly clothed as it had never seemed in life) and the front door where the breeze came softly in. The insects, which had been jarred into silence by the sound of the shot, took up cautiously where they left off.

My mind worked with a clear precision. With my free hand, I tightened the pins in my hair, smoothed my skirts and straightened my stocking seams. Amos would talk to the Wavells a while after supper. Then he would come home.

I thought over the Morgans one at the time, but with a distant, unreal emotion, as though they were people I had read about in a book. I had paid my debt to them and their debt to the world, when I fired the shot, and now I was free of them and a little weary of them too, as though the book had gone on too long. I was free and weary even of Louise who, as Amos had understood that day with Nathan and the hill people, was nothing but a dead woman, and we had all been betrayed— betrayed by wanting her, betrayed by having her, into the soft inaction, the too much talk that had marked the Morgans from way back until this night. I was free of them, and the measure and proof of my freedom was that I was alone. I had forsaken all others; my wedding night had come at last. I would face Amos Dudley alone.

I was not in the least afraid, and realizing the newness of this condition I knew that Dolly had said the truth: I had been for many years (perhaps since the April day I felt beneath my seat the swift contraction and collapse of the mare's stride and caught for a clear second the wild unleashed delight in the shouting face that broke through trained gait and trained control), afraid of Amos Dudley and what he would someday do.

He would have his chance now; his excuse lay on his own floor; his certain object sat quietly before him.

I was not afraid, but my heart picked up speed, racing faster and faster, like a bride's heart paced to the setting sun.

The Return: Amos

ALL MY life—or so long in my life it seemed like my life was hewed around them, and without them there wouldn't be any my life—I thirsted to see two things. One of them I'd seen once and wanted back, and the other I'd never seen and know now that I will never see, neither in this life nor after the fireworks. One was to see Ary's face again like I saw it first that day above the horse's mane, like a face not in the world, though it had been in the world all right, but was by her own will and nothing else whipped up clean above the world and outside, knowing she ought not to be out there with just men showing off that mare and in her own pride not caring, and in her own pride being proud of the mare, and of herself too, so that not even my pride in her which got so out of hand could quite manage to unsettle her. She was equal to me then and a little bit more.

And the other sight I thirsted to see was a ladder of angels.

If anybody wants to know which is worse—to want a thing back you had once, or to want a thing you never had—I'm here to say it's first one and then the other, and there's no telling which. For the times when I was lonely and turned back on myself (when Ary devilled me with so much family, or Dolly left me, or when Ary would listen without listening to my brag on business or the market or crop gain—she'd have a head for business if she wanted to, it's not being dumb; but it seemed like she said to herself once and for all, This is something I'm not going to put in my head)—those times I'd crack my eyeballs in the dead of night, going to lonely places, bayou, levee, or bogue, to see the bright ladder fall and the angels slide from rung to rung, slow as thick molasses dropping down. But when Ary and I came face to face in agreement or disagreement— and the truth of it is there's not much we've seen eye to eye on— I'd watch back off behind myself, watch and wait, for her face to burn white and cold as a star over frost, to be something not me nor a blooded mare run wild nor the eyes of a hundred planters and Syrians and Jews and niggers and Chinamen could put in the dust. But the years passed and she wouldn't be that again; I wore out with trying to bring it up in her. So when Joe Ferguson came and Dudley turned so fitful, as it had never quite stopped being since Thelma left, I begun to think that if I could latch onto the run of secret things as I had known them since the night on the Yocona River when the hand of God snatched me to kingdom come and back, that everything would fall in place along with me, and then the ladder would come down in some innocent way while I went along thinking about something else.

Then, too, I would have a son. I wanted a son more, I reckon, than I wanted the two sights I spoke of, but a son is a condition like money in the bank and the other is a thing to see. I would have traded my chances at the sights for the surety of a son; only the sights never seemed like a thing you could trade on, no more than you can swop off a pretty evening on the front porch and a good rest for equal value. That just happens and can't be jacked loose from what makes it.

But it did begin to sit right in my head that if I could just take one deep breath and swallow Joe Ferguson for what he claimed to be and, for all I wanted to know, was, then I would stand right at the criss-cross of the line of God that started in Yocona and the line of the devil that started with Thelma, being punished and blessed at once in Joe Ferguson, and it was right in the groin of that same criss-cross where I had a feeling the angels would come down. It set in my head, too, from the first, that Dinah and Joe would make a pair, and there needn't be any loose ends dangling, or anything to make the ladder sit catty-wampus, you might say, and have the angels falling.

It makes me laugh when you look at it that way—I could always laugh to myself about how much I wanted to see it. But then I came across a fellow once, up in the café on the highway, who got likkered up and told me how he used to dream about a town and honed to see it so, he covered Mexico twice looking for it and was heading for Florida right then to look some more. All-purpose cleaner salesman. He had a lean time in Mexico.

It's true that in pressing so close on the ladder, I forgot about Ary. Clean forgot her in that special way I had always kept her in mind, and that was right when she foxed me.

I walked in the front door that night after she had told me about Dinah and Joe in the afternoon (and still I saw how things could be all right, and how the bitterness of what had happened between them was right too, having happened in the bayou house where my own past lay in the old dust). I took three steps into the hall when I saw and took in what had happened, but it was not the thing that had happened that stopped me cold.

She sat in the straight chair with her legs crossed and the little gun hanging from one hand and her back growing straight up out of her seat, and above, way, way above, was her face. I saw it like a speck of a bird way up in the empty sky at a clear sunset and I saw it too like a leaf by the porch that the spyglass picks up when I study to see way off if the tractor's broke down. She had gone to some place way away from the gun in her hand, or the body on the floor, or the thing she had done. She was back where she was when the horse went round, but this time she was watching me.

While she watched and I stood there and the body lay between us on the floor, there came the sound of a car on the cattle gap. I jumped a foot, but she did not jump. "Sara's sent Nathan and Dolly for me likely," she said. "I was due back for supper."

And still she sat while the headlights slid on the smooth oak leaves and glanced off the porch, turning the drive. She did not stir. Her face was cut out of ice. I knew then she was not going to stir, that nothing could throw her now. I could prize the gun out of her hand, I could hold them behind the door while I hid the body in the closet, I could lock her up by force and lie; but the time would come when she would walk out calm as a breeze amongst them, carrying that face and say, "I shot Joe Ferguson," and she would be believed. So it was not anymore, I knew in that split second while the motor died in the yard and the headlights died and the car doors slammed—it was not any more what she couldn't do, but what I couldn't let her do, so I stepped over the boy's body and came close to her and hungered down on one knee.

"Ary," I said softly. "Ary. Give me the gun. I would beg all night, but you see there isn't time. All I got time to say is Please. Please, Ary?"

Her hand did not move, but a softness came in her face while the front gate slammed and steps crunched in the yard. Color grew right before my eyes in her lips and cheeks and her eyes burned so bright I could hardly stand it, but I remember thinking, I reckon that's going to have to go in place of the angels;

she had sure-God ruined my chances there. Then her hand
came up with the gun like there was all the time in creation and
she laid the pearl-handle in my hand.

"Thank you, Amos," she said, low and swift and almost to one
side, without any of the meaning gone, though, exactly like I
had moved a chair to suit her, or picked up something she
dropped.

That was how they found us: me with the gun above the body
of the dead, and Ary sitting in the chair, and that is how they
will always believe it was, and the kind of thing they always
thought was just like me to do.

Later I was mad at her. I saw that she had cheated me; I saw
the nature of it, and the heart. She had coined me to her own
use, the same as Thelma; it had taken murder to do it, and she
had gone that far, unregretful, with Dinah's damned pitiful lost
virtue to balance it off. But I did not think that at the time, and
in that time, forevermore, she had me.

How could I have kept her from what she did? If I had told
her what she tried to get at, told her all the long tale linking
back to the night in the Yocona River when I came near to
drowning to find what settled my heart, and did find it—was
found by it—what if I had told her that? She wouldn't have believed it, from the word go. She would have done the same.
Suppose I had told all the others, would they have acted different? Would Thelma have wanted a baby less, or Arney not
blamed me for letting her go, or Newt Simpson failed to say,
"What do you suggest, little Dudley?" blaming me for leaving
him alone, drunk, broke, and old, even when he knew I had
to go? Would Dolly not have tried to make me square with the
Morgans, so she would not have to choose? Would Joe have
stayed his distance from Dinah, or Dinah from Joe? No, I said
every time, and still say it. They would have done the same, or

more, if I had told them, giving them advantage. How can a man follow the way of his heart except by keeping it a secret way? Crooked as it goes, and far from home, he still must follow it, else he has no right to name himself a man.

And now she had ended that. Because just as sure as it is true that you can keep people ignorant, it's also true that you can't keep them harmless, and in finishing out my secret way I had had to count on them more than I knew, and that was where the way was lost, ended, over. I could not have Joe as a son and pay Thelma back, because Ary had killed him. I could not have Ary and deny her, because twice now she had showed me her face.

So it was over. I was left with a secret that had no more power, and with my heart, and where God had been there was nothing but a big silence. In the big silence, alone with his heart, what does a man do then? I can say that too, though it took no thought at the time. He does what he was brought up to do; he goes back to the way he was born knowing. He buries the dead as decent as he can; then he goes home. And in doing what he was brought up to do, if he is lucky—and I was born lucky—little kindly things may happen here and there.

When I came back from the river that night it was late and the house was full of more cousins of one kind or another: it seemed like they had been waiting in the bushes for the sound of the gun. They were all over the house; I stood alone in the empty hall and could hear them like rats in a seed house and couldn't see a one. What I saw was a little sooty sack on the hall table with twenty-eight green-molded silver dollars inside and a boy's account sheet that started with $9.68 for the Tabernacle collection and ended with $1.39 for a dress length for Thelma. I put the money back into the sack along with the sheet that split at the folds, and when I looked up, all the doors into the hall were cracked open and two or three cousins' eyes were stuck in every one. I whirled on my heel, shaking the sack in my hand at every eye I marked. "Arney never stole!" I shouted at the cracked doors. "Arney never stole!"

All the doors banged together and there was a great scuttling behind them, so that I was alone in the hall again with the sack and the account sheet and the twenty-eight silver dollars.

That was how I came to be driving late in the night along the highway dump, and the land that in night time might have been anything from so much water to so much concrete fell away on either side, and now and then a little light shone up from way off and down, like out of a pit. In one of those pits behind me I had left Ary and Dolly, not to say the others who didn't matter. never precisely meant to. They would just have to figure that out for themselves; I didn't have time to go back and explain things. And Nathan was there; I may have meant to scare him a little. Because when we got to the river bank in Joe Ferguson's '28 coupe, I rolled the body in the front seat and tied it to the wheel and never stirred the victrola nor records nor magazines nor anything from the back, except to draw the folding top up tight over them, and I looked down the long slope to where the river ran narrow and deep, heading for the Mississippi. There was a fisherman's path down to the edge, and I asked Nathan, "Well, will you pray for the funeral?"

And he said, "Yes, I'll pray."

I doubted if he had the wits to answer me, much less address the Lord; that coupe on the washboard had shook his top plate out twice to my knowledge. I put the car out of gear; it rolled into a dustbed and up the other side; the long slide pulled at it. I held it back.

"Why will you pray?" I asked Nathan. "What will you pray for?"

"For the rest of his soul," Nathan said.

"He never believed in any of that," I said. "Furthermore he's been lying a blue streak ever since I laid eyes on him two years ago."

"That is with God," Nathan said, and the car tugged us, eager for drowning, but I held though Nathan almost got flung up on the hood. He was my size by the tape-measure I reckon, but his job didn't run him to muscle.

"You got to know when to turn a-loose," I told him, "and mind out you do."

"Yes, indeed," Nathan said, and settled his hat and bit his plates together. I drew my hand across the dead shoulders at the wheel and straightened the collar so, woman-like, and thought it a pity there was no woman to set him nice. The car teetered, but I held on just one minute more.

"Where is he?" I asked Nathan. "What's happened to him?"

"It is with God," Nathan said, irritably. "For heavens' sake, Amos."

"Well, he's one of two places," I said, "and I think I know which one. But God is not going to snatch him out of hell because you prayed, or kick him out of heaven if you don't. So what you're praying for, is a mystery to me."

"It is," said Nathan, "a customary gesture."

"But customary for what?"

"For the family," Nathan said. I thought he might break out crying.

"Like that little flower-pot sprinkling you do and call baptizing," I said. "On little babies that can't do nothing but sprinkle back. Well. Pray ahead."

And I gave her a little shove and let go and she slid a little sideways like she was only teasing about wanting to go down, then the speed caught and righted her.

"Pray!" I said and gave Nathan a shove in the side.

"Oh, Lord—" I heard him start and then I couldn't hear him for the tearing in the brush and the long ripping splash of the water that burnt black silver the way when a fish jumped at night, and Joe Ferguson would lean to the boat's edge and say, "It's a trout, Mr. A.A. It's a trout, for shore." It was a handsome way he had of saying such things, with a boy's thrill coming out of him, smart and proud to be smart, and the water sucked, gulping, and two waves came up and met at a speed, spraying high, and Nathan said, "Amen."

He was gone before I was good through looking at the water, headed back into the brake by the river at a little scuttling walk that said plain as anything it was worth his reputation, not to say his job if anybody saw him down here, so I got right on his heels all the way home.

"If you just leave it up to God, how do you ever know if God does right by you?"

"It is a question of faith," Nathan said, and stumbled over a clump of sumac.

"But what's your proof?" I asked him.

"God is His own proof," Nathan said.

"But suppose God is no good?" I asked him. "Suppose God laughs?" He had to stop and catch his breath and I came even with him. "Suppose God cheats?"

He had a round, soft face, earnest like a little boy's. "Hush, Amos," he pleaded. I poked him in the chest with my finger.

"You talk about God," I told him, "three or four times a week for pay and a little on the side thrown in for free. But listen. I'll tell you my life story, Nathan. I was baptized in the same water with a drownded calf; I got my land by the will of God and the luck of a poker-playing Chinaman; I lived with a witch who went off pregnant, and that was her son or so he claimed, that's laying at the bottom of the Sunflower River. And added to that, I'm married to Ary Morgan. Now I'll just stand here and wait while you sort it out, good from bad."

Nathan moved off, a little uneasy. What right had a preacher, I wondered, to be uneasy around the truth? I caught his arm and pulled him around to me. "I saw a cat one time," I said and lifted my hand, "as tall as your shoulder, setting with front paws together and straight to the shoulder and eyes squint-closed, black except for a white blaze in the face. I saw him in the tail of my eye. And many another thing I've seen and heard tell of, since she left. They wait by every ditch and cross-road, and when he came with the story of the blonde woman he never saw that dropped him in Arkansas and died of a fever nobody could name, it didn't seem like no more of an unusual thing than I'd been used to for blows anyway."

"Now, Amos," Nathan said and broke my fingers off his arm one at the time. "You're just upset. Come on home and get a good night's rest."

"And added to that," I said, "I had no son. Not one would she give me except for death. Not one!"

I would have grabbed him again, but he was gone and kept a good pace ahead of me through the fields home, where he must have collapsed from over-exertion for I heard the women fanning him. I guess that's the most that ever happened to Nathan since his wedding night with Louise, which I have often wondered was so hot after all.

Yes, I could hear them fanning and fetching—and now and then a giggle (for that set of hers would find something to laugh at on Judgment Day)—and Nathan mumbling to Ary how I had gone clear out of my head and must have been so when I shot the boy; then they all got quiet and said that must be it, and so it was decided until they saw me through the cracked doors and I yelled over the money and that scattered them.

"It's come to a fine pass," I said to Ary (she had come behind me to the gate), "when a man can get called crazy in his own house and his wife don't say a thing but Uh-huh."

"You were there too," she said.

"I haven't got time to mess with them," I said.

"I guess I don't care any more," she said. "I don't care what they think. Where are you going, Amos?"

"Where the woodbine twineth," I said, "and the whangdoodle mourneth for her first born."

"No," she said. "Tell me."

"I got twenty-eight silver dollars in my pocket. That's all I know about in this world. I'm going back to Yocona first, then I'm going to find Arney."

"If you go back there, you might never come home," she said.

"It's likely," I said.

But I didn't find Arney. I didn't find Yocona either.

All I found was an empty waste full of raw dirt, soft and loose with no grass growing all around, with a deep hole blasted right about where I figured the house used to be and that old cedar where the little ones had a swing, and all the hills brought low. An arm of the dam they were building swung round about where the store once was and over across the river where the land lay smoother the scrub trees and brush had run all together, the way land will do when it knows the people are gone. The three pines by the river were gone. Far off I could see the rows of government barracks where the dam workers lived, all dark, and further up the lighted office where the trucks checked through. They had laid a gravel road to join way up on the raw end of the dam where I guess the niggers were tramping in the dirt loads and shoveling the gravel and small rock smooth. I couldn't see them from where I sat on the blasted-up tree trunk by the road. But the trucks came by me spewing gravel with the men sitting high like pilots, their faces set and sober and inward-looking and hardly colored at all—the way men look on a night shift—doing nothing but riding the yellow lights on the gravel and turning over slow in the mind whatever they fetched up from next to the heart.

It was chill. The trucks were all gone, I thought, until here come the cow's tail, treading down the gravel easier than the others, so that I thought even before the wheels began to wander like a broke bone in the socket, He's asleep.

I jumped on the running board and beat on the window.

He rolled down the window and crawled over to look at me.

"Who're you?" he asked me.

"Amos Dudley," I said.

"Jordan," he said, "Elmore Jordan." He called it Jerdon, the way people do. We shook hands through the window. "Much obliged," he said. "I aint been able to stay in the road since my wife died."

"When was that?" I asked him.

He counted. "Two weeks going on three. You don't work here?"

"No. I used to live here back before you ruined it."

"Don't look at me," he said. "M'self, I think it's a crime." He got out of the cab. "So you're another one, come back to look at where you used to live. You sho come at an unchristian hour."

"I was coming home," I said and something hard and suffocating rose in my throat. I had forgotten the feel of tears and the taste of them, but that's what it was. "I thought that if ever I saw this land laid low to ruin it would be from the fire of the Lord on the day when the saints marched in."

"Yeah. Well, this day and time Judgment Day waits for the

bill to go through Congress. Mr. Roosevelt just aint thought of it yet."

"Yeah," I said. "That's right. But me, I voted for it. Or rather for the man that did it."

"Then what did you think you were going to find, coming up here after midnight?"

"I didn't believe it. I hadn't seen it, so I didn't believe it. I thought the house would be left yet awhile. Or the store, empty. Or somebody's house. Or something."

"There was a lot of stout hills through here. This was the main basin on the plan they drawed. They aim to put the spillway right up yonder, you can't see at night, though. Lot of good fishing once they get it done."

"I don't want it done. I don't want it done at all." I said it loud, turning around, but the dam was way off and high and there was a little greenish-yellow light coming on that showed up a lot of ugliness the dark had covered up. The trouble with it all was being so big and bare that way, it made us both seem so little.

"It's done anyway," Elmore Jordan said. "Come on with me, fellow."

He said he was off by then, so he took me over on the highway to a café and ordered himself a big plate of eggs, then a chop of some café sort with mashed potatoes and gravy; then he said he was hungry so he had a piece of pie. He was a tall big-lunged man. I drank coffee. My stomach was weaving light and painful from hunger, but I kept saying I couldn't stop to eat, and why I couldn't say unless it was to go against Thelma and Ary who always threw up to you by the way they acted that the only thing a man really cared about was a full stomach. Both good cooks though.

"Yes, sir," said Elmore Jordon, "If you from the Delta, you ought to be right glad they've put all these hill rivers in harness. Dam the hills to save the Delta. That's what they say."

We had been cussing the government for going on two hours and it seemed like every conversation I'd had with anybody for the past thirty-five years, I'd had to join in on the same thing.

"It's our fault," I said. "We vote them in."

"The South can't do nothing," Elmore Jordon said, and shook his coffee spoon at me. "The South can't never do nothing until—"

"Until what?"

He leaned at me. "Split off," he said. "That's what we going to have to do. Just like before. Only this time do it quiet. Just leave."

"They got us too tied up," I said. "There's too many folks working for the government."

"Government can't last forever," he said. "Look how much debt we're in to now."

My stomach kicked up again. "Reckon I could get a beer?" I asked him.

"Sure. I'll have one with you."

One and my head went light, but my stomach set easy, so I had another one. Elmore Jordan had another one too.

"Yessir," he said. "There was fine folks living all up through here in the olden days."

"What's happened to all of them?"

"I tell you what's happened." He leaned again. "They died."

"They sure made a mess of raising children," I said. But that didn't sit well after I said it, because Ary wasn't any mess. "My big mistake," I told him, "was ever getting married."

"I used to say that. Then Roselle died on me. I tell you what, though. Without a wife a man don't have nothing to think about.

For long at the time, that is. I aim to get another one, quick as I can."

"I ought to spent my life," I said, "drinking a little bit here and yonder, working a little bit here and there, talking to folks just such as you and Arney that's gone and Joe Ferguson that's dead."

"Well, how come you didn't?"

"I got tangled up with God," I said.

He looked a little big-eyed, and it came over me I was pretty damned sick and tired of keeping shut-mouthed and close the kind of thing you got into by getting religion, and that too many folks for pay had made it out to be easy. So I told him about it. That's how it went: thirty or more years of keeping myself close around Ary for fear of that sharp little look she'd give and that thing or two she'd have to say, and the whole business would crumble like dry mud. And there it went, to the first man I was fool enough to drink with on an empty stomach.

"Seem like to me God done pretty well by you," he said, "though it's a fact I never heard of anybody else making business arrangements with the Almighty."

"I never felt right asking for a thing I asked for. Yet all I asked for I got. Up to the last. How come Him to let me go all my life? Here I am going on fifty-five years old."

"Maybe you'll get to live longer than most."

I thought that over. "Maybe so."

"You know," he said, and leaned at me, "I thought it a long time ago, and I'm going to say it now. I don't think there is any God."

"There is too," I said. "I aint that much of a prize fool."

"But take me, for instance. What would I do with a god if I had one? My wife was set on churches. Every Sunday that rolled I'd load her up and cart her into Water Valley to church.

Then the mail started to swell. All time after money. First it was a new pipe organ, then they got that; next it was new Sunday School rooms and they got that; then, God held me, they come close to going bankrupt. Don't ask me how a church goes bankrupt. I reckon they speculated too heavy on the Sunday School rooms and the pipe organ. So I says to my wife, Listen: that kind of church is too high-toned for country folks like us. (I was boring wells at the time.) Let's us go to the country church down the road here. We got in just in time for a revival. They shouted and prayed and so forth and me, I just set still. Ever'time my wife tried to get up I'd jerk her down. And sure enough, it wasn't long I had to wait. Here come the tin plates, and here come the preachers down the aisle selling Bibles and pictures of Jesus. I told my wife I'd just soon be a nigger and shout for free on the river bank. So after that she kept going and I kept staying at home. It was right before she died she said, Elmore, it weighs on me. When you was over in Alabama boring for that long spell, that Buchanan man used to call by right often— So I says, Don't worry about that none, honey; it's been twice since we married I done laid out on you. Then I says, Just out of curiosity, honey, how many times did you lay out on me? And she says, Twice. Well, church or not, what's the difference?"

"I never had time for churches either," I said.

"Well, God then. You believe in it. But look. You shot one man. Is that all?"

"That's all."

"I aint shot but one man either. Seems like I stay right about even with everybody."

"This aint getting me anywhere," I said. "I got to go down to the river."

"What you going down there for?"

"I'm fifty-five," I said. "But if it's all wrong, it's all wrong. I got to stop it someway. Who'd you shoot?"

"That Buchanan bastard."

I didn't know till later that he followed me. He told Ary—it was over to Dudley that he went, toting the sack of money that he fished out of the river where it caught on a stob—that he feared I was going to drown myself, that I talked right light-headed over the beer. Ary let that get out amongst the Morgans, and in the Delta to this day they'll tell you I went out of my mind once and might again. Ary let that get out and didn't care a bit, same as she let Nathan say I was off and never stopped him a time.

Elmore Jordan found Ary at the kitchen table drinking coffee and every now and then she'd pour a little whisky in to lace it. She gave him a drink straight, which he said was uncommonly kind (anybody else can give you a drink and you think that was nice, but Ary gives you a drink and you lick up the floor being grateful), and then they both sat down to the big dinner she had cooked for me to come back and eat. They had all the things I liked the most: roast hen and dressing and sweet pota-toes with marshmallows on top and a big glass dish full of tomato slabs and cucumbers and onions, all floating in vinegar, and rice and gravy and hot biscuits, coffee and buttermilk both, and coconut pie.

But I was far off, up beyond Toccopola on Henderson An-drews Creek.

After dinner they went back in the kitchen—Ary ran the nig-gers off. She said they had commenced acting like her life was their life and she wasn't going to put up with it. They kept on drinking coffee and whisky with the cotton gin growing crazy up the road: that's the way it will do when everything is still, like it popped into the same house with you and was rattling the roof: and Ary kept flying to the door, sure she'd heard a car. I asked her later did she want me home that bad, and she said she reckoned she was just nervous. And Dinah was there, sitting around nice and polite, or helping cook and wash up, which was something she'd never done before.

So then there were the three of them sitting around the kitchen table with the sack of silver dollars lying by the coffee pot and Elmore Jordan, being the kind of man obliged to keep talking to somebody, was telling Dinah some long tale or other, when Ary stepped in right in the middle of it and said:

"There's one thing certain. That money's got to go back in the Yocona River. And you," she told Elmore Jordan, "have got to go back to work." So she carted Dinah in to Sara's and the two of them put out for Yocona.

I reckon she got her shoes muddy there, tramping over a wild space at dark with a man she'd never seen before that day. But she made him show her the place—she said my tracks were still there—and stood in my tracks and threw the money and this time it sank, all the way down and gone, there where the old ford used to be and where I had stood that night and longed in my heart for my heart to want to throw it in. But there was still a difference, though I had come back to do it and to all intents and purposes had done it. In the day I first wanted to cast it, that little wad of paper and silver was all I had to name my own. So that moment I had that night to square myself with what I had done against Ephraim and Tabernacle and the name of Dudley and God was gone forever, and of such chances I guess a man is lucky if he has one in a lifetime. I'm looking for the man who had the chance and took it. I never have found him yet.

I went to find Ephraim instead and he was bent and squeaky

and rusty as an old hinge. I said, "Ephraim, I threw that money in the river." He never asked what money or what river. He just said, "That's a good place for it."

The next day was Sunday and it was way after dark when she heard a beating at the front door and ran slam into Elmore Jordan.

"I found him," he said.

They went back in the kitchen and Ary hooked up the coffee pot and fried him some sausage and eggs. He had a powerful appetite.

He had got his sleep out Saturday night when the crew was off work and Sunday morning he trailed me on up to where the Dudleys had moved out to, up into the hills back of Toccopola where the big trees grow amongst the rocks. He saw the baptizing down on the creek. It wasn't much of one, nothing like in the old days when the river ran between banks of folks and ladies standing in bright summer dresses with parasols and handkerchiefs held in one hand and the hymn books in the other, beating time in the sand with one foot and the other one braced not to topple when the children grabbed ahold of their skirts. And the preacher out waist deep and the saved going in dry and coming out with their clothes sucked to them while everybody sang, "Naked, wretched, poor, despised, Wash me, Savior, or I die."

This was just a little baptizing with nobody there much but Dudleys and the preacher Ephraim fancied and had salvaged out of Yocona with the family. Brother Harpis. It seemed like he was living with the rest of the family in Aunt Reesa's old two-story house with the dog run cleft through right up to the roof tree and the hill about to wash out from under it so that one side had to be propped up with a pole.

Ephraim said: "How come you been all this time and aint

ever washed your sins away like the Scripture says?"

"I reckon I just aint ever felt naked wretched pore despised before," I said.

"You took a mighty long chance," Ephraim said.

There wasn't anybody else for baptizing but Durley, Jr.'s three little ones. They shivered and shook and one of them cried. I picked him up, being wet too, and told him not to mind, I felt the same way. And for a fact, he wasn't hurt, he was just cocky and always pulling some stunt or other for folks to call him cute about and it hurt his feelings to get ducked that way. If he could have ducked Brother Harpis it would have been different. Or had on a swim suit. But the way it was, he felt silly and it didn't set well. It was truthful that I felt the same way. But I reckon that's what they want from you. If they can make you feel silly enough one time, you won't be apt to step so high afterwards. I don't know. I wasn't going to study about it any more.

We had to cut the singing short. There was a cloud blowing up from across the bottom land, and the hand-shaking went the rounds quick. Ephraim herded everybody up the road to dinner at Aunt Reesa's. Aunt Reesa had been cooking since daylight; she was too old and poorly to go to the baptizing and she was down in the back and walked with a cane and didn't have to bend over to smell anything on the stove.

Ephraim said: "There was a man hiding up in the brush during the baptizing. Is he a friend of yours?"

"That Jordan," I said. "For God's sake, don't let him in."

"Ought to ask him to dinner," Ephraim said.

But he wasn't there any more.

The thunder was knocking close and the clouds came in streamers first with the big ones rolling in behind. I hung back with Ephraim. He had to stop a time or two and pant on the

hill. It was so old he was now, with his face belted in wrinkles
and his eyes looking out from way down deep like an old turtle
half out of his shell.

"What you going to do, Ephraim?"

"The government tried to build us a house," he said and
panted. He climbed a little more. "I wouldn't take nothing from
them. I cussed the surveyors—" he stopped again and climbed
again and stopped—"I cussed the investigators—" he climbed
again—"I cussed the Vicksburg engineers and the dam crew—
I cussed all the alphabet they could send me." He sat down on
a rock. "But it didn't do no good. It's that Delta of yours. That
Delta that you went to. You got so much subsidy and parity
now, the government owns four walls of any house you live in."

Thunder rolled in the path. "Yes, Ephraim," I said, "but what
you going to do?"

"They bought my store," he said. "They bought my house
and land. Durley's got a school bus and no school to run it to.
The others had little pieces of land around. They offered us
money for all of it."

"You took it?"

I oughtn't to have pinned him down that way. It took the
grit out of him to say it and all he had left was grit for the
sockets of his bones to turn in. "I took it," he said.

The wind came and every leaf on the trees was laid flat as a
scared dog's ear. The lightning popped, but Ephraim sat there
on the gray rock doubled up, and never jumped.

"Durley and the young ones are dickering for some bottom
land. It was Aunt Reesa had to take us in. We got to start all
over again."

"Get up from there," I said, "before we both get blown to
kingdom come."

Then, as Jordan told Ary, he was headed for the house to

get out of the storm, scrabbling up the hill toward the house and as good a target as lightning would want when I came past him like a shot with Ephraim bundled up in my arms beating at me to let him down and all I gave Elmore Jordan was a shove which sent him down into the wind and it was a minute or two before he could get as far as the fence. We were gone in the house by then and the dog run was empty, but he could hear a lot of yelling and running around inside and about that time the wind boomed up full of thunder and every zinnia and marigold Aunt Reesa had was laid flat as a stick. He saw the tilted side of the house commence to grow higher than the safe side and he pushed at the gate like it was a stuck car and the palings splintered off in his hands; the wind was that strong. Then people commenced to pour out of the tilted side into the dog run and children jumped out of the second story above the dog run and people saw them in mid-air and snatched them and stood holding them and the gate came open all of a sudden on Jordan and pitched him on his face into the flower bed and the people in the dog run stood looking at him quietly and he looked back.

A little old woman, bent, came walking slow out of the tilted side with a walking cane in one hand and a plate of cornbread in the other: he could see the smoke rise from the bread. It was like she turned the house aloose because the wind boomed again and the lumber tore and half the house lifted up and before he knew it he was running back down the hill to where he left his car and pretty soon he caught on that the crashing he heard behind him was just his own sound in the brush.

So all the news Jordan had for Ary was that I might or might not be buried under a pile of kindling wood with twelve broke ribs and my nose mashed in. I don't think he had good sense. It was, though, he explained to her, an uncommonly strange sight and what with all he'd gone through about me for the past two days and what with his wife hardly cold, it unnerved him.

"I wasn't sure," he said to her, "that any of it was real."

"I know what you mean," she said. "But if I had had to drive a hundred and fifty miles every time I've wondered that in the past two years, I'd have spent most of my time on the road."

"Well, you know, Mrs. Dudley," he said, and helped himself to some more pork roast and cabbage and fried sweet potatoes, "I did take an interest in him."

"That's very kind of you," Ary said, and poured whisky in her coffee.

There was a gang of Morgans ventured in to see about Ary. They found her just before sundown sitting on the porch with her hair not combed since morning, an old housecoat wrapped around her, a bottle of whisky and a pot of cold coffee on the table, and a perfectly strange and awfully common man in a workshirt and no tie sitting with her like he owned the place.

She didn't even ask them in. "I don't need anything or anybody," she said. "I'm just sitting here waiting for Amos Dudley."

And she didn't explain about the man.

No matter what it cost me, it had done something for Ary, my taking that gun out of her hand. And I remembered when she told me that part of it, what she'd said when I left: "I guess I don't care any more. I don't care what they think."

"You know," Elmore Jordan said when the Morgans had packed up in the car again and gone, "if that old lady was cooking in that side of the house that fell in, wonder if they didn't get a bite to eat?"

"That would be terrible," Ary said.

But no matter how much I had done for her, taking away the gun, I guess we came out even, Ary and me. Because the time wasn't long in coming when I had to count on her not to plug me through the head with a .22 cartridge.

I wonder what she thought the next morning about ten o'clock when my car made the cattle gap slow and gentle for fear of spilling anybody. She was standing on the porch watching and Dinah was by her and Elmore Jordan, swinging in the swing.

Behind me, swirling off the highway was another car, an old beat-up '27 black Ford my youngest brother Mason owned. And his family was in it. Back of that was the school bus Durley had got stranded with, loaded down with furniture and mattresses and dishes and pots and Lord knows what all, together with any odd Dudleys that couldn't get in the other two cars. Aunt Reesa and Ephraim were riding up with me on the front seat, and Brother Harpis was in back along with the three little ones he had baptized, only I reckon he thought by now it would take more than creek water to wash the devil out of them. We stopped under the trees and commenced to unload. I had the tail of my eye towards the porch and I saw she was dressed up pretty that day and the longer she looked the more she was glad for it. A well-turned dress can cover a lot of flinching, and every Dudley that hit the ground she gave a little.

I came up the steps ahead of them.

"I brought them all home with me," I said. "I got too much land anyway."

"To stay?" she inquired.

"To live," I answered.

She did not say anything for a while.

"Be especially nice," I said, "to Ephraim and Aunt Reesa. It's Ephraim's pride. He's touchy about favors. It's the way the Dudleys are."

She still didn't say anything.

"I can sleep a lot of them down at the bayou," I said. "That is, until I can get a house started."

"You can't," she said. "I burned it down."

I wheeled around, staring out across the land. It was true. There in the tops of the big trees a black scar lay. It had not been there before.

"I didn't want any more foolishness about that bayou," she said. "Understand?"

"Yes, Ary."

She bit her lip. "Mr. Jordan here," she said, and nodded toward him, "wanted to see about living down there and working for you."

"All right, Ary."

Behind me they were milling at the gate. I wondered why they didn't come in. Then I saw what was holding them. It was her, the way she was holding herself, the way she was. "Ary," I said.

But she didn't hear me. She was gone down the steps past me, light and quick and free, the steps gone beneath her feet before they bore her weight and I stood, tighter than bolted iron, until I heard her at the gate, the sound of her voice, not the words, they were the same old words you used everytime when somebody special came to your house and you wanted them to know how glad.

So I turned to Elmore Jordan who was sitting on the swing by Dinah, and I said, "Dinah, aren't you ashamed. Run on down there and say hello to your Uncle Ephraim and your Aunt Reesa and all your cousins and uncles and aunts." Then I said to Elmore Jordan: "You come on back with me."

I took him out on the back porch. "You might have had some car expense," I said and gave him a twenty dollar bill which he took. He wanted to talk it out, but I said: "You might be looking for a wife and you might be looking for a steady job, but we sure don't know enough about you for Dinah Lee and I sure don't know enough about you for anything, which might be a good thing."

He grinned and looked at me sideways. "But don't you for-get, Mr. Dudley, I sure know a lot about you."

"Oh, that," I said. "You swallowed all that? I talk a lot when I drink and I can't hold a thimblefull. What did I say this time? Go on; what did I say?"

"Well," he hemmed, "I'd be willing to forget it."

"You can forget it if you want to, and you can remember it if you want to. Me, I aim to forget it. Now hit the road, son. You done made yourself entirely too convenient. I got sixteen Dudleys and a Baptist preacher to feed, and you eat too much."

So I turned him out. The likes of him had been a pitfall too often, like something you run over in the dark and wince for hitting and maybe hurting for fear it is worth more than you will ever be worth in a world that don't reason out too well.

Little Ned, the one that cried when the preacher ducked him, asked me the other day what happened to Uncle Ned that he was named for, and I said: "He's gone, son."

"Gone where?"

"Just gone," I said.

Then he wanted to know who Joe Ferguson was and what happened to him. Some young one he is, bright and quick on the trigger. He don't miss a trick. A great one for talking to the hands. So I said that Joe Ferguson was gone too.

That made two he knew about, Ned and Joe. But there were the others too: Arney and Thelma and Elmore Jordan and Drew whose guitar I broke and old Newt Simpson. All gone, like all the worthless of this earth who know something they won't tell you. I wonder sometime if God will go too, like they have, because He sure-Lord knows something that He won't tell and it took me a long time to find out that the only way to believe in Him is to give Him His right to be worthless too. He showed me a heap; but He held out on me about that ladder.

And Yocona is gone too and lies under water now, the same as the Delta used to, way back yonder, or so they tell me. There's water high up on the dam that I saw bare to the foot, and folks from around here go up before day and fish for perch and bream and bass and come back with strings to take pictures of. They say it's great sport up there. I don't know. I never have been.

www.ingramcontent.com/pod-product-compliance
Lightning Source LLC
Chambersburg PA
CBHW020557030726
47497CB00007B/1971